# Christmas in Tahoe

By Martha O'Sullivan

ISBN: 978-1-7367667-3-6

Christmas in Tahoe by Martha O'Sullivan

Cover and formatting by coversbykaren.com

To Uncle Marty for filling in all the gaps

# CHAPTER ONE

LAUREL REYNOLDS ALWAYS had a plan. For as long as she could remember, she went to bed knowing the next day's agenda. Even as a teenager—school, practice, hanging out with friends. College threw in studying, sorority activities and football games. Adulthood added work, domestic duties and social obligations. But now, for the first time in three decades of living, she had no idea what she was doing tomorrow, let alone the next day.

And she liked it.

But she was the only one. Her mother thought she'd completely lost her mind, her boss thought she needed an intervention and her best friend was convinced it was the divorce talking. And as Laurel watched the pastel haze suffuse the mountains and dusk fall over the lake, she had to admit that one had legs. Why, they had collectively argued, would the senior managing editor and heir apparent to publisher of *L.A. Digital* magazine, with a trendy apartment and a bright future, want to move to a sleepy little town in the mountains to write a novel.

Alone.

But that was all she wanted to do. Part of her had always wanted to be an author, but the rest of her, the practical, ambitious, realistic part, knew that was a pipe dream. It was nearly impossible to make a decent living as a writer in this day and age. She'd only landed the job she had because she'd fallen into a college internship, worked her ass off and stayed on after graduation for peanuts. Much of which had been facilitated by her ex-husband. She used to feel guilty about that; now she considered it paying it forward.

Laurel slowed her pace, anticipating the upcoming change in elevation. When she was a girl, the view from the curve on Lakeshore Boulevard wasn't as obstructed as it was now. Before the waist-high guardrail and sign prohibiting cell phone use, this had been her favorite part of the drive. She still remembered goosebumps erupting on her arms as the lake came into view. First it only teased, peering out from behind the forests of massive trees and panorama of snowcapped mountains. Then suddenly it emerged, a boundless expanse of cobalt blue, the crests of its waves gleaming like millions of tiny diamonds in the sunlight. And if Lake Tahoe could hold its own for millions of years, through droughts and wildfires, long, harsh winters and scorching hot summers, surely she could face her fear of failure and make something tangible out of the ideas that had been running amok in her head for what seemed like just as long.

By Christmas.

She found herself pulling onto the shoulder at the vista at the top of the hill. She got out of the car, zipped up her jacket and filled her lungs with the crisp, fresh mountain air. Walking to the lookout, she took in the lake with its rugged, rocky shoreline, the rows of bottle washer pines casting lengthening shadows over the water, the crashing of the waves in the evening wind.

Resting her forearms against the rail, she took a few deep breaths, shut her eyes and indulged herself in the summers of her childhood. The scent of sunscreen melded with pine straw and cedar filled the air, wall-to-wall sunshine warmed her cheeks and sand, coarse and silty, coated her toes. Squeals of laughter rose up from the beach where children buried each other in the sand and watched as sandcastles were washed away in the afternoon drift. Boats zigzagged the lake, towing tubers and skiers as jet skis skirted the shore, leaving a trail of white in their wake. Her mother stood in ankle-deep water, a hand shielding her eyes from the sun, making sure Laurel didn't venture past the buoys. Every so often a melody floated through the air as if on butterfly wings, its harmony as familiar to her as the voice that carried it.

She opened her eyes, damp now, and returned to the present. Clusters of lights dotted the mountainside and the docks were illuminated from below, awaiting the handful of boaters who would be out at this hour this time of year. The sheet of glass that was Lake Tahoe at sunrise was long gone, giving way to a steady pounding as the lake settled itself in for the night. And that ebb and flow, as comforting to Laurel as a lullaby, took with it the last little bit of doubt that she was doing the right thing.

She'd rented a furnished house in town, something that had taken some wrangling and persuading on her part. Most single-family homes here only leased annually, were partial to locals and preferred to have some mutual acquaintance or common thread between the two parties. When offering to pay over asking didn't move the needle, Laurel pulled the nostalgia card and

3

did a little name-dropping. After all, she'd spent many summers here as a child and wanted to return to her Tahoe roots. To those carefree, seminal, fundamental years on which she'd based her life. That, and oh, by the way, her grandmother was Ronnie Reynolds. And although the property manager didn't seem to be old enough to recognize the name, let alone appreciate the zeitgeist of Southern California in the seventies, Laurel had a feeling that the property owner was. In fact, she'd put money on it. She'd done her homework; she was a journalist after all. The little house on the corner of Village and Southwood had been owned by the same person since the sixties. A person who must treasure it enough to never have sold it in the last fifty years despite its value increasing tenfold. And that person was likely right around the age of someone who would appreciate the music and culture of Southern California in the seventies. In fact, it wasn't outside the realm of possibility that said owner had crossed paths with her grandmother or her mother back in the day, either here or in L.A. where he apparently lived. The leasing agent, her skepticism bordering on condescending, had finally agreed to humor Laurel and run the request by him.

So it had come as little surprise when she'd called back within fifteen minutes and in a considerably friendlier tone of voice, congratulated Laurel on securing the property for seven months at the advertised price and not a penny more. The only caveat was that the house was scheduled for some maintenance and repairs which likely wouldn't be completed until late May. That was fine, Laurel had insisted. She could put on her noise-cancelling headphones and escape into her writing hole, such as it was. By day's end, she had mailed a cashier's check for the deposit and signed an electronic lease beginning May first.

Which was tomorrow.

But for tonight she was treating herself to the best hotel in town, a nice dinner and a couple of glasses of wine. Straightening up, she let out a bolstering breath, tapped the top of the guardrail in farewell and left the sunset behind. She was still in that wistful state of mind when she arrived at the hotel ten minutes later. The lobby was an updated version of the way she remembered it, a refined, rustic decor of rich leathers and warm tapestries with lodge-themed rugs accenting the hardwood floors. Once in her room, she freshened up, changed into jeans and a cashmere sweater and headed across the street to the hotel's lakeside restaurant. She should be tired from the drive, but between the brisk evening air and the rush of making it to her intended destination, she felt more alive than she had in months. Her grandmother had always told her to listen to her gut, that anything was possible if she wanted it badly enough. And Laurel was about to see if Ronnie Reynolds was right about that too.

~~~

McGovern Scott walked into Hues of Blue loosening his tie. God, that felt good. The only thing he hated more than wearing a tie was wearing dress shoes. But he couldn't take those off, so he went with the lesser of two evils. Shoving the tie into the pocket of his suit coat, also among his least favorite things, he made quick work of the stairs. With an upward nod to the hostess indicating his intention, he made his way to the bar. Despite the calendar claiming it was shoulder season, the place was hopping. Whoever coined the phrase location, location, location must have done so here. Hues of Blue was the only lakeside restaurant and bar combination in town, with not only an upscale hotel but a high-end casino to boot. And the floor-to-ceiling windows with unparalleled views of Lake Tahoe didn't hurt.

There were a few empty stools scattered around the bar, but he set his sights on one at the far end, near the prep area and computer station. Not the most desirable spot to some, but it was close to the windows and he knew most of the staff, at least in passing. He'd spent the day with clients who had more money than he thought possible, so the idea of being around people more like himself was appealing. He'd barely settled himself in when a cocktail napkin followed by a beer in a frosted glass appeared in front of him. He didn't have to look up to know Mac was working.

"Thanks."

"Gov," Mac greeted, sliding a card through the reader on the side of the computer monitor and using a corner of it to tap the screen a few times. "I'll take the liberty of assuming it's a start-a-tab kind of night," he stated more than asked.

"What gave it away?"

"I bet there was a tie to go with that dress shirt and the suit looks almost as awkward on you as you probably feel in it."

"Hey," Gov mocked insult. He opened one side of the coat, proudly displaying the label.

Mac's gray eyes crinkled at the edges in amusement, accentuating the whiskers of time around them. "Big spender. What's the occasion?"

"Jack Brody is too damn good at his job, that's the occasion. We knock one teardown out of the park and suddenly he's the most popular contractor this side of Stateline. Dragging me to so many client meetings, I had to buy two new suits."

"Sounds like a good problem to have. How'd it go?"

"Oh, we got it," Gov told him with a good-humored snicker. "Who knew people could have not only three, but four homes, each one bigger than the other."

"So where's Mr. Wonderful tonight?"

"Probably halfway down the mountain by now." Gov took a sip. "New baby at home. I don't think things could be going any better for the guy. I told him to buy a lottery ticket."

"Good to hear. Brodys are good people."

"Can't argue with you there," Gov said and meant it. "How have you been?"

"Busy. Working. We've been short-staffed all spring. No one just comes for ski week and spring break anymore."

"Don't I know it. Didn't you tell me last summer that you were getting too old for the night shift?"

Now it was Mac's turn to snicker. "Yeah, well until I get too rich for it, I'll be working it." He laid a menu down in front of Gov. "I've got to make my rounds. I'll check back in with you."

Gov watched as Mac walked down the bar to greet a couple who'd just arrived, then went back to his beer. He grabbed his phone from his pants pocket and checked his texts, then scanned through his email messages. He was about to turn his attention to the menu, see if they'd changed it up any, when he saw her out of the corner of his eye. He actually felt his jaw drop, his

7

head tilt slightly forward in wonder. Later, he would realize he was trying to decide what was most captivating about her. Was it the auburn hair, flowing just past her shoulders in long, loose curls? Her bright, infectious smile as she conversed with the waiter? Or was it her coffee-colored eyes dancing in the soft light against her flawless porcelain skin? Even with the distance between them, the chatter of the bar all around him, he could somehow make out her voice. Velvety, a little husky, yet inviting and warm. He looked on as she handed her menu to the waiter, then nodded in reply at his parting words. Gov was still in a state of awe when he realized that Mac had returned.

"What's the verdict?"

Gov turned back around and sent Mac a blank look.

"A little dinner to go with that beer? Which you've hardly touched. Usually the first one goes down pretty easy."

"Ah, yeah." Gov looked unseeingly at the menu. Then he handed it back to Mac. "Actually, surprise me."

Mac chuckled. "Since we both know the offerings by heart, that's not much of a stretch for either one of us." He stowed the menu behind the bar and took his leave.

But Gov was already focusing his attention back to the redhead. From his vantage point at the bar, he had little more than a profile view of her. He couldn't imagine how beautiful she must be face-to-face when she looked this mesmerizing from the side. By now there was a glass of wine sitting on the high-top table in front of her. He watched as she intermittently sipped it and tended to her phone, her lips curving upward every so often as she typed.

Gov couldn't remember the last time he'd found himself so starstruck by a woman. He loved looking at women, no doubt about it, but just the sight of her actually *did* something to him, *moved* something in him. Like some mechanism he'd never known was there had been triggered. And he wanted to keep it on. Mac was nowhere to be found, so Gov got the attention of a passing waiter. Five minutes later Mac reappeared with a glass of wine in his hand and a confused look on his face.

"Did you order this?"

"Yes, I did," Gov replied readily, taking the glass from Mac and sliding off the bar stool. "Keep my dinner warm, will you?"

He felt Mac's gaze on his back as he made his way through the bar. Once he reached the woman he'd planned to give himself a moment to take her in, to selfishly indulge himself in her beauty, but she lifted her chin and gave him a curious look the second his shadow crossed her. He started to speak, flash that smile he'd been told was disarming, but froze. He prided himself on being smooth with women, cool under pressure, in control of any situation. But for some reason his tongue was tied and his mouth was unable to form enough syllables to string a sentence together. His eyes were working just fine though; he simply couldn't take them off of her. He'd been right; she was even more stunning up close. The begging to be touched curls accentuated her high cheekbones and her doe-like eyes were soulful and deep-set behind thick lashes. Her mouth was heart-shaped and just pouty enough to be sexy. And right now it was broadening into a nonplussed, closemouthed smile. She was staring at him,

9

eyebrows raised in anticipation and head cocked to the side inquisitively.

Finally, Gov heard himself say, "I thought you could use a refill." He set the glass of wine down on the table next to her half-empty one.

"Ah, thank you," she said, without taking her eyes off of him.

She wasn't going to make this easy. "May I join you?"

She exhaled a short breath of contemplation, then gestured with open palm to the chair across from her. "Sure."

Gov couldn't believe how happy that made him. He took a seat, setting the beer he'd forgotten he was holding down on the table. Now that they were one-on-one, he could see the tiny flecks of gold in her sable eyes, the splattering of freckles that dotted her nose, the subtle plumpness of her bottom lip. He could also see, as she cupped the glass in both hands and fidgeted her fingers a bit, that she wore no rings. He extended his hand. "McGovern Scott."

She offered hers across the table in kind, holding his eyes in hers all the while. Her soft, small hand fit perfectly into his. "Laurel Reynolds. Nice to meet you."

"The pleasure is all mine, Lauren."

She opened her mouth slightly as if to say something, but swallowed it. Instead, she took a sip of wine. "Hmm. Lovely. You have excellent taste."

"So I'm told. The waiter said you ordered the best Cab they had by the glass."

She slanted her head to the side. "I did. And this isn't it."

"No, it isn't. It's one of their signature reds. From a small vineyard in Amador County."

She thought about that for a moment. "And it's a Cab, not a Zin? From Amador?"

"Someone knows her varietals," Gov said, impressed. "It's actually a Barbera. The owner of the vineyard frequents the restaurant when he's in town. They usually keep some on hand for him."

She nodded at that, as if she understood how such things worked. Just as she finished another sip, the hostess appeared. "Ma'am, your table is ready." She glanced briefly at Gov, then back to Lauren. "Dinner for one, correct?"

"Yes," she confirmed, rising. Now Gov could take in the full-length of her, from the neckline of her sweater that showed just enough cleavage to make his mouth water, to the narrow indentation of her waist and the willowy curve of her hips. He had to stop himself from grunting appreciatively as he stood.

She picked up the glass he'd brought her and with a polite smile said, "Thanks again for the wine."

"My pleasure. Enjoy your dinner." He'd intended to ask for her number—after all she'd accepted the drink, wore no rings and was dining alone. But before he knew it she was gone, being led through the bar toward the restaurant. All Gov could do was watch as she walked past the stone hearth and then disappeared behind the mahogany doors at the far end of the room. He stood there for a long moment, still a little thunderstruck, until he heard someone ask if he was leaving. Shaking off the reverie, he answered accordingly, grabbed his beer and returned to the bar. There he found Mac and a fresh draft waiting for him.

"Well, that was short and sweet," Mac commented.

"Yeah," Gov grumbled, finishing the beer in his hand in one long pull and setting the glass on the bar, then sitting down. "They're a little too efficient at turning tables in the restaurant tonight."

Mac laughed without opening his mouth. "Just your luck. Probably scored some points with the Barbera, though. You're welcome, by the way. I opened a bottle for you."

"Duly noted. Ms. Reynolds seemed quite impressed. From the ten seconds or so I got to spend with her," he replied with a derisive snort.

Mac nodded speculatively. "I thought that might be her."

Gov, about to take a sip from the second beer, froze. "You know her?" he astonished.

"Not personally. Well, I knew her as a kid when they used to spend summers up here."

Gov put the beer down. "They?"

"I know I've got a solid three decades on you, but tell me you've heard of Ronnie Reynolds."

"I have not."

Mac shook his head in disappointment. "You're breaking my heart, man. Singer, songwriter, activist back in the seventies and eighties? She passed away not long ago. That's got to be her granddaughter, all grown up. Looks just like her."

The name didn't even begin to ring a bell. "And you knew her?"

"Everybody knew everybody around here then. I'd just gotten sober, Ronnie wanted to get sober. So she bought a place up here to get away from L.A. for a while. She sang a little in the clubs—Crystal Bay, the CalNeva—to keep her toe in it, make some money.

That's probably why it took her a couple of tries to get clean. She didn't have a support system or enter a program like I did. She had too many enablers for that, too much at stake for too many people. In the end it was the granddaughter who did the trick. Veronica wouldn't let her near the kid otherwise."

"Veronica?"

"Ronnie's daughter. Ronnie was married, albeit briefly, to Garry Reynolds, a big music producer in the sixties and seventies. I always got the impression that it was more of a merger than a marriage, but whatever it was, it produced a daughter, Veronica. He died in a plane crash years ago."

"What happened to the daughter?" Gov asked, oddly fascinated.

"She got caught in the growing up rich and famous trap. That's another reason Ronnie came up here. To get her daughter out of L.A., give her a shot at a normal life. But Veronica ended up pregnant anyway. Turned out to be the best thing that ever could have happened to either one of them, though. Gave them a common purpose, an incentive for Ronnie to get sober and a reason for Veronica to straighten up."

"So what happened to them?"

"Once Ronnie got sober, she realized her days on stage were behind her; she had terrible stage fright. She'd have to be buzzed to perform in front of people. But she could write songs and record them in the privacy of her own studio sober as a judge. So she concentrated on that, helped her daughter raise the girl, did a lot of charity work. Stopped spending summers up here about fifteen years ago now, only came up every so often and then rarely. Veronica took over most of the philanthropy work after Laurel grew up and Ronnie's health started to deteriorate."

"Do they still have a place here?"

"Naw." Mac shook his head. "Most of those quaint little houses are gone now, replaced by the multimillion dollar mansions that make up the lakefront side of Lakeshore between Country Club and Tahoe Boulevard."

"I wonder what she's doing here?" Gov asked himself as much as Mac.

"I couldn't tell you. Maybe feeling nostalgic or just passing through."

Gov was about to voice his vote for the former when his dinner arrived, ending the conversation.

"How'd I do?" Mac asked, as if he already knew the answer.

Gov looked down. "Bison. A little pricey, but an excellent choice."

"I figured you earned it today. Enjoy."

"Thanks. And thanks for the info. You're a wealth of information as usual. But just so you know, it's Lauren," Gov informed him, unwrapping his napkin and silverware. At Mac's confused expression he clarified, "Ronnie Reynolds' granddaughter. Her name is Lauren, not Laurel."

Mac, who had been about to walk away, turned to face Gov again. "If that was Ronnie's granddaughter, and I'd bet my bottom dollar that it was, her name is Laurel. I think some of your more primal senses might have kicked into overdrive and compromised your hearing."

Gov knew what he'd heard, but he wasn't going to argue with Mac. "If you say so."

"Oh, I do," Mac maintained assuredly. "I've never heard of any songs written in Lauren Canyon, have you?" With raised eyebrows and a glimmer in his eye, he left Gov to his dinner.

Gov could only watch him walk away, speechless for the second time that night.

# CHAPTER TWO

LAUREL SPENT THE next day settling into the rental house, right in the heart of town. It exceeded any expectations she could have had and considering she'd secured it sight unseen, she decided that was an auspicious beginning. First order of business after unpacking was to stock the refrigerator and pantry, so she headed for the grocery store. Like the hotel, it was a modernized version of how she remembered it. Smaller than the markets she was used to in L.A., but more than sufficient and much less crowded. Her last stop was the wine section, which brought the brutally handsome and charmingly awkward McGovern Scott to mind. She'd looked for him when she left the restaurant to thank him again for the wine. She'd enjoyed another glass of the Barbera with dinner and was surprised to find herself a little disappointed that he'd apparently left. The name of the vineyard had slipped her mind, so she perused the top shelf of the wine aisle, hoping one of the labels would jog her memory. When nothing did, she decided she'd call Hues of Blue. Her grandmother had been friendly with the bartender there. And although he probably no longer worked there, surely someone else could help her.

Once back at the house, she set the kitchen to rights. It was a bit dated, probably last remolded twenty-plus years ago, but was fully stocked with dishes, cookware and utensils and boasted late-model appliances. It was also spotless and Laurel intended to keep it that way. The only thing she hated more than cooking was cleaning up. Her meals would consist of heat and serve and takeout. Opening a drawer, she found a stack of menus from local restaurants. Pizza, Mexican and Chinese—perfect fare for vacationers exhausted from a day on the lake or locals too tired from the grind of life to make dinner. Flipping through the stack, she came across an old favorite, North Shore Pizza. Even the logo was the same; a cartoon-like depiction of a portly man in a white apron and chef's hat balancing a pizza in one hand while standing on a mountain peak. She wondered if the inside of the restaurant was also the same—red and white checkered tablecloths, handle back chrome chairs and of course, a jukebox. It was usually just the three of them in Tahoe and her mother made dinner most nights unless they went out for pizza and ice cream. They could do that here without issue. Even when one of Ronnie's songs came on the jukebox, no one seemed to notice. A familiar ringtone brought her back to the present. She slipped the menus back in the drawer and reached for her phone. "Hey."

"Hi, honey. I'm sorry I missed your call earlier. I've been on the phone all morning."

"Saving the world, no doubt."

"Trying to. All settled in?"

"Almost," Laurel replied, hanging her canvas bags on a hook in the pantry. "I just got back from Raley's."

"Ah. How's the house?"

"As advertised. And perfect for me. I was so excited I hardly slept last night."

"Me too. Mark was snoring like a freight train," Veronica said of her longtime boyfriend. "Too much wine at the auction. Does it to him every time."

"How'd it go?"

"Also as advertised. We surpassed our goal. The Ronnie Reynolds Scholarship Fund was the cause du jour."

That brought a smile to Laurel's face so wide it narrowed her eyes. "She would have loved that."

"Yeah," her mother agreed in a small voice. "I'm focusing on Music Education and the Arts this year. To commemorate what would have been her eightieth birthday."

"She'd be so proud of that. And you."

"I think so. But not as proud as she'd be of you for following your dream. If she hadn't, life would have been very different for the three of us."

"I know all of this is hard for you to understand, Mom."

Veronica didn't respond for a long moment. Finally she said, "Maybe at first it was. But there are certainly worse things than your daughter tucking herself away in Tahoe to write a novel. But I do worry about you there alone after everything you've been through lately. First the divorce, then Ronnie dying."

"I'm fine," Laurel told her. "You're welcome to come up anytime and check on me."

"Be careful what you wish for. I don't want to be a distraction."

"Don't put out a press release and you won't be."

"Very funny. Now, enough about me. What's on the agenda? And don't tell me you don't know. You can deny it all you want, but you're hardwired to have a plan."

Her mother knew her so well, always managed to get to the heart of the matter before Laurel realized what they were really talking about. She'd hated than about her as a teenager. She began with a sigh, "Since I've yet to write a word, let alone a chapter, I'm going to sit my ass down tonight and pound out a few ideas and see where they take me. And I just might have some fresh inspiration for my male lead."

"That's the spirit. Make sure he's tall, dark and conventionally handsome," Veronica replied, her voice dripping with disparagement.

"Grant was tall, Mom."

"He was six feet at best. Make this one lanky like a basketball player. With whiskey-colored eyes, close-cropped hair and a taut, chiseled chin."

She'd just described McGovern Scott to a tee. "I'll keep that in mind."

"Remind me why you married him again?"

"I can't remember exactly. I think it was the sex," she justified with a sly smile.

"Jesus, Laurel. I know we're close, but I'm still your mother."

"You started it."

"Since you clearly want to change the subject, I came across something that might interest you in one of Ronnie's drawers—a song she never finished. Just some random lyrics and incomplete chords on sheet music paper, but she was writing about Tahoe."

"She always said Tahoe saved her because she got sober here."

"*You* saved her, but yeah, Tahoe probably had something to do with it. I'll take a picture of the pages and send it to you. It might help jump-start the writing."

"Okay, thanks. I've been thinking a lot about our summers here since I arrived. Sleeping with the windows open to the wind chimes jingling in the breeze, going to the old-fashioned candy store and the ice cream parlor. I even found a menu for the pizza place we used to go to in one of the drawers in the kitchen. The one with the jukebox."

"Those were fun years, when you were little, Mom was finally sober and I was young. I'm so glad we made those memories together, as unintentional as it was."

"Unintentional?"

"Ronnie needed to get out of L.A. I think she knew it was the beginning of the end but wasn't quite ready to admit it yet. The sixties and seventies were catching up with anyone in the business who had actually survived them. And I was a handful as a teenager. Once she got us up there, I think she started to see the light at the end of the tunnel. But it took us a while to get out of that tunnel. In the end, it was you who finally got us out. So you really saved both of us."

"No, Mom. You saved *all* of us. You could have taken another path. But you were brave. You pulled yourself up by your bootstraps and by doing so forced Ronnie to do the same."

"Once I knew, I just…I just couldn't do anything else. It's the right decision for some women, but it wasn't the right decision for me. I wasn't even scared when I realized I was pregnant. Well, other than being scared of telling my mother. But she hugged me and we cried together and she told me everything was going to be all right."

"And it was," Laurel affirmed, feeling a lump begin to form in her throat.

"So much better than all right. You were the light of her life. Ronnie only had one stipulation."

"She was not to be called Grandma," Laurel put in through a watery laugh.

"Yep. She loved being your grandmother but no way was she going to answer to it."

They shared a sentimental moment before Laurel broke the silence asking, "Thanks for sending the song notes, but how will that help me write? I mean other than being special because of Ronnie."

"A song is just a story set to music. If she could write all those songs, teach herself to read music and play the piano with nothing more than a library book, then maybe her chicken scratch will help you dig deep and bring the story buried inside you to life. And maybe that's what really brought you back there, to Tahoe. Maybe Ronnie's up there, leading the band, guiding you. Maybe that's why I found the papers now, months after she's been gone."

"She always said I reminded her of someone she used to know."

"Yes, and she loved you best because of it. You are so much like her in so many ways."

"I always thought I reminded her of *you*," Laurel flabbergasted.

Veronica laughed from deep in her throat. "No, honey, you reminded her of herself. Before she screwed it all up. Think about it—only a narcissist names her daughter after herself. It's different for men somehow. Anyway, she was bound and determined not to let history repeat itself. It was a little late for me, but not for you. She always said she should have named me Laurel Veronica instead of the other way around. But her ego got in the way. That's why we named you Laurel, not so much for where it all began but for a new beginning."

Laurel, as taken aback by her mother's unassuming words as by her newfound encouragement, sat in stunned silence for a few beats. Finally, she said, "Thanks, Mom. You always seem to have the answer. Even before I ask the question."

"You were my answer, Laurel. To every question I ever had and to every prayer I ever said. Now, go write that book. Sleep with the windows open and let the melody of the breeze serenade you to sleep. Your answers, and your grandmother, are there, in the chimes."

~~~

Gov only had one regret about moving to Incline Village. No yard. There was green space in the common areas and courtyard of the condo complex, of course. Plenty of places for Boot to relieve himself. But he missed throwing a ball around with him in the privacy of his own backyard with a cup of coffee in the morning or a beer in the evening. Still, all things considered, it only made sense to live up here, at least for the time being. Commuting up the mountain in the summer was one thing, but Mount Rose Highway was unpredictable in the winter months. And those teardown projects that Jack kept acquiring as well as the subsequent build-outs often required his immediate and undivided attention. That, and being offered an inordinate amount of money for his house in Reno, which wasn't even on the market at the time, had made the decision to move a no-brainer. Real estate prices were just as inflated up here, so he'd decided to rent a condo until things leveled off. He'd sit on his equity, maybe dabble in the stock market a bit.

But that wasn't top of mind this morning.

He'd spent an hour at the bar last night alternating between eating his dinner and reading all he could find about Ronnie Reynolds. He'd grown up with the music of the sixties and seventies, his parents were baby boomers, yet he'd never heard of her. Wikipedia confirmed much of what Mac had told him. Ronnie Reynolds was born in 1943 in Oakland. Her father, deployed at the time of her birth, died in Europe before her first birthday. Her mother remarried when Ronnie was ten, until which time the two of them had lived with her maternal grandparents. Typical, in fact, unremarkable for the time. Her step-father had been an executive for I. Magnin, the now defunct department store chain. Her parents were active in the social scene in San Francisco and Ronnie had been quoted as saying that she was handed the American dream only to kick it to the curb. Caught up in the counterculture revolution, she flunked out of Berkeley after her sophomore year. Forced to move home, she begrudgingly took a job at the beauty counter of her step-father's flagship store. Years later she cited this as being a pivotal moment in her life. A cosmetic executive on a store visit saw her and offered her a modeling contract on the spot. She moved to L.A., spending her days in front of the camera in Beverly Hills and her nights in the clubs of West Hollywood. It was during this time she discovered, among other things, that she had a decent voice. She sang backup in a few bands, danced and drank the night away and sought pharmaceutical intervention to function during the day. She eventually met and married Garry Reynolds, who produced her first album, which yielded several big hits and made her a household name overnight. Together they had a daughter, Veronica. Ronnie's career struggled on and off after Reynolds' untimely death, leading to speculation that he had sold the proverbial sizzle and she was nothing more than a glorified lounge singer. She became the subject of tabloid fodder and eventually fell off the Hollywood radar.

There were a few photos of her from the seventies, when Ronnie would have been in her thirties, and the resemblance to Laurel was striking. But there was no mention of her or of any connection to Tahoe. The article did mention Ronnie's dedication to charitable organizations later in life, addiction recovery and the Arts in particular, and that her daughter had joined her in championing such causes in recent years. Once home, Gov downloaded a couple of her songs from the early days and while they didn't sound familiar, her songwriting credits were. She became quite an accomplished songwriter in the eighties and nineties. She died at her home in Beverly Hills last year surrounded by family.

Well, Laurel Reynolds had quite a pedigree. His was equally as impressive, but far less dramatic. His roots were buried deep in Nevada, in the gold and silver that had forged its history and in the politics that had shaped it into the Nevada of today. Some of his earliest memories were of panning with his grandfather McGovern in the foothills around Virginia City and along the shores of the Truckee River. His mother's family had chased gold and silver all the way to the American River and had eventually backtracked and settled in Reno. The Scott side hailed from Carson City, where generations of career politicians had a hand in everything from advocating homesteading to legalizing gambling to drafting water conservation legislation. Considering the largest silver discovery in U.S. history was found in the mountains near Carson City, Gov's ancestors had likely stumbled across each other long before his parents met at the University of Nevada in the late seventies. This lineage had given him a deep appreciation for the land and the basin, for the opportunities it presented and the respect it commanded. It had also given him a great upbringing, a solid education and for as long as he could remember, a desire to build things.

His father had no interest in going into politics, something that no doubt disappointed Gov's grandfather as well as many others in Carson City. Instead, he earned an engineering degree and spent his career preparing regulatory documents, applying industry standards and performing safety inspections. And unlike his own father, he was home for dinner most nights. Gov's mother had returned to teaching when he was in middle school, after having used some of her years at home to get a master's degree. She'd taught English Literature at the high school for twenty years. His parents retired a couple of years ago and now split their time between Palm Springs and Reno.

"Come on boy, time to go in," Gov called to his yellow Lab. The adjustment to a condo would have been much harder for Boot if the unit hadn't been on the first floor. At least there was a decent-sized patch of grass for him to roll in and a patio on which to sun. And Gov took him to the dog park a couple of times a week. The dog obeyed without hesitation, running through the open slider in search of his breakfast. Dog owner duties fulfilled, Gov freshened his coffee and grabbed his phone off the kitchen counter before opening the refrigerator. It seemed that Boot would be eating better than he this morning, he realized with a disappointed grunt. He put the grocery store on his mental to-do list as his mother's phone rang for the third time.

"Good morning," she answered, a little out of breath.

"Running another marathon, Mom?"

"I was outside watering my flowers and didn't want to miss you. Your sister programed my ringtones so I know who's calling. It's like a lazy version of Caller ID."

Gov had to smile. The rest of the world had been doing that for years. "Good to know. Now you can avoid me."

"Don't be silly, McGovern. You're my favorite son. How are things there?"

"Fine. Still chilly in the mornings. When are you coming home?"

"When it's no longer chilly in the mornings. Probably in a couple of weeks. The older I get the more I appreciate your grandmother leaving me her house here. She was definitely on to something, moving here in her later years. Grandpa didn't like it much, but she wore him down."

"Like with most things. Hey, have you ever heard of Ronnie Reynolds?"

"Yes, of course. Hasn't everyone?"

"Why haven't I?"

"I couldn't tell you. I saw that she died recently. Such a shame. I used to see her around Incline sometimes when we'd stay at the lake in the summer."

"You did?" Gov astounded.

"Yeah. And since we were attached at the hip in those days, you likely did as well. Her daughter and granddaughter too. I never said anything to them; celebrities who come to Tahoe do so to escape all the notoriety. Otherwise they'd go to Vail or Aspen. But your father's mouth would water at the very sight of her. She was absolutely stunning, a true natural beauty. With the voice of an angel on top of it. I practically had to pick his chin up from the floor one time when we were out for pizza."

Like father, like son, Gov thought. "How old was I?"

Sheryl Scott thought about that for a moment. "Ten, maybe? Summers got too busy once Kenzie was in high school to spend much time up at the lake, so before that. Why do you ask?"

"I met her granddaughter at Hues of Blue last night. Mac gave me the lowdown."

"Well, Mac would know. He and Ronnie were friends long after she stopped drinking. She'd supposedly go there late-night to try out a new song while he closed, to get a feel for how it would sound in a big, open room. They had a baby grand piano in front of the window in those days and she'd treat whomever was still around to a little show."

How could he have no recollection of this? "Do you remember the granddaughter?"

"I do. She was a little younger than you, looked more like Ronnie than her mother; Veronica favored her father. But the girl had that signature auburn hair, those big brown eyes. Even then, you could tell she was going to be a knockout."

"I'll say," Gov muttered under his breath.

"What, honey?"

He shook off the reverie and changed the subject. "Nothing. So Kenzie came for a visit?"

"Yeah. Matt is still deployed and she wanted to see us again before we go home. He'll be back in July and they're planning a trip to Disneyland before the kids go back to school."

"Is he still planning to do twenty?" Gov asked of his brother-in-law.

"At least. It's in his blood. They really like Southern California and would like to stay here or at least end up back here down the road. We'll see if the Marines agree."

Gov had the upmost respect for Matt and the generations of servicemen he came from. At least being stationed at Twentynine Palms allowed Kenzie and the kids to spend more time with his parents during the winter months.

"It's so strange that you brought up Ronnie Reynolds," his mother was still talking. "Dad and I went out to dinner last night and one of her old songs was on the radio in the car on the way home. I hadn't heard it in ages. He mentioned how we used to see them in Tahoe."

So much for changing the subject. "A lot?" Gov couldn't help but ask.

"Who would have thought, in unassuming Incline Village, but yeah. And I don't remember thinking much of it; lots of famous people had homes up there. But the Reynolds were different. I used to see Veronica at the grocery store, the library, the gas station. Other celebrities might employ people to do all those mundane things for them, but they were just like everyone else. The condo we rented was a few doors down from their house. Veronica would sit on the beach and read while the girl, I don't remember her name…"

"Laurel," Gov supplied.

"Yes, of course. Like Laurel Canyon. Anyway, Laurel would play on the beach with other little girls or wade in the water at the shore. Veronica was a much younger mother than I and she'd often be right in there with her. Ronnie would come out occasionally. She wore these long, flowing Bohemian-style dresses and had about a hundred bracelets up and down her arms. Seemed like Veronica and Laurel spent their days at the lake and then they'd all go out to dinner as a family in the evenings. When I think about it now, it should have been a bigger deal. Ronnie was probably in the house writing songs we'd eventually hear on the radio. But somehow it wasn't."

"I wish I remembered some of that."

"Well, you were a rough and tumble little boy interested in playing sharks and minnows and building sandcastles and unimpressed by celebrity. Speaking of building, how's work going?"

"Good. I'm busier than hell but glad I made the move. Jack Brody is great to work for. He doesn't suffer fools gladly and is a big fan of autonomy. Not a micromanager like I had before. And since it's a small, family-owned business everyone is all-in, wears whatever hat is necessary. I like that."

"To hear Dad talk, it won't be small much longer. Even in retirement he's heard that Brody & Sons is becoming the go-to for remodels and new construction on the North Shore."

"We'll see. That stuff has the tendency to wax and wane. But looking at the next five years, I don't see it slowing down much. Our biggest challenge is finding skilled workers and retaining them. And Jack's sister Moira, who really runs the place, is pregnant. That's not the kind of position that can be outsourced, so it'll be all hands on deck when she's on maternity leave."

"How nice. Please congratulate her for me. Not only do I remember Moira Brody as being one of my best students, but she and Lindsay Foster, whose family also had a house on that part of the lake, were likely among the gaggle of little girls who played on the beach with Laurel Reynolds those long-ago summers. What a small world." Before Gov could weigh in on that his mother put in, "Oh, that's Dad. He must be done with golf. I'm meeting him for an early lunch at the club. I'll let you go."

Gov bid his mother good-bye and decided he was going to make the world a little smaller yet and somehow manage to see Laurel Reynolds again.

# CHAPTER THREE

LAUREL HADN'T REALLY lied to her mother; she'd simply answered on the fly. But once she'd said the words out loud, she had no choice but to sit down with her laptop and jot down a few ideas. She'd decided after reading the notes from Ronnie's unfinished song, as if part of her didn't already know, that all roads led to Tahoe for the setting. After only a few days here she already felt more at peace. The rental house was on a quiet residential street, surrounded by comparable homes and a small townhouse community. The backyard was large and wooded and she could sit at the table on the deck, listen to the birds declare spring had sprung and write to her heart's content. She'd taken several creative writing classes in college and the common theme had always been to write what you know, what you like to read. But her college internship and subsequent career path had taken her in a different direction. Human interest pieces, travel segments, interviews with local personalities, informative stories of historical or social significance. The decade she'd spent in the trenches at *L.A. Digital* had left very little time for personal creativity. After all, she'd had deadlines to meet, freelancers to manage and advertisers to please.

But now she had no excuse.

She enjoyed reading women's fiction, specifically romance novels with a modern twist, characters to whom she could relate and a happily ever after ending that was earned rather than guaranteed. Love, commitment and fidelity in the midst of heartache, disappointment and anything else life might throw your way. That narrative hit a little close to home, so she decided to start by creating the hero and heroine. Build the story around her characters instead of tailoring them to fit into the mold of a typical romance novel.

She also recalled from undergrad that the building blocks of fiction, from romance to thrillers to sci-fi, was universal; goal, motivation, conflict. She had seven months to write a book. That was doable, right? She immediately pulled up her calendar and began to calculate. Say a chapter a week for a roughly sixty thousand word novel. That brought her to early fall. Then a month or two for editing. Was she going to self-edit? She'd cross that bridge when she came to it. Cover art, formatting, front and back matter. She could call in some favors for that. Anything was better than a blank page, so she'd start with the hero. She knew her mom had only been half-joking when she suggested that he be the complete opposite of her ex-husband. But maybe she had a point; her hero being the antithesis of Grant could be therapeutic.

Grant Hurley was the quintessential Southern California stereotype; a blond, blue-eyed surfer with a man bun who'd been born with a silver spoon in his mouth. Laurel had met him on the beach in Santa Monica the summer before her senior year at UCLA and had fallen for him instantly. She hadn't had much experience with men, just one high school romance and a couple of relationships in college that never went anywhere. Grant was also a student at UCLA, but they had never crossed paths and had no mutual acquaintances. Not so much due to the size of the school, Laurel had later learned, but because Grant rarely showed up for class. He came from a long line of UCLA alumni and his family was both proud Bruins and staunch contributors. He was older than her, a fifth year senior, and already had the position of his choice in his family's publishing business waiting for him upon graduation.

Laurel was convinced he was the love of her life. She slept with him on their second date and he gave her her first orgasm. And many more after that. Even thinking about it now sent a shiver of desire down her spine. He had a phenomenal body and was an incredible lover. And he knew it.

Since he came from money and stature himself, he was not at all intimidated by Ronnie's fame or their home in Beverly Hills. He'd grown up on Carbon Beach in Malibu and had been surrounded by celebrity and wealth his entire life. His parents were lovely, proper and sophisticated without being haughty. They were older, closer to Ronnie's age than her mother's, and had three other children. Grant had been their bonus, his father would say. The publishing empire had been in Grant's father's family for generations and his parents entertained and traveled frequently in its stead. Grant was used to a wide berth, an inexhaustible bank account and the luxury to indulge in whatever struck his fancy. And to Laurel's surprise and delight, for a time at least, that had been her.

They'd celebrated college gradation together with a month at his house in Maui before she started her internship at *L.A. Digital* and he his job at one of the other publishing houses under the family umbrella. Eventually they moved in together, to a house in Santa Monica that Grant's family held as an investment property. Laurel worked long hours, not only to learn the business, but to prove herself as more than just Grant Hurley's girlfriend. She wanted to earn her own way and gain the respect of her co-workers. But Grant did not. He'd roll out of bed to surf around the time she was leaving for work. He got into the office around the time she was choking down lunch. And he somehow always made it home before she did in the evenings.

He asked her to marry him one New Year's Eve on a private yacht docked off Catalina Island. They made love all night on the deck of the boat, with no one else on board to hear their screams of passion. Laurel thought she'd died and gone to heaven. They married in a small ceremony later that year with the Pacific Ocean as their backdrop.

Then Grant got bored. He might have been bored before, but she liked to think that was the first time he'd actually acted on it. Grant had the kind of sex appeal that constantly attracted women. Some would stare unabashedly, some would discretely indulge in him out of the corner of their eye and some would actually come on to him despite a wedding ring on his finger and a woman by his side. But Laurel trusted him, tried not to think much of it. She was used to it.

She'd heard rumors at work about him being a notorious player. When she'd asked him about it, he'd dismissed it with a "Yeah, right. They wish." So she'd let it go, but that little voice inside her head would occasionally remind her that where there's smoke there's fire. Sometimes he'd be overly indulgent, showering her with jewelry, flowers, candlelit dinners out of the blue. She'd wonder if it was more guilt than romance talking. She knew she should confront him about it but the good times were so good, she didn't want her un-substantiated paranoia to ruin them.

Then one day a friend at work pulled her aside. She'd come to *L.A. Digital* from the publishing house where Grant worked and kept up with people there. She'd heard about an editor who claimed she was pregnant with Grant's baby. Laurel told her she was crazy and stood by her husband, but inside she knew it was true. Grant denied it of course, threatened to have both wom-en fired for libel. So Laurel went to Grant's office when she knew he wasn't there to see for herself. The woman tearfully admitted that they had been sleeping together on and off for years. Once Grant found out she was pregnant, he wanted nothing more to do with her. He'd denied responsibility, called her a gold digger and an opportunist. She was waiting until the baby was born to have a paternity test performed and pursue legal action for support.

Backed into a corner, Grant was regretful at best. He didn't beg Laurel for forgiveness or promise such an indiscretion wouldn't happen again, but instead reiter-ated that he loved her and only her. The superfluous *women* were just a distraction, a hobby so to speak. They didn't mean anything to him; he just wasn't a one-woman man. Take it or leave it.

Laurel left it.

The divorce was quick and relatively painless. They had a prenup, of course. Not that Laurel wanted or needed Grant's money. But she did want and need her job. Either his reach didn't extend that far or he didn't care enough to have her terminated because other than being the subject of some gossip, it was business as usual at the office. Devastated, she moved home with her mom and Ronnie for a while. Grant eventually married the mother of his child, likely at his father's insistence, to legitimize the heir. As far as she knew they were still married, for what it was worth.

But a walk down memory lane does not a writer make, so Laurel forced her mind back to her hero. He would be tall, dark and handsome with a slightly asymmetrical face and a perpetual five-o'clock shadow. And he'd work with his hands. Grant had been small in stature everywhere but below the belt, so this guy would have big, strong hands, callused from a lifetime of work. His muscular build would be the result of an active lifestyle, not hours in the gym. His nose would be proportional but a little crooked; he'd been in a fight in his younger, rebellious years. And he came from a hardworking, middle-class family. He'd had to put himself through college and was better off for it.

His eyes would be a rich brown, the color of aged whiskey, with a touch of smokiness around the rims. His hair would be a shade darker and short with enough texture for a woman to run her fingers through it. His appearance would be stylish and tidy, yet still rugged and masculine. He'd wear boots and sport a tan, no matter the season. He'd smell like the outdoors with a hint of spice. Comfortable in his own skin, he'd carry himself with confidence and pride with no need for arrogance. He could make a woman feel like she was completely out of his league while simultaneously undressing her with his eyes. He'd loved many, but was still looking for the one. And once he found her, he would never let her go, never give her up. He would love her and only her. She would know this deep in her soul, not because of the things he said, or the gifts he gave or the places he took her, but by the way he loved her. By the way he held her eyes across a crowded room. By the way his hand rested at the small of her back, in reassurance and protection, not possessiveness or control. By the way he reached for her in the night and pulled her close. He'd want everyone to know she was his and he hers, most importantly her. He was an accomplished lover, generous and patient, more interested in her pleasure than his own. And when it was his turn, she took him to heights he'd never imagined, let alone reached before. Once he gave himself to her, it was for forever. He saw no one else, longed for no one else.

Laurel stopped typing and let out a jagged breath. Her heart was racing, her hands were shaking, her stomach reeling. She was taking a few restorative pants, striving for calm, when she heard someone clear their throat. With a jolt she looked up, and standing there in front of her was her hero.

~~~

With a couple of projects at the mercy of the Tahoe Regional Planning Agency, Gov decided to use the morning to check out the Baker house. It had been a rental for decades and for the majority of that time Brody and Sons had helped the leasing company manage it. Jack's late father had used this type of income stream to supplement the business when he was first getting the company off the ground. The Brodys had bigger fish to fry these days, but the owner had been a loyal and lucrative client over the years. Brody and Sons had remodeled the kitchen and updated both bathrooms, which had eventually led to other jobs in the neighborhood and beyond. They were under a verbal contract of sorts to perform or outsource annual maintenance and repairs. A new tenant was moving in and Jack had asked Gov to make some time this week to survey the property so Moira could schedule whatever work needed to be done.

Gov arrived at the house late on Wednesday morning and decided to evaluate the exterior first. The day was warm and spring-like, so he left his jacket in the truck and grabbed his sunglasses and iPad. It was so beautiful out that he felt a little guilty for leaving Boot at home. The old boy would love the wooded yard covered in autumn's forgotten leaves. First order of business would be to get rid of them, though. Wildfire season was upon them and leaf litter made for perfect kindling. He made a note to that effect and took in the front of the house. The trim and door could use a fresh coat of paint, but the cedar shingle siding appeared to be in good shape. He added that to his list and continued to circle the house, making his way around to the back. Pushing his sunglasses up on his head to take a closer look, he was debating if the window panes also needed paint or just a good scrubbing when he saw what could only be an apparition in his peripheral vision.

Sitting there on the deck, laptop open on the table in front of her and mouth agape was none other than Laurel Reynolds. Her hair, more strawberry blonde than auburn in the bright sunlight, was pulled back in a tie at the nape of her neck leaving only a few strands to frame her face. Her umber eyes, saucer-like and unblinking, stared at him in astonishment. Her chest was rising and falling in short, shallow breaths and she seemed to be trying to collect herself, something to which Gov could relate. Time stood still for a few silent beats until he finally managed, "Good morning. I'm sorry if I startled you." He closed the space between them in three strides and continued, "I'm here to assess the property for the owner."

She pushed up from behind the wrought iron table and let out a deep breath. Closing her laptop, she approached him, crossing the deck and stopping at the top step. She was wearing what Gov thought of as yoga pants and a loose-fitting sweatshirt that exposed one shoulder. One very sexy shoulder that he would love to put his mouth on. "No problem," she said with a tight-lipped smile. "The leasing agent said someone would be by, but that I would get fair warning."

"I guess that's on me. I didn't realize anyone was living here yet." He extended his hand in greeting. "McGovern Scott. We met the other night at Hues of Blue."

She stepped down one step, bringing them almost to eye level before accepting his hand. "Yes, of course. It's nice to see you again."

"Likewise." She was within a few breaths of him now and he could feel his pulse begin to race, his palms begin to sweat. He forced himself to let go of her hand. "If I'm interrupting, I can come back another time."

"Not at all. So you work for the leasing company?"

"No. I'm with a contractor in Reno. We help maintain the property for the owner."

She nodded in understanding. "I see."

"You're the new tenant?" Gov asked, wondering if she heard the hopefulness in his voice.

"That I am," she affirmed. Then after a short pause, added. "Well, this is convenient. I wanted to thank you again for the wine. I had another glass with dinner."

"My pleasure, *Laurel*," Gov returned, drawing out the name. "It's the least I could do after getting your name wrong."

"You ordered the wine before we exchanged names, but nice try," she laughed.

"And you decided not to correct me?"

"It happens all the time," she replied with an easygoing shrug. "But who did?"

Gov took a moment to consider his answer. He didn't want to come off as a stalker, but what else could he say? "The bartender. Apparently he's an old family friend."

"He's still there?" Laurel asked incredulously.

"Mac? Yeah. He'll die in that place."

"Mac. Yes, of course. I meant to ask my mother his name. I was going to call Hues of Blue because I couldn't remember the name of the wine. I'd like to pick up a bottle."

Done, Gov thought. "He said your family used to summer up here."

She nodded. "My grandmother had an affinity for the Sierra."

"Mac mentioned she passed away recently. I'm sorry."

A sad smile crossed her face. "Thank you."

Silence hung in the air for a few blinks during which time their eyes seemed to be intangibly attached. Finally Gov cleared his throat and said, "So you work remotely?"

She glanced over her shoulder at the laptop. "Something like that. I wanted to get out of the rat race for a while."

"Well, there's no better place for that than Tahoe."

"I couldn't agree more. I already feel more inspired," she said with a wide grin that revealed two perfectly shaped dimples at the corners of her mouth.

"What do you do?" Gov asked, wanting to keep the conversation going.

Pulling her sweatshirt up a bit higher on that sexy shoulder, she considered a moment before answering. "I'm in publishing. But I took a bit of a sabbatical."

"Again, you've definitely come to the right place."

"I guess we'll see," she said as her phone starting ringing behind her. "I'd better get that. Feel free to look around."

"I'll come back another time to finish." Gov heard himself say, reaching into the front pocket of his jeans. "Here's my card if you have any problems."

"Thanks," she said, accepting the card before turning around to retrieve her phone.

"Sure." Gov stood there for a moment, admiring her backside as she bent over to grab her phone from the table. She gave him a parting wave and then spoke indistinctly into it.

Returning the gesture, Gov took his leave and finished surveying the exterior of the house. Once back in the truck, he shot Moira a quick email as to his findings. On his way to his next stop, he gave the office a call.

"Brody and Sons Construction."

"Hey, Moira. It's Gov."

Moira Webster laughed a little. "I know."

"Right. I always forget about your Caller ID."

"I usually answer before I read the screen, so don't feel too bad. What's up?"

"I went by the Baker house this morning. I just emailed you my observations."

There was a short pause and the sound of keystrokes. "Yep. I got it. That's all this time?"

"I only got to the exterior. The new tenant is already in."

"Oh, I didn't realize that. There's usually plenty of time in between. Sorry if I sent you on a wild goose chase."

"No problem." That was a gross understatement. In fact, he owed her one. "I left my card if she has any problems."

"Okay. The property manager did a walk-through after the last tenant vacated and said everything was in operating order, so we should be good."

"I can always stop back by. It's right up the street from my place."

"I'll leave that up to you."

Now he owed her two, Gov thought. "I'm heading over to the Lakeshore Terrace project now to see how the Pre-Grade Inspection is going."

"You don't have to check in with me, Gov. Jack knows better than to hire someone I have to babysit, especially in light of recent developments. We all have plenty to do without having to keep track of each other."

"Old habits die hard. Speaking of recent developments, how are you feeling?"

"Great. I'm eating everything in sight and Paul is waiting on me hand and foot," Moira said of her husband.

"Sounds like my sister when she was pregnant with her first. Her husband was deployed for most of her second pregnancy, so that was fortuitous on his part. My mom had to take over for him."

Moira chuckled. "I'm sure she didn't mind a bit. Is she enjoying retirement?"

"Loves it. My parents are in Palm Springs for the winter. She wanted me to extend her congratulations to you. She said you were one of her best students."

"She was on of my favorite teachers. Please tell her I said hello."

"I will," Gov replied, then asked on a whim, "You spent a lot of time in Incline when you were growing up, didn't you?"

"Yes, skiing in the winter and at the beach in the summer. Why do you ask?"

"The woman renting the Baker house. My mom thought you might know her."

"Is she from Reno?"

"No. L.A., I think. But apparently she used to spend the summer here when she was a girl. She'd be around your age."

"What's her name?"

Gov shoved the truck into park in front of the construction site. "Laurel Reynolds."

"Laurel Reynolds..." Moira repeated in a faraway voice, as if mentally rewinding time. "Not off the top of my head. But most of my summer days at the lake were spent at my friend Lindsay's house."

"So I'm told. My mom remembers her family from the summers we rented a condo on the same beach."

"And this Laurel Reynolds is back in Incline, renting the Baker place?"

"Yeah. Taking a break from the rat race," Gov informed her, grabbing his hard hat off the passenger seat.

"Must be nice. I'll ask Lindsay if she remembers her."

"If you think of it. I just thought it was an interesting coincidence," Gov remarked, getting out of the truck. "I'll get back over there to check out the rest of the house later this week."

"If you have the time."

"I'll make the time." In fact, he was already looking forward to it.

# CHAPTER FOUR

LAUREL COULD DENY it all she wanted, but she was programmed to have a plan. So she decided she'd write everyday but still treat the weekend a little differently, make it special somehow. Since today was Saturday, she'd do more exploring than writing. She didn't bother to set an alarm here; she had the Sooty Grouses and the Mountain Chickadees for that. It was still too cold at night to sleep with the windows open, but their birdsong managed to wake her up every morning around the same time. She'd grab some coffee and a sweatshirt and head out to the deck with her laptop. She'd start by skimming over what she'd written the previous day, to get her head back in the story, before writing anything new. But there was a problem with that routine the last few days.

And his name was McGovern Scott.

She had yet to name her hero when he suddenly appeared before her, all tall, dark and handsome, in an unbuttoned flannel shirt over a white t-shirt and blue jeans broken in in all the right places. And ever since then she couldn't seem to get him, or his name, out of her head. So for now her hero would be called "Scott" as a placeholder until she could delve further into his character and come up with a more suitable name. But she had a feeling that McGovern Scott's image would not be so easily replaced. It was ingrained in her mind as deeply as the scuffs on his weathered leather boots appeared to be.

After collecting herself following his pop in on Wednesday, she'd devoted the rest of the day to the setting of the novel. She'd been researching the Tahoe area online, but needed to bring all those facts and figures to life. So the last two mornings, after a couple of cups of coffee and something small to eat, she'd walked the length of Lakeshore Boulevard and back. Today she'd planned to hike the Tunnel Creek Trail up to Monkey Rock to get some broader views of the lake, but decided to give her body one more day to acclimate to the elevation. Instead, she found herself at the public beach. The gate was open and the beach deserted but for a few people milling about by the shore. Laurel knew this part of the lake well; their house been just up the beach a little shy of Crystal Bay. Ronnie had found herself in a writing slump in the mid-aughts and had panicked and sold the property. The house had been subsequently torn down and the land combined with several other lots to make way for two large estates.

It was a warm and sunny day but Laurel knew the water would still be ice cold. The price of the lake never freezing was that it rarely reached seventy degrees, even in the dog days of summer. She made her way down to the shore and looked across the water at the mountains in the distance. The dramatic ten thousand foot peaks, the craggily switchbacks, the triple-tiered forested hillsides never ceased to amaze her. She made a mental note not to forget about the California side of the lake, for herself as much as for her book. Maybe if her mother came up for a visit they could go to Truckee for lunch and shopping one day, then take the long way home through Tahoe City and South Lake Tahoe. Once or twice a summer, Ronnie would rent a boat and they would pack a cooler and head over to Emerald Bay for the day. Laurel hadn't thought about that in years. It would be the perfect spot for a meet-cute.

She sat down on a nearby bench and removed her shoes and socks, then walked through the cool sand to the water. Rolling up her joggers, she stuck in a toe, then a foot and eventually the other. She trudged through the surf, shuttering a little as the lapping waves spit spindrift on her ankles. She took in the opposite side of the lake again for a moment more before turning around to face the shoreline. In her mind's eye it was any given summer day of her youth. Beachgoers with chairs on their backs and coolers in their arms searched for the perfect spot. Crowds packed picnic areas and filled volleyball courts under the towering trees. A crisp, woodsy scent laced with the sweetness of pine straw floated through the air. All under a sky so preternaturally blue it almost hurt your eyes.

She grabbed her phone from her jacket pocket and dictated into it, trying to do the picture in her head justice. When she was done, she let out a long, pensive breath and headed to shore. It wasn't until she was back at the bench that she realized she was no longer alone. An older couple, likely in their late seventies, was standing near the water. He was in khaki slacks and a green windbreaker, she in yellow linen pants and a white sweater. Even in the breeze, the woman's gray hair was perfectly coiffed and Laurel could see that she was wearing the same bold shade of red on both her lips and fingernails. The man wore a checkered newsboy

47

cap that reminded Laurel of a character in her favorite Christmas movie. She watched them walk hand in hand closer to the water. Stopping just short of the surf, the man pointed out something across the lake to the woman. She nodded in recognition, then rested her head against his shoulder. He leaned down and kissed the top of her head.

Laurel found herself enthralled with them. Not just by the affection they clearly shared for one another, but by the obvious contentment they felt within that affection. She wondered how long they'd been married. Fifty years? Sixty? Did they have children? Grandchildren? Great-grandchildren? There was something about the way he looked at her; something about the way she smiled up at him. It was one of the sweetest, most endearing things Laurel had ever seen. Comfortable and familiar, without being tiresome and stale, after what was likely a lifetime together. How was that even possible?

She'd never imagined she and Grant that way, decades from now. She certainly hadn't expected to end up divorced at thirty, but she'd also never thought about the two of them in their golden years. Maybe she just hadn't gotten that far. Or maybe because it had always just been Ronnie, her mom and herself. No father, no grandfather, no man in the picture. Everything she remembered about Ronnie's love life came from the rags in the grocery store checkout line. Not that Laurel had ever thought to ask. Her mother hadn't dated much until she started seeing Mark when Laurel was a teenager. And as much as Mark was around, he never stayed overnight at the house, let alone lived with them. That had likely changed when she was away at college, but even now he and Veronica maintained separate residences. Why her mother didn't marry him, Laurel had no idea. He had asked her a million times.

She shook off the reverie and refocused on the couple. They'd started walking slowly down the beach, still hand in hand. She wondered if they lived in one of the estate homes; they had an elegant, classy look about them. Or maybe they were here on vacation; perhaps Tahoe held some special meaning. They could be from the Bay Area; maybe they had a second home here and were in town to open it up for the summer. Leave it to an only child to entertain herself by making up scenarios in her head. No wonder she'd become a writer, she muttered to herself.

Laurel watched their retreating backs for another few moments before retrieving her shoes and socks from under the bench. The walk back to the house was quick and after tidying up a bit and throwing in some laundry, she got back to work. She pounded out a few paragraphs based on her dictation and reread yesterday's writing. She'd settled on Whitney for her heroine's name. It was contemporary but not too trendy and since Mount Whitney was the tallest peak in the Sierra Nevada, she thought the connection was clever.

The walk by the lake had made her nostalgic and since she'd promised herself to make the weekend different somehow, she decided to order from North Shore Pizza for dinner. Tahoe had an early to bed, early to rise vibe, so Laurel called in her order right at five when they opened. Being here also meant being on Tahoe time and delivery would be at least an hour, which was fine with her. She used the time to shower and put on a little makeup. She wasn't going anywhere, but realized she'd hardly done any primping in the week she'd been here and was actually starting to miss it.

And that impulse proved to be rather fortuitous.

She hadn't been asked for a credit card number upon placing her order, so when the doorbell rang she grabbed a twenty and a few singles to cover the tip from her purse. But when she opened the front door, instead of the gawky teenager she'd expected, she found herself face-to-face with McGovern Scott. He was wearing a mischievous grin and a San Francisco Giants ball cap and holding a pizza box and a bottle of wine.

"Did someone here order a pizza?"

She could do nothing but stare at him blankly, open-mouthed and wide-eyed. Finally, she managed, "Yes, as a matter of fact, I did."

"Sorry for the delay. They're really backed up to-night," he informed her nonchalantly, smiling all the while.

Laurel cleared her throat needlessly. "No problem." She wasn't sure what to do next. Pay him? Surely he didn't work a side job delivering pizzas. He was gain-fully employed. So she held out her hands to take the pizza. "Thank you."

"My pleasure. But if I hand you the pizza, I might drop the wine and that would be a crime. Can I come in?"

Laurel had to give him credit; he was resourceful. And very, very smooth. "Of course," she replied, step-ping back to give him room to pass. She watched him walk straight back to the kitchen; he obviously knew the layout of the house. And God, he had a sexy butt. She followed him.

He set the pizza on the island while carefully support-ing the wine under one arm. Then he turned to her. "I was at North Shore, picking up a pizza. I heard your or-der being called in. Joe and I go way back; his dad and my dad played football together in high school. Any-way, I thought I'd save them the trouble and deliver it myself." He gestured over his shoulder with his thumb. "I live right down the street."

Such a Tahoe thing to do. That would never happen in L.A. "How nice of you. But I didn't know that North Shore sold wine by the bottle." She nodded toward the bottle he now held in his hand.

"They don't. I was planning to stop back by this week-end to schedule a time to check the rest of the house. I had Mac put one of these aside for me. I swung by the bar and grabbed it." He closed the space between them in two easy strides, then handed her the bottle. "You said you liked it and it's hard to come by."

He was wooing her and she found herself not minding one little bit. She looked from him to the bottle, then back to him. "How thoughtful. Thank you, McGovern."

He flashed her that killer smile. "My pleasure, Lau-rel. And my friends call me Gov."

"Thanks, Gov. But where's your pizza?" she asked, nodding to the lone box on the island.

"In the truck, hopefully not attracting a bear."

"Right, I have to get used to that," she replied, not sure if he was kidding or not.

"Just don't leave your kitchen window open when there's food out and you'll be fine. And be sure to latch your garbage can tight on pickup days. Otherwise keep it in the garage with the door shut."

"Okay, I'll remember that. Thanks."

They stood there for a long moment, staring at each other. Finally Gov said, "Well, I'll let you get to that pizza before it gets cold. Give me a call as to a good time to do the interior inspection. You have my card." With a tight nod, he started to walk out of the kitchen.

"Gov?" Laurel heard herself say.

He immediately stopped and turned on his heel. "Yeah?"

"This was all so nice of you. Would you like to stay for a glass of wine? I mean, unless you have to get that pizza home," she finished purposefully.

He held her eyes in his for a few loaded clicks, then said, "If I had to get that pizza home, I wouldn't be here."

She nodded as the weight of his response passed between them. "Then why don't you grab it from your truck? We can eat together on the deck."

"That'd be great."

"I'll open the wine and let it breathe. Maybe throw a salad together."

"And I'll go disappoint that bear and be right back."

Fifteen minutes later they were sitting at the table on the deck with the bottle of wine and the pizzas. Laurel had found some melamine plates in the laundry room cabinet and a big bowl for the salad. It was cooling off with the setting sun and she thought about offering for them to eat inside, but didn't want to give him the wrong impression.

Or did she?

"So, how's the sabbatical going?" Gov wanted to know.

"Good. I can't remember the last time I felt this relaxed," Laurel told him and meant it. "I was afraid I might get a little stir-crazy, but so far so good."

"You said you were in publishing?"

"I'm an editor at *L.A. Digital* magazine," she answered, taking a sip of wine. It felt as smooth as velvet sliding down her throat. "I mean, I was. I took a leave of absence."

"Burned out?" Gov asked around a bite of pizza loaded with pepperoni slices.

"No more than usual. In fact, the fire in my belly is as hot as ever. It just seems to be fanning a different kind of flame."

"Such as?"

Laurel let out a contemplative breath. How much should she tell him? What did he already know about her? Mac had likely filled him in on her family tree. And of course, there was always Google. "I'm writing a novel."

He thought about that for a moment. Then with a speculative nod said, "I can see that. You have an intuitiveness about you."

"I do?"

"Yeah. You think about what you're going to say before you say it. Unlike myself," he added with a grin. "My mom was an English Lit. teacher. She could always tell which students grasped the material by the analogies they used in their essays. Not just drawing generic conclusions to finish the assignment, but actually understanding the concepts. I bet you were like that in school."

She had been. Laurel sent him a wary look. "You know this is only dinner, right? Flattery won't get you any further than that."

He laughed. "Yeah, I know. It's just an observation. So what's your novel about?"

"A writer at loose ends who swears off men," she told him with a facetious grin.

"Great," he scoffed, rolling his eyes. "Seriously."

"Seriously. But I'm just getting started. The protagonist is an aspiring novelist who has just gotten out of a long-term relationship. One she thought would go the distance. To top it all off, she loses her job and subsequently her apartment. With nothing left to lose, she escapes to a cabin in the mountains in search of a fresh start."

"And?"

"That's as far as I've gotten."

"No Yang for the Yin?"

"Not yet," Laurel lied.

"Well, keep me posted," he said, his eyes dancing with humor. "Let me know if you need a prototype or something."

If he only knew. But she answered offhandedly, "Will do. So how about you? All I know about you is that you work for a contractor and your mom was an English teacher."

Gov began with a shrug. "I'm from Reno, I went to undergrad at UNR and got my master's degree at Stanford. I worked in the Bay Area for about five years until the obscene cost of living finally did me in. I took a position with a commercial real estate firm and moved back to Reno. They got bought out by a conglomerate a few years ago. My position was secure, but the corporate structure and managerial hierarchy didn't work for me. Now I work for Brody and Sons Construction, a small family business you've likely never heard of. I'm an engineer by degree, like my father, and have an older sister. She's married to a Marine and has two kids. "

"That's nice. And I actually have heard of Brody and Sons," Laurel commented. "Their name and number is on the emergency contact sheet as well some paperwork in one of the kitchen drawers. What do you do for them?"

"I'm the head foreman, second in command to Jack Brody in the field, third string in the office. But make no mistake; Jack's sister actually runs the place. I've been there for about two years. Jack needed help after his father passed away since neither of his brothers were interested in going into the family business. He's got more work than he knows what to do with, especially lately. I wanted to get out of the corporate world and back into the field, so it works well for both of us."

Could he fit her hero's bill any more perfectly? Laurel amazed, wondering if that was good or bad. "So you like it?" she inquired, taking a bite of pizza.

"Love it," Gov affirmed with a nod. "I moved to Incline last year to be closer to the jobs. Most of what we're doing now are multi-year projects like teardowns and build-outs so I was working up here most of the time anyway. I sold my house in Reno off-market. We're renting a condo for the time being."

Laurel felt her heart fall to her stomach. She swallowed hard. "We?"

"Boot and I," Gov hurriedly explained, sitting up a little straighter in his chair. "My yellow Lab. Condo living has been a bit of an adjustment for the old boy, but he's a trooper."

"Got it," Laurel said, wondering if he heard the relief in her voice. And if it surprised him as much as it did her.

"How about you? I mean other than writing the great American novel and being an editor?" He refilled both of their glasses, killing the bottle.

"I'm from L.A. I graduated from UCLA with a journalism degree." She paused for a moment, then decided to rip the bandage right off. "I'm recently divorced."

"I'd say I'm sorry to hear that," Gov replied, unfazed. "But if you weren't I doubt we'd be sitting here like this."

"No, we definitely wouldn't be."

"But I'm sorry you had to go through that. You don't get to thirty-five without seeing a buddy or two get divorced. From what I understand it's like a death in the family, with similar feelings of sadness and loss."

Who was the intuitive one now? "Thank you. And yes, it's a different kind of grief."

"How long were you married?"

"Two years, but together for eight, give or take."

Gov nodded. "That's a long time. About a quarter of your life, I'm guessing."

"Just about," Laurel confirmed around a sip of wine. "But I don't regret it; the relationship or the divorce. My grandmother used to say whatever doesn't kill you makes you stronger. And I'm starting to see that she was right about that, among other things."

"Yes, mothers and grandmothers have a way of always being right, I've learned. But how so?"

"I never would have had the courage to do this before. To leave my job, pack up my life and come to the mountains to chase a dream. Especially a dream that I didn't dare utter out loud until a few years ago," she told him, realizing she'd never actually articulated that before. "And all by myself on top of it."

"Well, I'm glad you did," he said with a warm smile.

"How about you?" She could feel the wine going to her head and took another bite of pizza in an attempt to counteract it.

"Me? Never been married, never even been close."

"Interesting."

"Is it?" he remarked, lifting his eyebrows.

"Very," she replied, leaning back in the chair. "You don't seem like a ladies' man, yet I have a feeling you are no stranger to female company."

"Like I said, intuitive. I guess I haven't met the right one to take that next step with," Gov said, taking a sip of wine. "But I'm open to it. I have nothing against commitment."

Their eyes locked and held over the top of his glass for a few beats. Laurel could feel her cheeks begin to burn and her heart begin to race. She wondered if he noticed. She took another sip of wine.

"Well, I'd better get going," Gov started talking again. "Boot will be crossing his legs by now."

She watched him push up from behind the table and begin to tidy up, condensing the pizza slices into one box and throwing the used napkins in the other. Shaking off whatever spell had come over her, she stood and started collecting the plates and silverware. "Thanks, but I've got this. You get home to Boot."

"It'll just take a second. It's getting dark and I don't want you out here alone. You don't want to find yourself on the business end of a mama bear coming out of hibernation. It's that time of year."

"For a guy from Reno, you sure know a lot about Tahoe," she noted, stacking the salad bowl on top of the plates and following him inside.

"They're kind of one in the same, if you take advantage of it. And my family did. We spent time up here every the summer when I was a kid."

"So did we." Laurel set the dishes in the sink and began covering the salad bowl with plastic wrap. "But you already knew that."

He finished breaking down the empty pizza box. "Yeah, I already knew that."

"What else do you know?" she asked, meeting his eyes.

He laid his hands on her shoulders and turned her to face him. "I know I'd like to get to know you better. I know I'd like you to get to know me better. But most of all, I know I'd like to kiss you."

Laurel felt her arms drop to her sides. His mouth was within a few breaths of hers now, hovering in anticipation. His eyes were at half-mast, focused on her lips as if constructing a plan of attack in his mind. He leaned in a little closer and she could smell the spring night on him. Her heart skipped a beat. She hadn't shared a kiss, let alone anything else, with a man in over two years. And she had a feeling that was about to change.

He went in for the kill slowly, as if testing the waters, sampling. First he only drew her to him and laid his lips on hers, held them there. After meeting no resistance, he began to lavish her with long, full kisses. She responded in kind, giving as much as she was taking, wanting more than she could give. His entire mouth was covering hers now, moving over it thoroughly, devouring her little by little. His lips were wet, his beard rough, his tongue hot. She could taste the tanginess of the wine laced with the sweetness of the tomato sauce as he inched his way inside her mouth and his tongue began to mingle with hers. Her hands went up his back and she began to weave her fingers through his hair. His arms were circling her waist now, clutching her against him. She pressed her body to his as his tongue explored her mouth deeply, passionately, desperately, as if starved of it.

He left her mouth on sawed-off breaths and licked a silky trail down her throat. She felt a tug of want in the pit of her stomach when his tongue found that sensitive spot just below her earlobe. She cradled his head in her hands as he reached the hollow notch at the base of her neck, sending arrows of need shooting through her. She wanted his mouth on her, his hands on her, his hardness inside her. He was kissing his way down to the valley between her breasts and she could feel herself start to quiver with long-forgotten dampness below.

And then he stopped.

They stood there for a few moments, crushed against the kitchen counter, their chests rising and falling in serrated breaths. Finally, Gov lifted his head and met her gaze. His eyes were dark and fierce and filled with the same urgency she felt between her legs. "Laurel, I'm sorry. I lost my head."

"I'd say we both lost our heads," she managed as her breathing leveled a bit. "You have nothing to be sorry about."

"Yes, I do. I'm extremely attracted to you." Panting, he inched out of her embrace and rubbed a frustrated hand at the nape of his neck. "I should have known better than to start something."

"I was a more than willing participant." She reached up patted his hair down a little at the forehead. "As you'll see when you look in the mirror."

He brought her back to him. "Can I call you tomorrow?"

She nodded. "I'd like that."

"In the morning?'

"Sure."

"Like first thing in the morning?"

"Yeah," she chuckled.

He slid his hand into hers. "Are you free tomorrow night?"

"I am."

"Let's plan on dinner then. I'll make a reservation."

"That'd be great."

They walked to the front door hand in hand. He opened it, then turned back to her. "Thanks for a nice evening."

"Thank you. For the pizza and the wine. It brought back a lot of old memories."

"I'd like us to make some new memories." He let go of her hand but his eyes remained pinned to hers.

She swallowed hard. "Me too."

He tilted her chin up and laid a tender kiss on her mouth. "I'll see you tomorrow."

"I'll look forward to it."

She looked on as he got into his truck and pulled away with a parting wave. Once he was out of sight, she closed and locked the door, then leaned back against it.

Well, the weekend had definitely been different. She touched her swollen lips. And it wasn't quite over yet.

# CHAPTER FIVE

GOV HAD NEVER been told he talked in his sleep, so when he woke up to the mutterings of his own voice it took him a few seconds to get his bearings. He was, unfortunately, alone in his bed. Which meant only one thing; he'd been having the most incredible dream. Laurel was on top of him, riding him as he grew as hard as he'd ever been inside her. Her head was thrown back in rapture, her coppery curls cascaded down her back in a silky waterfall and her hedonic moans were filling the room. She was coming again and again, begging for him to thrust harder, to push deeper, as she drenched him over and over. Finally, unable to hold out any longer, he howled her name and exploded into her just as she collapsed on top of him. It was a climax like no other, a gratification like he'd never known, a release so mind-shattering it left him boneless.

And wanting more.

Sitting up in bed, he let his eyes adjust to the predawn light and trudged an agitated hand through his hair. He had to get a grip on himself. He'd come very close to losing control last night. He hadn't been that aroused without having sex since he was a teenager. Probably before he'd actually even had sex. He'd had a lot of sex since then, but none like the sex he'd been having in that dream. The problem was that was all it was, a dream, so it didn't count. Standing, he grabbed yesterday's shirt off the floor and gave Boot a gentle nudge. He was still asleep at the foot of the bed, snoring like a bear. Gov immediately envied him. He would trade anything, save the dream he'd just had, to be able sleep like that for three more hours. Instead he headed to the kitchen to make coffee.

As the coffee maker sputtered and steamed, Gov turned his attention to his phone. Shit. It was Mother's Day. Too late to send a gift, not that Sheryl Scott would expect anything from him in a timely fashion anyway. Hopefully, Kenzie had sent her flowers or chocolates or something and had done him a solid by signing his name. Which his mother would, of course, see right through. She'd thank him for the gift right before telling him what it was. But Mother's Day also meant dinner reservations would be hard to come by. With any luck most mothers preferred to be taken out to brunch, Gov reasoned and started scrolling on his phone for options. It was too early to call anywhere and Open Table showed nothing decent available until nine o'clock. He knew Mac could always squeeze them in at the bar, but that wasn't an ideal setting for a first date. He needed a quiet table, somewhere where they didn't feel rushed, with enough privacy for them to talk and get to know each other on a more personal level. Last night had started out that way but had quickly escalated to something sexual, almost carnal. He wanted to date Laurel Reynolds, not just sleep with her. And he wanted her to know that.

He poured himself a cup of coffee and stared out the kitchen window. The sun was up now, drenching the basin in unrelieved golden light. So she'd been married. For a couple of years. And with the guy for the better part of a decade. Gov had trouble relating; he'd never been in a romantic relationship anywhere near that long. But it did make him wonder what had suddenly gone wrong, after all that time together. She didn't say; he didn't ask. Did it matter? Not at all, he decided and concentrated on what he did know. For one thing, the ex-husband must be a complete and utter fool to let a woman like Laurel slip through his fingers. Unless she'd wanted out. No, Gov thought, her eyes said otherwise. They'd grown melancholy when she spoke of the marriage, but not forlorn. So she'd accepted that the relationship was over and was ready to move on. With him and starting tonight if he had anything to say about it. So he really needed a damn dinner reservation. He'd offer to make something here—he was a decent enough cook—but that seemed like too much too soon, staying in on a first date. Reno had a plethora of dining options, but he didn't want to make the trek down the mountain if he didn't have to. In a perfect world, he'd secure a quiet table by a window where they could bask in the alpenglow over a bottle of wine and have a proper meal. He'd like to enjoy some wine himself, so he didn't want to venture too far from home.

Gov heard sounds of entry and turned to see Boot standing at the bedroom door. "How about a long walk this morning, old buddy? We'll kill two birds with one stone; get our juices flowing and come up with a game plan for tonight." Gov drained his cup before setting it in the sink and returning to the bedroom to get dressed, talking to Boot all the while. "I might have to ask you to be flexible about your bedtime routine tonight. Like real flexible," Gov told him, grabbing the leash and shoving his phone in his pocket. "Tell you what, we'll get your business out of the way, then head for the dog park." Boot's eyes danced as he panted with excitement. Sometimes Gov swore he understood what he was saying. "After that, if I can't get someone to answer the phone at some of the finer establishments in town, we'll pop in a few places." Gov bent down and attached Boot's leash to his collar and gave the dog's head a good rubdown. "Who could say no to this face?"

Everyone, apparently. The restaurants were slammed, overbooked from open to close. And Gov had another problem. He didn't have Laurel's cell or a way to reach her. He'd texted Jack to see if the house had a landline, but he was unable to help. He dealt with the management company directly and they were closed on Sundays. The White Pages listed a dozen Bakers in town, none of whom lived on Southwood. That was a long shot anyway; why would the owner pay for a landline in a rental when everyone had a cell phone these days? Then Gov got a lucky break. He was driving home, intending for he and Boot to drop by Laurel's to touch base about tonight, when he noticed the receipt from North Shore Pizza on the truck console. And stapled to that receipt was two order slips with their names and numbers on them.

Bingo.

He'd figure out the when and where later, but he called Laurel to ask if six o'clock would work. The call immediately went to voice mail and instead of leaving a message he texted her to that effect. She replied that would be fine and that she was looking forward to it. And she wasn't the only one, Gov thought as he dialed Mac's cell.

"Make it quick," Mac groused.

Gov could hear the din from the restaurant in the background. "Well, Happy Mother's Day to you. Busy day?"

Mac ignored the the rhetorical question. "Let me guess. You want another bottle of the Barbera."

"For starters. But I really need a table for tonight."

Mac laughed sardonically. "Where? Some place they don't celebrate Mother's Day?"

"I know it's a big ask."

"Could this have something to do with a certain redhead?"

"No rust on you. I'm flexible on the time."

Mac let out a calculated breath and after a few seconds of dead air said, "Come in around seven. Things should be settling down by then. I'll squeeze you in somewhere, but it might not be pretty."

Gov clenched a victorious fist in the air. "Thanks. I owe you."

"I'll add it to the list."

"At least I'm a good tipper."

"Relatively speaking."

"Seriously, Mac, thank you. I really appreciate it."

"Yeah, yeah, yeah, I know. But I'm not just doing it for you. I'm doing it for Ronnie." He paused, then finished on a softer note, "The girl could do worse."

~~~

"Happy Mother's Day," Laurel said into the phone, sucking in her cheeks and studying herself in the bedroom mirror. She'd lost some weight and was starting to look a little gaunt.

"Thank you," Carli Harper replied. "Maybe someday I'll be able to say the same to you."

"Don't hold your breath," Laurel told her best friend. "Did you get breakfast in bed?"

Carli laughed without opening her mouth. "Hardly. Zack had a gig last night. He's still asleep."

"The life of being married to a professional musician."

"Yeah. But I knew what I was getting into. Ronnie made sure of that."

"How are you feeling?"

"Fine. I'm through the first trimester so not as tired. But with two kids under five, it really doesn't matter if I'm tired or not. Life goes on."

"It actually sounds pretty quiet there," Laurel commented, twisting her hair into a makeshift bun on the top of her head, then letting it fall.

"The boys are watching *Dinosaur Train*. I bribed them with my parents' pool. We're going over there later for an early dinner. Dad and Zack are in charge of that, so Mom and I will sit out back and relax while the boys swim."

"That's nice. Wish her a Happy Mother's Day for me." Hearing Carli's plans made her miss her mother. She felt bad about not seeing her today, especially with Ronnie gone, but Veronica had insisted that Laurel stay the course in Tahoe. She and Mark were flying to Vegas tonight anyway. He had business there first thing in the morning.

"Will do. And since I have a temporary reprieve and we haven't spoken in a couple of days, tell me everything. Anything new with the tall, dark and handsome handyman?" Carli wanted to know.

"Turns out he's a lot more than a handyman." Laurel brought her friend up to speed. "So I didn't just call to wish you a Happy Mother's Day. I don't know what to wear."

The sound of running water ceased and Laurel imagined Carli holding the phone in the crook of her shoulder while she dried sippy cups. "Where are you going for dinner? I haven't been up there in years, but I assume Tahoe is still pretty casual. Classy, but casual. Surely you brought a little black dress just in case?"

"I don't know where we're going. It's a Sunday night in what used to be considered shoulder season so who knows what all is open. And yes, I brought a black dress," Laurel told her, walking over to the closet.

"The black shift dress, the epitome of classy casual."

"With what shoes? Wedges, flats, slip-ons?"

"Wedges. You have that Sam Edelman with the gauzy sleeves that is length-appropriate but still shows a little leg. Did you bring that one?"

"I did," Laurel answered, pulling it out and holding it up in front of her. "But what if we end up at a beachfront place with plastic tables and chairs on the sand? I don't want to appear presumptive."

"Laurel, even the beach bars on that side of the lake serve Rombauer. Overdress to impress."

She hung the dress over the closet door and grabbed her black wedges and placed them on the floor beneath it. "You're right. I don't know why I'm so nervous."

"Hmm, let's see. Maybe because you haven't had a first date in about ten years?"

Carli was right and Laurel knew it, but she couldn't stop herself from saying, "Neither have you."

Now her friend laughed wholeheartedly. "True. But that's what happens when you marry your high school sweetheart and have a couple of kids. Plus the stay-at-home mom dating scene isn't what it's cracked up to be."

Part of Laurel envied her friend's life and part of her didn't know how she did it. But Carli was happy and that was all that mattered. "Okay, so the black Sam Edelman with wedges," she said, ignoring a call from an unfamiliar number.

"And—hold on," Carli interrupted herself to address her older son, "Nick, hands to yourself," she called in a firm voice. "Sorry, where were we?" she asked, returning to the conversation. "Oh, yeah, accessories. Small black purse, like a crossbody. Functional but still appropriate for evening and your diamond studs. That's it. No necklace, bracelets, etc."

"That's easy. Do you ever miss working?" Carli had been a buyer for a chain of department stores. "Sometimes I forget how good you are at it."

"Thanks. And yes, sometimes. But most of the time I'm too busy to miss it. And it'll be there when the kids are older. Between the cost of childcare and Zack's schedule, it wouldn't be worth the hassle. I feel fortunate we have the choice; many families don't."

They spoke for a few more minutes, mostly about Laurel's progress on the book and the beginnings of a plan for Carli and her family to come up for the Fourth of July weekend. "The kids would love the fireworks. Apparently it's gone high tech with drones. They don't set them off from a barge in the middle of the lake like when we were kids."

"God, I've haven't thought about that in ages. I'll try to make it work. And I have to say, I thought you were crazy at first, but this was the right thing to do. I can hear it in your voice."

"Thanks. Even my mother seems to be on board now."

"Well, that says something. I've got to go round up the troops. Have a great time tonight."

Laurel caught herself smiling. "I just might. Thanks for the fashion advice."

"My pleasure. In exchange I want all the gory details so I can live vicariously through you."

"As if you'd change a thing."

"I wouldn't. And that's another thing I hope to share with you one day."

After they hung up Laurel walked outside and sat on the deck for a while, thinking about what Carli had said. Could she honestly look back at her life with Grant and say she wouldn't change a thing? She'd experienced all the typical feelings of inadequacy a woman does after infidelity. Could she have presented herself better, been more attractive? More adventurous in bed? Been a better life partner? Money had never been an issue between them, so that didn't apply. They'd never discussed a timeline for having a family; neither one of them seemed to be in a hurry. Yet here Grant was, married with a toddler. She hadn't thought much about becoming a mother, she'd just assumed the time would eventually come. But now she couldn't fathom parenting with Grant any more than she could have imagined the two of them like the older couple on the beach. She also couldn't imagine counting on him the way Carli counted on Zack, from putting all her financial eggs in one basket to pausing her career for the good of the family to letting him sleep in on Mother's Day because he'd had a late night. And not thinking a thing of it. But maybe that's what had been missing from her marriage. That sense of teamwork, the one for all and all for one, the not mine or yours, but ours mentality. In her defense, Grant had an example of marriage and she had not. Yet, he'd still managed to screw it up.

Speaking of marriage, McGovern Scott had admittedly never even been close, but not because he was at all opposed to the idea. By all accounts he came from a solid family and was presumably looking for the same. She suddenly wondered what he must think of her. Being divorced at her age, coming from celebrity, leaving a good job to chase a dream. Growing up where she had, as much as Ronnie and her mom had tried to shield her from it, divorces and affairs and pretenses had been the rule rather than the exception. But Ronnie had told her more than once that they would be that exception, she would see to it. And Laurel felt like they'd done a pretty good job of that. She had nothing to be ashamed of.

Returning to her phone, Laurel checked her texts and was surprised to find one from Gov. He'd been the unfamiliar caller, she realized, taking note of the number. Normally she would have found that unsettling since they hadn't exchanged numbers, but he had numerous connections in town. Between the pizza parlor and his employer, it wouldn't be hard for him to track her down. Her spirits instantly lifted and she felt a little giddy as she texted him back to confirm their evening plans.

She attempted to start a new chapter with no avail. So she went back over her notes, tried to add some details for the setting and firm up the background stories on her protagonists. That's when Laurel realized she'd spent considerably more time on the hero. In fact, she couldn't even form a visual of Whitney in her head. Was she blonde? Brunette? Redhead? Did her eye color mirror that of the hero? Complement it? Contrast it? Had she been unlucky in love before or had this been the love of her life? Was she realizing she'd been going through the motions in the relationship or was she truly heartbroken? Whitney was a California girl, that much Laurel knew. But should she buck convention and make her a dark-haired, brown-eyed beauty, or go with the blonde, blue-eyed, perpetually suntanned stereotype? Did that insult the reader? And why had she sworn off men? Infidelity? Sudden change of heart? A dark past rearing its ugly head? Or was that part of the mystery of her? Something that would evolve with the story as Whitney built a new life.

The next thing Laurel knew it was time to get ready. Her nails were a mess, so she started there, shaping them and throwing on a coat of clear polish. She took more time than usual with her hair—the high desert climate here was definitely her friend—and the Tahoe sun had weaved in some blonde highlights. She put on black lace panties to match her favorite bra. For no particular reason, she told herself.

She was ready by five-thirty, dressed to the nines and smelling of lavender and rose oil. She poured herself a glass of wine, then debated if she should set a second glass out for Gov. Would they have time for a drink here or need to get going? She hadn't thought to get an appetizer to offer, let alone have beer or hard liquor on hand. She sipped the wine carefully, as not to smudge her lip gloss, and paced around the kitchen. She felt ridiculous, like a schoolgirl going to her first dance, not a grown woman going out to dinner. She had no sooner walked to the powder room to check her reflection for the umpteenth time when the doorbell rang. Pushing down the butterflies in her stomach, she headed down the hall with the distinct feeling that she, like her inchoate protagonist, was also starting over.

# CHAPTER SIX

GOV ARRIVED AT Laurel's just before six feeling pretty good about himself for pulling this whole thing together. Sure, he'd have to put up with Mac's ribbing for a while, but that was a small price to pay to share the evening with Laurel. As was wearing dress pants and a button down shirt for the third time this week. And he'd checked off the rest of his to-do list in short order. He'd sweet-talked Charlene into squeezing him in for a quick trim, gotten the last decent bouquet of flowers at the grocery store and picked up a nice bottle of Cabernet on sale. Sundown should be around eight, so they had time for a drink here before heading over to Hues of Blue. No rush there either; as long as they were near a window by seven-thirty they could take full advantage of the sunset and subsequent alpenglow. He unfurled himself from the truck and stepped out into the lush spring evening. The air was warm, the sky was cloudless and the waning sunlight filtered through the aspens, casting an iridescent glow over the basin. He walked to the passenger side and grabbed the flowers and wine off the seat, then headed up to the front door with a spring in his step. He felt so much better about things, so much more in control of his emotions than he had last night and was determined to keep it that way.

But the second he saw Laurel, he knew that would be impossible.

She was wearing a black dress that let her breasts peek out just enough for Gov to taste them with his eyes and a hemline that hit mid-thigh. Her hair was sexily disheveled and seemed longer, resting at the curve of those voluptuous breasts. The thought of running his fingers through that hair and burying his face in that cleavage made his heart race and his cock throb. Her skin had taken on a shimmery luster, mimicking the evening light and her smile was heartfelt but tentative as she looked at him from behind bottomless chestnut eyes. She smelled intoxicating, feminine and fresh, like thousands of flowers blooming at once. He wanted to douse himself in her scent, gather her in his arms and hold her until she melted into him and they became one. Then he realized she was talking. Gov shook off the stupor. "Hi," he returned around a gulp. "Laurel, you look incredible."

"Thank you. You clean up quite nicely yourself."

He stepped inside and after she closed the door said, "I come bearing gifts." He handed her the flowers, still in their cone-shaped wrapper. "This was the best I could do. Mother's Day and all."

"They're beautiful. Thank you," she replied, accepting the bouquet. "I think I saw a vase in the pantry. Come on back."

He indulged himself in her sculptured legs and firm butt as he followed her past the living room and down the hall. Once they reached the kitchen he set the wine on the island, then looked on as she searched for a vase and went to the sink to fill it. He shoved his hands in his pockets for safekeeping.

"I just poured myself a glass of wine. Do we have time for one together before we go?" she asked, gesturing to the open bottle and two glasses on the counter next to the sink.

"Sure. Our reservation isn't until seven. To be honest, we don't really have a reservation. Mac is squeezing us in."

"How nice," she said, turning off the water. She dried her hands and grabbed a pair of scissors out of a drawer. She removed the cellophane and superfluous greenery, then cut the stems at a diagonal before placing the flowers in the vase. She set them on the counter and started fussing with them needlessly. Her hands were shaking and Gov could all but see her heart beating outside of her chest.

"Laurel. Stop."

After a few silent clicks, she met his gaze. Her eyes were agog and full of apprehension. She swallowed hard and pressed her lips together. He turned her to face him and tilted her chin up with his index finger. "I'm nervous too. And I'm never nervous."

She blew out a cutting breath and gave him a weak smile. He leaned down and laid a gentle kiss on her lips. She circled his neck with her arms and fell into him as he drew her to him. He kissed her deeply, thoroughly, then simply held her. She rested her head on his shoulder and he could feel her heartbeat start to settle, then sync with his. They stood there in silence for a long moment. Finally, she said, "Thank God. I thought I was the only one."

He angled out of her embrace. "I'm pretty sure we're in this together, if that makes you feel any better."

"It does. It's just been so long since I've…" her voice trailed off as she searched the kitchen for the words, "had a date. Or anything else."

He met her uneasy gaze with a sure one. "Me too. And there's no need to rush into anything. I'm not going anywhere."

"I know. But I find myself in a hurry anyway. That's new for me."

"I'll take that as a compliment. Now, let's have some wine to calm our nerves and then get over to Hues of Blue. You can't go wrong there at sunset. There's not a bad seat in the house." He paused, then finished on a lighter note, "Tell me you're a sunset, not a sunrise, person."

"Definitely sunset. If it wasn't for the birds, I'd sleep until noon."

"Good to know. Feel better?"

She nodded, then gave him a peck on the lips before turning her attention back to the flowers. She set them on the kitchen table, then poured him a glass of wine. "Let's go out on the deck. It's such a lovely night."

They sat at the table as the day wound down and the breeze picked up. It lifted Laurel's hair just enough for Gov to get a good look at her neck. God, he'd love to get his mouth on it and work his way down. All the way down. He pushed away the thought and they chatted colloquially for a bit. Just before seven, Gov suggested they get going. "Even if we end up eating at the bar, we'll want to cull out a spot in front of the windows for the sunset. We can stand if we have to."

They locked up and Laurel turned on a few lights. "This is the first night since I've been here that I've gone out in the evening."

Gov had every intention of her making that a habit. But he only said, "It's always a good idea to be cautious, but this is a safe area. An occasional speeding ticket or a drunk and disorderly is about all that keeps the cops busy around here."

They exited through the garage and Laurel closed it behind them using the outdoor keypad. Gov opened the passenger side door for her and helped her into the truck. Once he was behind the wheel he asked, "How do you like the Range?"

"There's not much not to like about it. It was Ronnie's—my grandmother. Mom didn't see any point in it going to waste, especially with me coming up here."

"You called her Ronnie?"

"Yeah. It's a long story."

"I'd like to hear it."

She cocked her head to the side and gave him an amused smile. "Maybe, if you're a very good boy, I'll tell you. But I have a feeling you might already know," she said, pointing to his phone sitting in the cupholder.

"You can't believe everything you read, especially online. Besides, Google didn't say anything about you and that's what I'm interested in," Gov told her and meant it. He shifted gears and backed up using the camera on the dash. "If it wasn't for Mac, I wouldn't have even known to look."

"I'll have to thank him for enlightening you," she said with a waggish grin.

"He'd love that. To be honest, I didn't know who your grandmother was. Apparently I should be shot."

"That's going a little far. Maybe just tarred and feathered."

Stopped at a light, Gov looked over at her. Her eyes were shining with humor. "You're enjoying this."

"I might be. But there's not as much to tell as you may think. You might be disappointed to learn how normal my childhood was. And that, like the lack of information on the Internet, was not by accident. The real story is the work it took to make it that way."

Gov took that in with a thoughtful nod as they drove through town. They both commented on the unprecedented growth and influx of wealth that Tahoe had experienced in recent years. Ten minutes later they were walking into Hues of Blue. Laurel paused just inside the entrance at the top of the stairs and let out an appreciative sigh.

"It never gets old, does it?' Gov remarked.

"There's no view of the basin quite like it." She turned to face him. "It's nice that you feel that way too, since you've lived here all your life."

"Anyone who doesn't needs to get their eyes checked." He clasped one hand in hers, then gestured in front of them with the other. "Shall we?" They walked down the stairs to the hostess stand. They were welcomed by a young woman wearing a hospitable smile that quickly became a confused frown. "I'm sorry, Gov. I don't see a reservation for you. You usually sit at the bar, don't you?"

Before Gov could reply, Mac appeared. "They're with me, Casey," he informed the hostess. "Last-minute booking. I'll take it from here." He grabbed two menus from behind the podium. "Right this way, folks."

He was going to pay dearly for this one, Gov thought as they followed Mac to the back of the restaurant. He'd never been in this section before but had a sneaking suspicion that the small table angled in the corner near the bay window hadn't been there this morning.

Mac was all smiles as he pulled out a chair. "Miss?"

"Thank you, Mac," Laurel said, sitting down.

"Ah, my reputation proceeds me. It's a pleasure to see you again, Ms. Reynolds."

"Laurel. Likewise. You haven't changed a bit."

"Oh, not much changes around here," Mac replied around a laugh, then sobered. "I was so sorry to hear about Ronnie. She was a one of kind."

"Thank you. She was quite fond of you."

"The feeling was mutual. Please pass on my condolences to your mother."

"I will," Laurel promised. "She'll likely be up to visit this summer. I'm sure she'll want to stop in and see you."

"I'll look forward to it," he said, handing her, then Gov, a menu. "Enjoy."

"Thanks, Mac," Gov told him, settling into his chair.

The older man put his hands on Gov's shoulders from behind, then leaned down and whispered in his ear, "I need a new putter, want to add a mallet to my bag. Jimmy in the pro shop has one set aside for me. And tip your waitstaff, especially Mary, big. She's staying late for you and helped me drag this table out of storage."

Gov nodded in acknowledgement as Mac took his leave. He'd actually expected worse.

"What was that all about?" Laurel asked over the top of her menu.

"Nothing. He just wanted to make sure we knew about the specials tonight."

She held up the menu insert. "They're right here."

She didn't miss a trick. Gov pretended to peruse the menu. "Huh. How about that?"

"Gov," she said, reaching across the table and laying her hand on his, "thank you."

He lifted his gaze to meet hers. He felt the emotion swirling in her eyes catch in his throat. He nodded and squeezed her hand. "You're welcome."

Just then Mary, one of the restaurant's long-tenured waitresses, appeared with a bottle of Barbera. "Hey, Gov," she greeted. "Funny to see out here. You're usually in the cheap seats."

"No cheap seats here, you know that. Laurel, this is Mary. Mary, Laurel."

"Nice to meet you, Laurel," Mary said with a bright smile, opening the wine and pouring Gov a sample. "What brings you guys in tonight?"

As if she didn't know, Gov thought, taking a sip, then nodding in approval. "Laurel's new in town and I thought I'd introduce her to one of Incline's finer dining establishments."

"Good answer. But here it's really all about the people," she replied, filling their glasses, then setting the bottle on the table. "And the sunset." She gestured toward the window. "You'll have a bird's-eye view. I'll be back in a few minutes to check on you."

After she left, Laurel gave Gov a mischievous look and said, "Do you know everybody?"

"Just about. I know Mac and he knows everybody," Gov answered with a tip of the head. "The show is starting." They looked on as the top half of the golden sun slid behind the jagged peaks, leaving behind a fusion of pastels that glowed like millions of fireflies converging on a summer night.

"Absolutely breathtaking."

"I'll say." But Gov was looking at her, not the alpenglow. Laurel looked like a celestial goddess in the luminous light. He had to stop himself from touching her to ensure she was real.

"Why don't we watch it every night?" she asked, turning to him.

Gov forced himself back to the real world. "Life gets in the way," he answered with a shrug. "And we take it for granted, like so many other things."

"Yeah," Laurel agreed. Their eyes met and clung for a long moment before the lights came up in the restaurant. "I need to be better about that."

"We all do."

She smiled and took a sip of wine. Mary returned and took their orders and topped off their glasses. After she left, Laurel said, "Okay, shoot."

Gov sent her a blank look. "I'm going to need a little more to go on."

"What do you want to know? It's only fair; you told me about your family, your background, your job."

Gov looked deeply into her eyes. "Laurel, I'm interested in you because of you. Not because Ronnie Reynolds was your grandmother." He was also interested in the idiot ex-husband, but he'd keep that to himself.

"I know. But that would be like you talking about your childhood and not mentioning your parents or your sister. It's impossible."

"Then start at the beginning," he suggested with a shrug. "That's what I did."

Laurel took a moment to gather her thoughts, then began, "I was born to an unwed, seventeen-year-old mother who grew up in L.A. during a time that romanticized rebellion and encouraged experimentation and came from such. Her parents divorced when she was young and her father died a few years later. Her mother was a former model, an incredibly talented singer, a celebrity for time immemorial. She was also desperately insecure, uncomfortable in her own skin and suffered from impostor syndrome. But at the same time she was a committed, loving and selfless mother. She struggled to be present for her daughter while trying to make it in the unforgiving and often cruel world that is show business. She was doing everything good enough but nothing well." Laurel paused and took another sip of wine.

Gov already knew some of this, of course. It was a matter of public record.

"My mother spent her formative years on the road, touring with Ronnie. She had nannies and tutors, lived in hotels, rarely had a home-cooked meal. But Ronnie tucked her in every night before the show. Sometimes Mom would wake up in the morning and find Ronnie asleep next to her still dressed up from the night before. She did as much of the parenting as she could, but still carried tremendous guilt for the life they were living. She became increasingly distracted and nervous on stage. She started drinking before the show, during the show, after the show. The habit carried over to their stints at home, which were becoming longer and longer as Ronnie's career struggled. One summer my mother spent a few months with her grandparents in San Francisco; it was Ronnie's first attempt at rehab. It didn't stick, but it did get her thinking. When the therapist told her to go to a happy place in her mind, she found herself in Tahoe. She had gone there with her parents a few times as girl. So she bought a place up here, where she could go to regroup, recharge, try to get and stay sober. By now my mother was in high school and a little precocious." Laurel took a deep pull of water, chased it down with more wine. "She never really outgrew her flower child roots."

"Hence, your name. Laurel, like the canyon," Gov interjected, deciding they were going to need another bottle of wine.

She lifted her eyebrows in approval and surprise. "Right. You've done your homework. Having said that Mom started to see the error of Ronnie's ways, some of them anyway. Not that she necessarily wanted to. She was having a good time. She had a cool mom, some newfound teenage freedom, plenty of spending money. But the more she was at home the more stable, yet somehow unstable her life became. She was attending school regularly for the first time, joining clubs, going to dances. She was also going to friends' houses, seeing how their families were structured, how they interacted, the way their homes were run. Remember this is Beverly Hills, so being the daughter of a celebrity doesn't make you special. She also discovered that boys thought she was cute and she was drawn to that male attention. As well as all the forbidden fruits teenagers are curious about." Laurel was pausing to take a breath when a waiter appeared and placed a salad in front of each of them. Gov ordered another bottle of wine. After a couple of bites, Laurel asked, "Bored yet?"

"Not in the least. Go on. I have a feeling we're getting to the best part."

She acknowledged that with a smile, then continued, "But unbeknownst to my mother, Ronnie had a plan.

All she needed was a few more good years, another Top 40 hit or two and she could get them out of the business, give Mom a normal life. The problem was that she had developed terrible stage fright over the years and couldn't perform unless she was buzzed. The first summer they came up here she relapsed, but she still sold out six nights a week. So who cares, right?"

Gov nodded in response. The question was obviously rhetorical and reiterated what Mac had already told him. Just then he appeared with their second bottle of wine, already open. "Mary is taking a little break. I think we're past the ceremonial tasting at this point in our relationship," Mac told Gov, dispensing the wine and swapping out the empty bottle for the new one. "I'm sure your dinners will be right up."

Once he was gone, Laurel picked the story back up. "By now, my mother was sixteen. She'd been seeing a boy from school behind Ronnie's back. One night they went on a car date. One thing led to another and voilà!" She pointed her index fingers inward.

"That's been happening since the beginning of time." Gov waved off the editorialization. "And frankly it's about the least remarkable thing you've said so far."

"True enough," Laurel snickered in agreement. "To hear my mother tell it, she had a sneaking suspicion right afterward. She saw the boy a few more times, but once he realized *that* wasn't going to happen again, he dumped her. His family moved away shortly thereafter and she never saw him again."

"So he doesn't know about you?' Gov couldn't imagine not knowing his father. Or not knowing that he was one.

"No." Laurel shook her head. "To a man that probably seems selfish and cruel, but remember this was over thirty years ago. It wasn't as accepted as it is now to have a baby alone and keep it. And if you're the teenage daughter of a celebrity, there are some added layers of risk. Scandal, blackmail, even kidnapping. Still, after I was born, my mother did try to locate the family with no avail. She found out a few years later that my father died in a car accident at age twenty-one. End of story."

"And you never wanted to find his family? Your grandparents? Any half-siblings?"

"Oddly, no. I was perfectly content with Mom and Ronnie. And Rosa. She was our housekeeper."

Just then their dinners arrived, suspending the conversation. They talked easily over cedar plank salmon and braised short ribs, garlic mashed potatoes and roasted asparagus. Gov told her about growing up in Reno, about being a bit of a loner in high school until he made the baseball team sophomore year, his father's aversion to politics, his mother coming from the early settlers of Nevada. Family camping trips, summers at the lake, panning for gold with his grandfather.

"That sounds like a wonderful, normal childhood," Laurel said between bites.

"I never really thought about it, but I guess it was. Pretty boring compared to yours. I couldn't wait to get out of here. Then I couldn't wait to come back."

"Mine wasn't nearly as colorful as you may think. People always thought of Ronnie as a force of nature, but it was really my mother who called the shots after I came along. She claims I saved them, but she literally and figuratively saved all three of us. Something clicked in her once she found out she was pregnant. She laid down the law; no more relapses for Ronnie and no more excuses for her. Ronnie got sober once and for all, Mom got her degree and they both dedicated themselves to our family. Ronnie gave up the stage and started writing songs; Mom took care of me and helped Ronnie run things behind the scenes." Laurel went on to say that neither her mother nor herself had inherited Ronnie's musical genes and that Ronnie had considered that a blessing. "She didn't want my mother, let alone me, to go into the business. They wanted me to have a regular life out of the spotlight. Fame and fortune isn't always what it's cracked up to be."

"I'll have to take your word on that." Gov said, as their dinner dishes were cleared. "I have it on good authority they succeeded with the normal life thing though. Which brings me to a confession of sorts. "

Laurel's face fell a bit, but she managed to catch it. Straightening up in her chair, she seemed to be steeling herself against whatever he was about to say.

"I knew some of that. Some from Mac, some from a Google search, some from my mother."

Laurel's stoic expression instantly relaxed. Gov wondered what she thought he was going to admit to. "Your mother?" she bemused, as coffee was served.

"As a girl, you used to play on the beach here in the summer, right?"

She shrugged indifferently. "All the time."

"My family rented a condo on that same beach every July. My mom would stay with us and my dad would come up for long weekends. She said we used to see you guys around town and that Ronnie and your mom were always lovely, didn't expect any special treatment, didn't want to draw any attention to themselves. She also said you were friends with some local girls."

"Thanks. And yes, it was sometimes just Mom and I, but whoever was out on the beach that day would play together. And sometimes Carli would come up with us."

"Carli?"

Now Laurel's eyes softened and began to shine. "My best friend, Rosa's daughter. Rosa didn't live with us; she had her own home and family."

"You'll have to tell me more about that too." They'd talked predominantly about her mother and grand-mother and barely scrapped the surface about her. "Anyway, my mom used to take my sister and me to the beach and she'd see you guys. She said you and your mom would be out there from morning until night and that Ronnie would come out from time to time."

"Mom was more like an older sister in many ways. We used to bury each other in the sand, build sand-castles, play Barbies in the water. She never really got to be a kid. Summers in Tahoe served more than one purpose; it was also a chance for Ronnie to give my mother the childhood she'd missed." She paused for a moment and sipped her coffee. Then she shot him a look from under her lashes and said, "You told your mother about me?"

Shit, Gov thought. He'd walked right into that one. He cleared his throat. "Not in the way you think. The night we met, after Mac scolded me for not knowing who Ronnie Reynolds was, he told me some stories. I asked my mom about it the next day since we spent so much time up here then."

Just as Laurel opened her mouth in reply, Mary came by with the check. It was then that Gov realized they were the only ones left in the restaurant. "All done, folks?" she asked hopefully, handing Gov a leather folder. "I can cork the rest of the wine."

He took the hint and settled the bill. They walked out through the restaurant hand in hand. The waitstaff was changing out the tablecloths, the waitresses were cashing out their tips and Mac was wiping down the bar. It made Gov wonder if this was when Ronnie would come by and try out a new song. What a treat that must have been for the staff as they closed down for the night. When they were out in front waiting for the car to be brought around, Laurel turned to him and said, "Thank you for dinner. It was lovely." She reached up and gave him a peck on the cheek.

"My pleasure. The conversation was even better than the food. And the food here never disappoints."

"Anything else you'd like to know?"

"Yeah." Gov looked down at her and matched her playful grin. "Why did you call her Ronnie?"

Laurel threw her head back in laughter and leaned against him. "That'll cost you another dinner."

Just then the valet returned with the truck and helped Laurel inside while Gov took the wheel. They rode in companionable silence and once they got to Laurel's, Gov grabbed the wine from the backseat and walked around to the passenger side. But Laurel was already out of the car, standing there waiting for him. She was staring at him expectantly, her eyes gleaming in the moonlight, her mouth curved upward in a shy smile. He swallowed hard and said, "I'll walk you up."

She put her arm through his and as they walked up the driveway to the garage. Punching in the entry code, she asked, "Would you like to come in?"

Yes, Gov thought, I would. I would like to come in, kiss you like you've never been kissed, carry you to bed and make love to you all night long. But he heard himself say, "Just for a minute. I need to get going."

"Sure," she said, sounding a little disappointed. Or was that just wishful thinking on his part?

They walked through the laundry room and into the kitchen. Laurel put her purse on the island and Gov set the wine next to it, then turned to her and gathered her in his arms. "Thanks for a great night. I'd like to do it again."

"Me too." Her voice hitched a bit.

He lowered his gaze to her mouth and leaned down to kiss her, reminding himself to take it slow, pace himself this time. That proved to be undoable because she met him halfway and unleashed her mouth on his. Hers was hot and greedy and he surrendered to it, returning the want and need in equal measure. He slid his hands down her back and glued them to her buttocks, trying to keep himself in check. But she wreathed his neck and pressed his body to hers, pinning his burgeoning erection to the vee between her legs. His tongue found hers and began to feed until there wasn't a shared breath between them. He left her mouth on reluctant, shotgun breaths and buried his face in her hair. He had to get a grip. He could feel himself starting to surge.

Laurel dropped her arms to his waist and fell into him. They stood there in silence, their heavy breaths filling the sultry air, her breasts heaving hard and fast against his chest. He wanted them in his hands, in his mouth, under him. He wanted her out of that dress and naked, her legs coiled around his, her cries of passion in his ear. He wanted to bury himself inside her and make her come over and over, like in his dream. By now her breathing had leveled and her heartbeat had settled. Considerably. "Laurel," he murmured, leaning out of her embrace. "I—" he cut himself off. She was snuggled against him, her arms still wrapped around his middle, her head nestled in the crook of his shoulder. Her eyes were completely shut, her dark, feathery lashes resting on the tiny creases beneath them. Her mouth had taken on a crescent moon-like shape, as if she'd dozed off mid-smile. She'd reminded him of a goddess earlier, now she looked more like a cherub. He couldn't help but laugh. He'd never put a woman to sleep before. Well, that would put an end to things for the evening. He stroked her cheek with the back of his hand. "Laurel," he repeated softly.

Her eyes fluttered open and she gave him a confused, startled look. The she straightened up and shook herself awake. "Oh, God. Did I fall asleep?"

"I think so."

"I'm so sorry," she flustered, throwing a mortified hand over her mouth.

"I'll try not to take it personally," Gov replied around a chuckle.

"It's not you! I wanted to…I was enjoying…"

"I know. It's okay. It's late and we had a lot of wine." He grazed his lips over hers. "I need to get going anyway. Boot will be waiting."

She gave him a dismayed look and laid the palm of her hand on his cheek. "Gov… I don't know what to say. I'm so embarrassed."

"You can make it up to me. What are you doing tomorrow?" He took her hand in his and started walking them out of the kitchen.

She shrugged. "Everyday is kind of lather, rinse, repeat for me."

"I need to run down to Reno first thing, but I'll be back mid-afternoon. How about I come by around five-thirty? We can take Boot for his evening constitution, he'd love this neighborhood with all the old-growth trees, then grab something to eat."

"That'll make up for me falling asleep like that? Something we might have done anyway?"

"No, but it's a start."

"Okay," she told him with a giggle. Then her face grew serious and she put her arms around him. "Thank you again. For everything."

Gov held her close and kissed the top of her head. "My pleasure. Well, almost," he teased. He opened the laundry room door and took his leave through the garage. She watched him get into the truck and they exchanged a parting wave before she shut the garage door and disappeared into the house. Gov sat there for a long moment, thinking. Hearing about Laurel's family had made him think about his own. He threw the car in gear and headed for home, remembering a game his mother had made them play at dinner when he was growing up. They all had to go around the table and say what they'd learned today—good or bad. He used to roll his eyes and make a smart aleck remark half the time, earning a dirty look from his father. But occasionally in his adult life he'd thought about that at the end of the day, what he'd learned. And today he'd learned that in only one week's time, he'd fallen in love with Laurel Reynolds.

# CHAPTER SEVEN

LAUREL WAS OF two minds the next morning. She was still incredibly embarrassed about falling asleep like that. But she was also incredibly excited to be seeing Gov again tonight. He'd seemed unfazed by the whole thing, laughed it off in fact. She already knew she liked him, there was something so real, so endearing about him. But that feeling of safety, comfort, compatibility was much harder to come by. She found herself trusting him already. She'd literally fallen asleep in his arms. He could have easily taken advantage of her. Had she let him, would she have woken up this morning with regret along with a wine headache? If she was being honest with herself, no. She wanted him; he clearly wanted her. And that reality usurped her stomach and spun around like an ambivalent top of delight and uneasiness. She was a little rusty in the sex department.

Slow down, she told herself. The last time she'd let herself get caught up, she'd ended up divorced after a decade-long investment. And she was only here for a few months. She'd be gone before Christmas, maybe by Thanksgiving, depending on her progress. The last thing she was looking for was a relationship. She'd come to Tahoe for a fresh start, to pursue a dream and achieve a goal, not fall in love.

That brought Laurel up short. Was she falling in love with Gov? Surely not; she'd only known him for a week! She knew so little about him, yet felt like she knew him so well. They'd talked about their families, their formative years, their careers, but hadn't gotten to previous relationships, let alone her marriage. He hadn't asked about Grant or what happened between them. Should she volunteer the information? Gov appeared to be genuinely interested in her and not at all put off by her failed marriage or her storied family tree. In fact, he seemed wonderfully indifferent to both. He was almost too good to be true.

She had been raised to be cautious, but not paranoid, about that. So many people had an angle in the world she knew, the world she'd grown up in. That was why she hadn't given an express purpose for taking a leave of absence from work. She could see the headlines now—*The Real Ronnie Reynolds Story*—granddaughter writes tell-all. The tabloids would have a field day with even the hint of a scandal, trying to profit by exploiting her loss. Nothing makes more money than making something out of nothing, as Ronnie used to say. How disappointed they would all be to realize that Laurel's novel had nothing to do with her infamous grandmother. Her writing career would be over before it began.

Speaking of her writing career, she needed to get back to it. She'd been contemplating Ronnie's discombobulated lyrics. She'd had the chorus pretty well firmed up—*Once Tahoe got hold of my heart she never let go, like a lover from long ago, who keeps comin' back around, making sure nothing keeps me down*. It made Laurel wonder if Ronnie had taken a lover here back in the day. Surely she hadn't been celibate for the rest of her life after her divorce, although she would often say she had enough trouble of her own without borrowing any from a man. Maybe she'd had a fling or two here and writing about it soothed her soul, brought back those beloved memories, pulled at her heartstrings in all the right ways.

There's an idea. Maybe Whitney and "Scott" had crossed paths in Tahoe in the past. But something had kept them apart, came between them and then life took them in different directions. But had they been lovers? Or was it unrequited love? A one-night stand that should have been more? Or a full-blown romance? Maybe they'd come full circle in their lives, both finding themselves back in Tahoe. Not unlike Ronnie or even herself.

Laurel forced her mind back to the matter at hand, focusing on Whitney. She could see her now in her mind's eye—a strawberry blonde, blue-eyed beauty, tall and slender but with a little meat on her bones. She liked characters who emulated real people, especially female characters. Even if the story ended in happily ever after, which obviously didn't always happen in real life, readers could better relate to a woman with a typical body instead of an unrealistic supermodel type. Someone like themselves, someone they could identify with, someone to cheer for. Someone with flaws, hopes, dreams and a whole lot of moxie. Like, she realized, her mother and Ronnie. And she'd like to think, herself. So Whitney would be a California girl 2.0, beautiful and accomplished, able to stand on her own two feet, but still looking for someone with whom to share her life. A partner to lean on and vice versa, raise a family with and grow old with. And walk on the beach with after years of having each other's back. So the archetypal fairy tale but for today's woman. Whitney wanted it all, was willing to work for it and could do it alone, but she didn't want to. And she was strong enough to admit it.

Morning became afternoon and Laurel found her mind drifting to the evening and the delight and uneasiness in her stomach was joined with trepidation. She got up to stretch her legs and walked around front to check the mail. It was mostly junk, clothing catalogues and local advertisements. But it did make her think about what to wear tonight. She knew Carli would be busy with the boys at this time of day, so she'd have to dress herself like she did every other day. They were just walking the dog, so jeans and a t-shirt would surely do. Gov had technically bought her dinner twice so she should probably offer to reciprocate. Walking inside to the kitchen, she opened the freezer and took stock. Slim pickings but she'd picked up a frozen lasagna to have on hand. She transferred it to the refrigerator and confirmed that she had a couple of bags of salad mix. The corked wine from last night was in the pantry and she had a couple of other bottles as well. She didn't have any bread to make garlic bread, but surely this would be enough.

Feeling a little more in control with having a plan, Laurel stowed her laptop and notes in the bedroom she was using as an office. The room was the smallest of the three bedrooms, with only a twin-sized bed, a chest of drawers and a corner desk and chair, but it was more than sufficient for her needs. She'd wanted to create some kind of physical separation between her writing and the other aspects of her life. Otherwise she'd be a slave to her computer all the time. It was bad enough that she made notes in her phone every time an idea popped into her head. It seemed that some days she couldn't turn the story off, but when she sat down to write she couldn't get anything of consequence down. She wondered if Ronnie had ever felt that way about songwriting.

With dinner defrosting and writing done for the day, Laurel showered. While her hair air-dried, she put together a salad and made some dressing with olive oil, red wine vinegar and spices. If the lasagna didn't turn out, at least the salad was relatively foolproof. If worse came to worst, they could always order a pizza. Like herself, Gov had declined dessert the previous night, so she wasn't going to worry about that. There was always ice cream in a pinch. She put the finishing touches on her hair and applied a little makeup. Just mascara with a dusting of eyeshadow and lip gloss as the sun did most of the work for her here. She'd chosen raw-hem ankle jeans and a white t-shirt and sneakers. She grabbed a jacket and set it by the front door.

And then she waited. Not because Gov was late but because it was barely five o'clock. She poured herself half a glass of wine from the bottle she'd opened last night; she didn't feel right drinking the Barbera without him. She got out placemats, napkins and silverware, another wine glass and two water glasses. She set the table on the deck, using the flowers from Gov as a centerpiece. And then she waited some more. She checked the lasagna's progress, reread the baking instructions, shook the cruet of dressing, touched up her lip gloss and fluffed her hair. She poured herself another half glass of wine and wiped down the counters needlessly, wondering if she should have picked up a dog toy for Boot. Of course not, she scolded herself. He surely had plenty of toys and would be more interested in all the new smells in the house.

She felt a sudden rush of heat and touched the palms of her hands to her cheeks. For some reason, she was burning up. She was contemplating that when she saw a flash go by the kitchen window followed by a resonant voice. The flash came to a screeching halt and a dog with yellow fur and a muscular build appeared. He seemed to momentarily debate resuming his flight, but lowered his head and retraced his steps, trotting this time, in response to what could only be Gov's command.

Laurel started laughing. Hysterically. She'd spent the last thirty minutes driving herself crazy and it had taken the delightful antics of a mutinous dog to bring her back to her senses. She was getting all worked up about going for a walk and serving frozen lasagna. Ronnie was probably looking down at her with equal parts disappointment and frustration, wishing she could tell her to get over herself. Laurel dabbed the corners of her eyes with the edge of the dish towel, then hung it on the stove handle and went to the front door. She was still feeling amused when she opened it to Gov coming up the walk. He was wearing jeans and a Stanford University sweatshirt and carrying a paper grocery bag that was filled to the brim. He gave her a big smile and held her eyes in his for a long moment, then greeted her with a kiss. "Hi."

"Hi," she returned, feeling her stomach jump and her heart swell. Her eyes were still locked on his when she heard a soft whining at her feet. She tore her gaze away from Gov and looked down at the biggest, sweetest set of puppy dog eyes she'd ever seen. She kneeled down and petted the dog's flaxen head laced with gray. "You must be Boot. Making a break for it, were you?" Then she stood and met Gov's eyes again. "Come on in."

Boot on his heels, Gov obliged. When they were in the kitchen, he set the bag down on the counter and took her in his arms. He captured her mouth and kissed her longingly, as if it had been years, not hours since he'd seen her. The capricious top in her stomach started spinning again, winding the uneasiness and trepidation from earlier into a spool of joy and need. And then it hit her. She really was in love with him. She was in love with a man she'd known for a week, in the last place she would have expected, where meeting someone was the furthest thing from her mind. She left his mouth on ragged breaths and fell into him. He tightened his arms around her and stroked her hair.

"Laurel?" His voice was but a whisper and a little shaky. Did he feel it too? "You okay?"

She shook off the revelation and put on a smile as she leaned back. "Yeah."

He gave her a concerned look. "You sure? I didn't mean to—"

She cut him off by placing her index finger over his mouth. "You didn't. I mean, you didn't do anything I didn't want done. I'm just a little overwhelmed. I wasn't prepared…" her voice trailed off as she reached for the words. "You're very unexpected for me, that's all. I didn't come here to…" My God, what had she almost said? "Meet someone," she finished quietly.

He let out a deliberate sigh, then laid his forehead against hers. "I know. But now that you have, before we go any further, you should know that I don't do things halfway. Falling in love chief among them. Which puts me in a bit of a bind as I'm falling in love with you. So if you're not up for that, I'd like to know now." He straightened up and found her gaze again. "So I can find a way to change your mind." His tone was serious but his eyes were smiling, like when he'd shown up at her door with the pizza.

And suddenly she knew. She loved him, she trusted him, she wanted him. And it was okay. She jumped back into his arms and squeezed him tight. "I don't do things halfway either. So I guess we're in this together, like you said last night."

He ran his hands up and down her back, pressing her to him. "Good to know. Now that we have that out of the way, we have a dog to walk." He gestured with a nod to Boot, sitting patiently at their feet. He let go of her with a final peck on the mouth. "I brought provisions, for us and for Boot," he informed her, turning to the grocery bag. "He watched me pack it up, so he already knows what's in here." Gov produced two plastic bowls and a bag of dog food as well as a bottle of wine and a package of sliced meats and cheeses. "After we get Boot settled, we can we figure out dinner over wine and what people now call a charcuterie board." He displayed the deli box complete with nuts and a sleeve of crackers. "It's what my mom used to call cheese and crackers with cold cuts."

"Mine too," Laurel laughed. He was so proper, so cute, so funny. She pushed away the increasingly familiar feeling that he was too good to be true and told herself to go with the flow. "But I have dinner covered." She went over to the refrigerator and opened it, proudly pointing out the lasagna and salad. "I made a salad and defrosted a lasagna. All we have to do is bake it."

"Great," he said, bending down to leash up Boot. "I'd say we make a pretty good team."

"Yeah," Laurel agreed, as the realization hung in the air between them. "I'll just go grab my jacket."

Ten minutes later they were leaving her neighborhood and heading up into the hills. It was a beautiful spring night, perfumed by daffodils and freshly tilled soil.

"How's the writing going?" Gov asked.

"It's going. I finally have my main characters established. I'm working on the backstory. You know, the why and how we got here. I think they may be rekindling an old flame. Something kept them apart and now that obstacle is gone. But is it worth the risk to try again? Baggage and all?"

Gov yanked gently on the leash, reminding Boot to stop sniffing and do his business. "So have many years passed? Are they basically different people? Has life worn them down?"

Laurel thought about that. "No, not necessarily. They've both been hurt, unlucky in love. And the timing was off before."

"If life has taught me anything it's that timing is everything."

"Yeah." She cleared her throat. "How was your day?"

"Busy. I spent some time in the office this morning doing some brainstorming with Jack," he answered as they stopped to let Boot relieve himself. "Then came some damage control on a project in Crystal Bay which required getting rebar from point A to point B in the eleventh hour."

"Sounds…stressful."

Gov untied one of the plastic bags attached to the leash. "More annoying than anything. If everyone would stop to think and follow directions, supplies would get where they need to be without issue. Why would a house that is framed, roofed and roughed-in need coils of rebar?"

"I couldn't tell you," she replied, not having a clue what he was talking about.

Bent over to pick up after Boot, he gave her a clever look. "But you're not supposed to know. It'd be like editing your manuscript after the book is published. It just doesn't make any sense."

That she could relate to. "Got it."

He stood and threw the bag into one of the trash cans scattered along the trail. They walked in companionable silence for a while until Gov said, "Oh, I almost forgot about this." He reached into his back pocket and pulled out a small white envelope. He handed it to her. "Speaking of timing."

Laurel opened the envelope to find a photograph of four little girls huddled together on the beach. She remembered that swim suit, she was probably six or seven. Carli was next to her and on the other side of her sat two other girls, one blonde and one with raven curls. She tried to place them, and that summer, in her mind. "Where did you get this?"

"From Moira, my boss. She's the dark-haired one. Remember I told you we used to frequent that beach? So did Moira. I asked her about it because you guys are around the same age. You said whoever was out would play together. Moira doesn't know who took the picture; she's moving and was going through some boxes and found it. She took a picture of it for herself and said you can have that one."

"How nice of her. I have so many memories of summer days like this, but not of this one in particular. I wish I could remember her. Please thank her for me." Laurel looked over at Gov with raised eyebrows. "So you told your mother *and* your boss about me?"

"I just may have," he admitted with a smug grin. He slowed his pace and leaned over and kissed her. "I think Boot's had enough. Let's head back."

By the time they got home, the evening light was dwindling. Gov put out Boot's food and water while Laurel popped the lasagna in the oven. Then she got out the wine from last night. "Ronnie always said to serve the good stuff first." There was about a glass of the Barbera left for each of them. They arranged the charcuterie on a plate and took it to the outside table. After Boot ate and acquainted himself with his new surroundings, he laid down in the back corner of the deck and went to sleep.

"So does your novel have a title?" Gov asked, leaning back in the chair and stretching out his legs in front of him.

"Just a working one. *Christmas in Tahoe*."

Gov gave her a puzzled look. "It's a Christmas book?"

"No," Laurel told him with a shake of the head. "Not really. It's going to culminate at Christmas. It was actually Carli's idea. She's said since I've always wanted to write a book and I've always wanted to spend Christmas in Tahoe and since I was going to Tahoe to write said book, I should name it that, at least for now. She thought it would be good karma."

"Can't have enough good karma."

"I think it's more irony than karma since I'll be gone by Christmas. But I appreciate where she's coming from."

That seemed to throw Gov a bit, give him pause. But surely he knew the terms of her lease. He cleared his throat. "Tell me more about Carli. Your eyes light up whenever you speak of her."

Laurel felt the smile in her heart spread to her face and amplify. "Carli and I have been best friends since kindergarten. She used to come to work with her mom and we'd play in the afternoons. She went to a different school at first, but eventually Ronnie wore Rosa down and she let Ronnie pay Carli's tuition where I went to school. Ronnie actually had to give Rosa a conditional raise to cover it. Ronnie said it would make everybody's life easier. So from second grade on we went to school together, hung out at my house after school and were basically inseparable. She's an only child too, although she has a slew of cousins. She's a stay-at-home mom now with two boys and a baby on the way. We're hoping for a girl this time. Her husband is a musician who works crazy hours and sometimes spends weeks on the road. Rosa retired a few years ago to help Carli when Zack is gone for long stretches. We all went to high school together—Carli, Zack and I. They've been together since we were fifteen."

"That's nice that it worked out for them," Gov said, clearly impressed. "Most high school romances don't. And now we're getting somewhere—to you. I feel like we talked about your mother and grandmother more than we talked about you last night."

Was this Gov's way of asking about Grant? Not that he even knew his name, let alone their history. But she

supposed he deserved to know about the most significant romantic relationship of her life. So over lasagna
and salad and another bottle of wine, she told him. Everything. From meeting Grant on the beach to falling
madly in love, to traveling the world with him, to living together and finally getting married. From a college
internship that became an entry-level job that led to a
senior managing editor position and potentially, eventually to publisher. To the womanizing, the little voice
inside her head that she tried to ignore and Grant's initial denials. His immature, unapologetic attitude, his
indifference to saving their marriage and most of all,
his inability to see that his infidelity was the problem.
To where he was today, married with a toddler.

"Wow," Gov said as they put away the leftovers and
loaded the dishwasher. Boot had made himself comfortable on the couch in the family room and was snoring away. "I don't know what to say. I'm sorry doesn't
cover it. But he's the big loser here, in every sense of
the word." He put his arms around her from behind.
"And I hope his loss is my gain."

Leaning back against him, Laurel dropped the dish
towel into the sink and raised her arms to link his neck,
bringing him closer. He was kissing her now, nuzzling
her neck with pecks and licks as his arms moved from
her waist to just below her breasts. She heard herself
moan a little as the ache of anticipation began to rise
inside her, then settle in the pit of her stomach. It had
been so long since she'd felt this way, so long since
she'd wanted to. She covered his hands with hers and
slid them up to rest on her breasts. Gov let out a sigh
of appreciation as she tipped her head back and closed

her eyes, indulging herself in his touch. She wanted to completely immerse herself in him. And he in her.

"Laurel." Her name left his lips on choppy breaths. "I want you. Desperately."

She turned around and met his eyes. They were dark with desire and swimming with want. She responded by commandeering his mouth, moving over it slowly, sensually, then outlining his lips with her tongue. She felt a shudder run through him and it tugged deep in her core, then radiated through her. Suddenly his hands were everywhere—raking through her hair, roving her back, scooping her buttocks— as he pushed her against the sink and seized her mouth. It was as if he couldn't kiss her enough to satiate himself.

"Is that a yes?" he gasped in a stringy voice. "Because I'm getting to the point of no return."

She answered with a murmur of agreement as he picked her up and carried her out of the kitchen, down the hall and to the bedroom. She couldn't help but laugh a little.

"What?" He put her down on the bed and laid down next to her.

"It's just funny that you knew which room was mine. Even in the dim light."

"I know the house. And I've been thinking about you." He stoked her hair. "Imagining you and me, in this room, in this bed. All the things we would do. All the things I want to do to you. I've wanted you since the second I laid eyes on you."

"You've been thinking about us, here, like this?" Laurel amazed, feeling need flood her again. "Tell me. Tell me what you want to do to me."

Gov rolled on top of her. "I want to do more than tell you, I want to show you. And once isn't going to be enough." He kissed her as if with his whole body. "I've never wanted anyone the way I want you."

"Prove it," she challenged.

He started with her mouth, biting, pulling, nipping, then covering it completely with his. He feasted, igniting a passion long dormant, as the yearning spread, consuming her pelvis as the demand to be filled with him began to grow inside her. She loved having his weight on her, loved how the slightest brush of his fingertips left tiny flames in its wake, loved the way his hands roamed up and down her body, searching for a place to start. She stilled them by guiding them under her shirt and bringing them to her breasts. Then reaching behind her back, she unhooked her bra. Her breasts tumbled into his eager hands. "Just as beautiful as I imagined," Gov muttered in awe, grazing them with his fingertips. He made quick work of her shirt, then his, throwing them off the bed. Then he buried his face in her cleavage. "I can't wait to taste them, to taste you, all of you." His tongue made circles around one nipple, then the other. He took a breast in his mouth and while fondling the other, sucked, lapped, caressed. She could already feel the pull deep in her stomach, the wave of desire building, the crest of pleasure forming. She felt like she was in a marathon and part of her desperately wanted to get to the finish line, but the other part didn't want the race to end. She ran her hands across his shoulders and down his arms, even stronger and more muscular than she'd imagined. Her heart skipped a beat at the thought of how virile the rest of him must be. Even through the denim he was as hard as a rock, rising to meet her. The realization put every cell in her body on high alert.

Licking his way up her chest and throat, Gov returned to her. He cradled her face in his hands. "I'm not going to last long. I want you too much. But I promise I'll make it up to you. Do we need to take precautions?"

Laurel shook her head. "I never went off the Pill. In terms of other things, I had myself checked out after Grant, just in case. There hasn't been anyone since."

Gov seconded that with a nod. "I haven't been with a woman in over a year. I've always used a condom unless I was in a long-term relationship, of which I've had two. The last one ended almost seven years ago. But I have some. It's up to you, whatever you're comfortable with."

She touched her lips to his then said, "I trust you. I want to be with you. I want you, all of you, inside me. I want it to be just you and me."

"I want that too." He started to say something else, but swallowed it. "I never have before, not like this, but I do now." His hands went down to the waistband of her jeans. He unbuttoned and unzipped, then helped her shimmy out of them as she kicked off her shoes. Laying the palm of his hand over the lace-covered triangle between her thighs, he murmured, "I can't wait much longer to make love to you."

"Then don't." She slid her hands under the thin strings at her hips. Down and off the thong went, seeing the same fate as her bra and shirt. She started to unhook his belt buckle but he quieted her hands with his.

"As soon as you touch me, I'm going to explode. Let me touch you first." Laurel felt the ache in her pelvis begin to spread as his fingers found her. "You're so wet, so soft, so ready for me." He explored her, layer by layer, fold by fold, crease by crease. She squirmed beneath him as he made circles with his fingers, driving her up as the arc of gratification took hold. Faster and faster they moved, darting in and out, as she swelled and seeped. Suddenly waves of pleasure vibrated through her, overtook her, consumed her. She peaked audibly, then fell, tumbling back to earth as her body went limp, leaving her spent and breathless.

Gov stilled his hand, then crawled back on top of her. "That was so hot. I almost came watching you. I wanted to keep going, but I won't last. I need to be inside you now." He kicked off his boots, then his jeans and briefs. She gasped out loud when she saw his erection. She hoped she could take him, he was so well-endowed. He entered her with a long, throaty moan, instantly filling her. "I'll try to go slow. I want us to come together." He began moving inside her, slowly at first, then rocking his hips harder with each thrust, as the tip of him found the most remote part of her. Up on his knees now, he bore down on her, then held taut, then pumped again, pushing them both to the edge. Throwing his head back and muttering endearments, he began to fly above her. "Come again for me. I can't hold out much longer." She tried to move with him, answer him in passion, but fresh spasms were inundating her body as she rode another wave of satisfaction. She climaxed, even bigger this time, obliging him just as he growled into the darkness and emptied himself into her.

~~~

"Am I crushing you?" Gov asked in a muffled voice. He was laying on top of her, his head buried in her hair, his arms wrapped around her, his legs entwined in hers.

He was, but she didn't mind. "No," she managed, lifting her arms to link his neck.

"Good," he replied, tightening his grip around her. "Because I don't think I can move."

"Move? I can hardly draw breath."

He pushed up on his elbows and smiled down at her. "I'd say I'm sorry but I'm not," he said with a kiss. "In fact, give me an hour or two and I'll take your breath away again."

"You don't need an hour or two to do that." The words escaped her lips before she considered the weight they carried. She'd agreed with more than returned the sentiment when he'd professed his love for her. She owed him that, she knew. She threaded her fingers through his hair, something she could do for hours. She loved having his arms around her, loved the way he was built, the way he moved, on her, with her, in her. She loved feeling him laying against her, wanting to love her again, but willing to wait. And the way he loved her was so true, so natural, so real. He was the kindest, sexiest, most generous man she'd ever known. She brought him closer, to indulge herself in his taste, his scent, to feel his naked body pressing against hers. She'd just had two mind-blowing orgasms and that wasn't enough. She wanted him again. Her hand found him, wrapped around him, and began to fondle him.

"Laurel," he groaned, dropping his head into the crook of her shoulder. "My God, Laurel."

She stroked him lovingly as he grew ramrod straight and engorged in her hand. He attempted to find her center, but seemed paralyzed by her touch. And that just added to the rush. She used both hands on him, rubbing him up and down, fast then slow, with her thumb working that sensitive tip, as he began to ooze. She'd never felt so empowered, so desired, so wanton, knowing she could do this to him. And she was close to coming again.

He laid a trembling hand on hers. "I'm begging you, please. Please let me be inside you." His voice was a broken rattle and came from deep in his throat. "I'm about to blow."

Easing him aside, Laurel climbed on top of him and received him in one determined thrust. She tightened around him as he grasped her hips and pulled her down to take the full-length of him. His erection was so large that his mere presence inside her aroused parts of herself she never knew existed. She'd never wanted a man again so quickly after climaxing, never thought it possible. Up on her feet now, she picked up the pace, increasing the friction as she soared above him, her hair strewn around her as if blowing in a headwind, his moans of contentment intensifying and driving her higher. Every molecule in her body was tingling with fresh, raw craving, reaching for that ring of fulfillment, chasing that glorious release. And when it crashed down on both of them, they shattered together, sharing it as one.

# CHAPTER EIGHT

IF GOV WAS a smoker, he'd need a cigarette. Or ten. Or a pack. That was the best sex of his life. Times two. And he wanted to make it three…thousand. They were still joined, with Laurel collapsed on top of him, matching him breath for breath, heartbeat for heartbeat. His arms were around her waist and he moved his hands up and down, skimming her back with the tips of his fingers. "You okay?"

She lifted her head up and shook her hair out of her face, then looked down at him from under heavy-lidded eyes. "Okay would be a gross understatement. I'm still vibrating inside."

"I aim to please."

"That you did. Three times. Yourself?"

"Never better. That was amazing. You are amazing."

"You sure?" she challenged, rolling off of him "That doesn't sound like okay, let alone amazing."

"Yeah." Gov conjured up a smile, but inside he was reeling. He'd never felt this way, been in this situation before. She'd been married, but for him this was uncharted territory. He was trying to come up with something to say other than *I think I love you, like really love you* when he heard the sound of approaching footfalls. He shifted his gaze to the doorway. Boot sat back on his haunches, cocked his head and stared at them inquisitively.

And suddenly Laurel, propped up on her elbows next to him, started laughing. He'd never heard her laugh so wholeheartedly before. Her chest was quaking and her giggles were filling the room as she stared at Boot. Gov couldn't help but start laughing himself.

"I think someone is looking for you," Laurel put in after a moment of shared amusement. "And he might be a little jealous."

"This is definitely a first for him."

"He doesn't normally go on dates with you?"

"No," Gov told her, his gaze locked on hers. "But then again none of this is normal."

Laurel nodded in understanding. "Does he need to go out or just want some attention?"

"He was probably wondering where we were. He shouldn't need to go out for the night yet." Gov stopped short. Did she want him to stay over? He cleared his throat. "Actually, let me go see. Can I get you anything?" he asked, getting out of bed.

"I'll come with you. I could use some water."

Gov got into his jeans and sweatshirt, then turned back to Laurel, intending to help her retrieve her clothes. But she was already out of bed and in her jeans, grabbing a sweatshirt out of a drawer. She threw it over her head, braless.

"We're just going to stay home, right? No bra required?" she asked, turning to face him.

Gov went to her and took her in his arms. "As far as I'm concerned, you can go braless all the time. As long as we're together. Alone together, that is," he quickly qualified. "No freebies for anyone else."

"No. No freebies for anyone else."

"No anyone else for me, Laurel. That's how I roll. The only way I roll."

"Me too." She hugged him tight. "Can you stay?"

"I want to. But only if you want me to."

She sniffled into the crook of his shoulder. "I do." Her voice was thick and full of emotion.

"If I stay I want it to be all night. The first of many nights."

"If I didn't think you'd stay all night, didn't think there would be a tomorrow night, I wouldn't ask you to stay at all." She leaned out of his embrace. "In fact, I wouldn't have slept with you to begin with."

"I might not have let you. And that's a first for me."

"You said once wouldn't be enough. I held you to it."

"You didn't have to. I love you, Laurel," he heard himself say, struggling a little to hold her gaze.

"I know. I can all but see it, rolling off you in waves. I love you, too. I can't believe it, but I do."

"As long as you believe me, that's the most important thing. We can work on the rest."

"Deal," she said, as Boot joined them. "Where does Boot sleep at home?" she asked, shifting her gaze downward.

"Wherever he wants. Usually in his bed in my room."

"I can get a pillow and blanket together for him. We can make up a little bed over there." She nodded toward the corner.

"Full disclosure, I threw his bed in the truck. Just in case."

"Pretty sure of yourself, huh?"

"More like wishful thinking."

"The best kind. Let's get some water and something sweet. I have some ice cream in the freezer."

Yet another reason to love her. "Ice cream girl, huh?"

"All day long."

"Let me guess. Chocolate?" Gov asked as they headed for the kitchen with Boot on their heels.

It was full dark now and Laurel flipped on the overhead lights. "The more chocolate the better. Throw in some brownie mix and top it with chocolate chunks and I'm a goner."

"I can get behind that. No peanut butter swirl?"

"Peanut butter is meant for sandwiches. It needs jelly to really shine. Chocolate can stand on its own two feet. No condiment needed."

Gov had to laugh. She was such a trip. So insightful and intuitive, yet still so openhearted and funny. As she got out a tub of double chocolate fudge brownie and bowls, his mind started to wander. If she had such an affinity for ice cream, he'd be glad to let her lick some off of him. And vice versa. He wondered if she had any whipped cream, the old-fashioned kind in the red can with the cool dispenser. The mere thought got his blood pumping again, to one organ in particular. Suddenly he needed some air. "Boot might need to go out after all," he decided out loud. "I'll take him and grab his bed while you do that."

"Okay," she replied, retrieving an ice cream scoop from a drawer.

He walked out front and took in the cool night, as the crickets chirped and the waves crashed in the distance. While Boot sniffed around, Gov exhaled deeply, once again finding himself striving for calm. The incredible sex was one thing; he could chalk up the first time to not having been with a woman for a year. And that encounter had been strictly business; a booty call with an old friend. No strings, just two people satisfying a physical need, wanting to scratch that itch for intimacy and release. But the second time, the instant Laurel touched him, he'd almost gone off the rails for the want. He'd been able to keep himself in check, but he'd been dangerously close to flipping her over and taking her with the force of a runaway train. Over and over, like in his dream. He hadn't recovered like that, let alone preformed like that, in such a short interval since he was in college. But she was so sexy, so responsive, so giving. He'd never felt that connected to a woman before. He could feel her orgasms building as if they were his own. And when she came, it gave him as much pleasure as his own did. He simply couldn't get enough of her and he didn't want to. And he genuinely liked her. Not just loved her, liked her. She could be his friend, his lover, his partner, his...wife? That was another first. He'd never thought in those terms before. Added to which he'd known her for barely a week. Maybe there was something to love at first sight. But that had to be a two-way street. She had obviously felt that way about her husband and they hadn't been divorced that long. And she was only here through the end of the year. He wondered how set in stone that was.

"Gov?" Laurel's voice came from behind, pulling him out of his thoughts.

"Yeah," he said, turning around.

She was standing at the front door, looking at him expectantly. "You guys okay? The ice cream is melting."

"Yeah," he told her with a smile. "Boot was exploring. I'll get the bed and we'll be right in."

She nodded in acknowledgment and closed the door all but a crack.

"Boot! Come on boy!" The dog followed Gov to the truck, probably thinking they were going for a ride. He grabbed the bed and led Boot back into the house, where he found Laurel in the family room sitting on the couch. There were two bowls of ice cream and two glasses of water sitting on the coffee table in front of her. The TV was on and she was flipping channels.

"Sorry," Gov said, throwing Boot's bed on the floor next to the couch and joining her. The dog immediately plopped down and made himself at home.

"No problem," she said, handing him the remote."Have at it. I forgot the spoons." She got up and headed for the kitchen.

Gov clicked on the guide and out of habit scrolled to the sports channels. The Giants were playing, but Laurel probably wouldn't like that, so he bypassed the game as well as the hockey playoffs in search of a more date-friendly choice. *Sweet Home Alabama*. Perfect.

Laurel came back into the room just as the movie came back from commercials. "*Sweet Home Alabama*?" she laughed, sitting next to him and handing him a spoon. "Isn't baseball on? The season just started."

"Yeah, but I thought you'd like this. I'll have a hundred and fifty more chances to watch the Giants play this season. Hopefully more."

"And as much as I like this movie, I've probably seen it a hundred and fifty times. Parts of it anyway." She leaned over and kissed him on the cheek. "But thank you. You're sweet. I actually think your Giants play my Dodgers tonight."

Gov fell a little deeper in love. "They do. At home."

"Well, put it on then," she said, around a spoonful of ice cream. "That's something we can both enjoy."

He was enjoying watching her lick ice cream off of her spoon. It made him wonder what else she could do with that tongue. And what he could do to her with his. He turned on the game, then picked up his bowl and took a couple of bites. When the inning ended, he said, "Care to make a wager?"

She met his gaze. "Sure. Ten bucks on the Giants. But nice try."

"You might be too smart for your own good. But I was thinking of a more personal bet. No cash involved." Putting a spoonful of ice cream into his mouth, Gov swallowed and waited for the insinuation to sink in.

Her eyes widened and began to sparkle. "What did you have in mind?"

"I'm up for anything, but I do like what you're doing with that spoon."

That seemed to surprise, then entice her. She licked the spoon again, demonstratively this time, and swallowed hard. Then she said, "So this bet of yours, it would be mutually beneficial?"

"Definitely. A win-win for all involved."

She put her bowl on the table and crawled onto to his lap, straddling him. "Promises, promises. But I'll bite. What did you have in mind?" She licked her lips provocatively, then bit the middle of the lower one and latched her eyes on his.

Gov set his bowl on the couch next to him. He rubbed his hands together to warm them, then found her breasts under her sweatshirt. He cradled them in his hands and using his thumbs, began to make circles around her nipples, bringing them to point. She started grinding against him, lithe as a cat, producing a similar result with his cock. He felt himself begin to grow.

"So what's the bet?" she asked breathily.

"Whatever you want. How about who goes first?"

She stopped moving and looked down at him, clearly intrigued. "Who goes first for what?"

Gov stilled his thumbs, but kept hold of her breasts. "I'd say first to come, but that's left to chance and more fun together, especially if I can get you there beforehand and it's a twofer for you. So how about first to taste the other?" He couldn't get the image of her licking ice cream off the spoon out of his mind.

She stiffened a little, making Gov hope he wasn't moving too fast for her. That was such an intimate thing for some women and he didn't want to rush her. He was about to backpedal, put the ball in her court, when she suggested, "How about we taste each other together. You know, since the bet is supposed to be mutually beneficial, a win-win."

That did it. He was done, pushed over the edge. He was going to lose his mind if he didn't have her, like that, right now. He pulled her down to him and took her mouth in a long, hard kiss. "God, yes. I can't wait to get my mouth on you. I can't wait to feel yours on me."

"Then what are we waiting for?"

He stood up and with her legs girdling his middle, supported her from the bottom as she began to lick his neck. Hopefully he could hold back long enough to please her, he thought, feeling himself harden. Just having the tip of her tongue on his skin seemed to throw him into a frenzy of carnal debauchery. How would he be able to keep it together when her mouth was on him? He carried her to the bedroom and set her down on the bed. He made quick work of his clothes while she got out of hers. Sitting among the rumpled sheets with her legs crisscrossed in front of her, she extended her arms in invitation. He joined her, wrangling himself on top of her and easing her back on the pillows. Her legs curved around his and he held her against him for a long moment, indulging himself in her. He'd never wanted to hold a woman almost as much as he wanted to have sex with her. If this session proved to be as extraordinary as the other two, she might ruin sex for him if it didn't work out for them in the long run. He was starting to realize that he'd never really made love, never really experienced intimacy. He'd only enjoyed the physical aspects of sex.

"Gov?"

He raised his head and looked into her eyes. "Yeah."

"What is it? Did you change your mind?"

And then it hit him. He was never going to change his mind. She was it for him. She was the love of his life. And somehow he would convince her that he was the love of hers. But he pushed that down and said, "I couldn't change my mind if I wanted to. I was deciding where to start."

Her hand found him. "Right here. I'll get things going right here."

Gov felt his heart start to race as she took him in her hands and began to stroke him. Top to bottom, under and around and then the very tip of him. His head dropped down between her breasts and he muttered superlatives as she used her thumb and fingertip to bring him to full-mast. If she kept this up, they'd never get to the bet. "Laurel, I want to taste you. I want you to taste me."

But she kept going, alternating between lightning fast and torturously slow. The next thing he knew, she was pushing him off of her and making her way down to his cock. She gripped him with one hand while the other guided him into her mouth. He went completely out of his mind as she took the length him and began to suck. Her hands caressed while her mouth worked his shaft. Up and down, around and around, using tongue, teeth, lips. He could feel the pressure building inside him, his pulse pounding fiercely, his muscles go slack. He didn't want to come like this, to do that to her, but he felt powerless, as if controlled by some intangible force lacking decency and restraint. He was teetering on the edge of reason, desperately trying to keep hold of his moral compass and not let the animal in him take over. He was leaking readiness, buckling in her wake and he was pretty sure she knew it. Finally, he tapped her head and managed, "Laurel, I can't hold off any longer. I have to have you now." She released him, slithering up to him with a wolfish grin. Positioning her beside him, he entered her from behind. He pressed his palms against her breasts, bringing her against him, and forged himself inside her. Her moans mingled in the air with his as they fell into an instinctive, visceral rhythm. She grew as wet as he was hard and just as she tightened around him and spasms spiraled through her, he let himself go and erupted inside her.

~~~

Laurel woke to the smell of coffee brewing for the first time in…forever. Likely since she lived with her mom and Ronnie. She made coffee every morning, but was rarely treated to waking up to it. But apparently waking up to freshly brewed coffee meant not waking up with Gov because she was alone in bed. She couldn't remember the last time she'd had sex three times in the same night, let alone had that many climaxes so close together. She could tell herself it was because she had been in a bit of a dry spell, but she knew it was more than that.

She'd only had one sexual partner before Grant, so him knocking her socks off shouldn't have come as such a big surprise. Come to think of it, she could remember the last time she'd had a night like last night. The night they'd gotten engaged. That had been incredible. But last night had been an entirely different kind of incredible, a deeper level of intimacy, more than just an exceptional sexual experience. She'd never felt so connected to a man before, so in sync, so bonded. She could see Gov's love for her in his eyes, taste it in his touch, hear it in his voice and most of all, feel it in her heart. She'd yet to know him for two weeks, but was as sure of him as if it had been two years.

She'd woken in the night and found herself in his arms, turned into him. His breathing was soft and steady, almost mellifluous, and there was a hint of a smile curving his lips. She'd touched his face, feeling the coarse whiskers of his five-o'clock shadow scrape against the back of her hand. He'd roused a little, made a few noises and then pulled her close and gone back to sleep. She didn't know how long she stayed like that, staring at him, until she fell back to sleep.

Yes, she did.

She sprang up in bed as the memory came rushing back. The chimes. That's when she'd heard them, just before she drifted off. After their third interlude, they'd gotten up to check on Boot and turn off the lights. The night was warm and Gov asked if they could leave a window cracked in the bedroom. She had yet to do that and feeling safe with him beside her, she'd gone to sleep to the gentle stirring of the cool night breeze. But as she was falling back to sleep, it wasn't the rustling of the breeze that had soothed her, but the peal of the wind chimes. She'd seen them near the back window, but hadn't thought about them again since that conversation with her mother when she'd first arrived.

Ronnie.

She was processing that, trying to get her head around it, when Gov appeared in the doorway with a steaming mug of coffee in each hand. He was wearing jeans, zipped but not buttoned, and a clever grin. "There she is," he said, approaching her with Boot in tow. He handed her a mug and bent down to kiss her. "Good morning."

He had such a sexy chest. Broad and ripped with just a smattering of hair. "Good morning. Thank you." She took a sip.

"My pleasure." He sat down next to her. Boot made himself comfortable on the floor at the foot of the bed. "Sleep okay?"

"Like a rock star." She matched his facetious tone. "Yourself?"

"Never better," he responded around a sip of coffee. "I wasn't sure if I should wake you. It's almost nine. I didn't know what time you usually get started. Seems like even when I can sleep these days, I don't. But I did today." When she didn't answer, he waved a hand in front of her face. "Laurel?"

"What?" she asked, realizing Gov was talking. It occurred to her that she hadn't slept that soundly in years. Like at least two. Okay, Ronnie. I'm getting the message, you can stop now. "Sorry. I mean, yeah. Wait, what did you say?"

Gov set his cup on the nightstand and scooted closer to her. He laid the palm of his hand on her forehead. "Are you okay? You look a little pale."

She could do nothing but stare at him in awe. He seemed genuinely concerned, almost alarmed. "I'm fine." She let the smile in her heart spread across her face. "I was just thinking. What were you saying?"

"Nothing. Just about sleeping in. But I have to say, those wind chimes take a little getting used to. "

Laurel felt her face fall. "You heard them too?"

"Vaguely, off and on. I know it's white noise and all, but I'm just not used to it." He gave her that killer grin. "But it's nothing I can't get past. The company is certainly worth it," he added, taking her mouth in a telling kiss.

But Laurel was too shaken up to return the kiss properly. Something bigger than Ronnie was going on here. Gov immediately pulled back. His winsome expression fell. "Listen, if this is too much, too soon for you, we can slow it down. Last night was—"

"Incredible," she cut him off, coming out of the daze. "Absolutely incredible." She set her cup down next to his and laid a hand on his cheek. "You are absolutely incredible." She leaned in and kissed him, hoping it would reiterate her words. "And I'm…" Her eyes searched the room for the word and coming up empty, went back to him.

"Scared?"

How did he know? She nodded.

"Me too."

"You are?" she astonished.

"Actually, I'm terrified."

She swallowed hard. "Of me?"

"Yeah, of you. Of this." He shrugged. "Of all of it."

"Gov, why?"

"Why?" he drawled, jerking back a little. "Well, for starters, I've never been here before. I've never been anywhere remotely *near* here before. Jesus, I hardly recognize myself." He stood up and running an anxious hand through his hair, began to pace. "I've never told a woman I love her after knowing her for a week! Hell, I don't think I've ever really loved anyone before, not like this anyway. I've never cared more about a woman's pleasure than my own, which honestly makes me more of an asshole than I had considered myself to be. And I've never wanted to strangle a man I've never met because of something he did long before I even knew you existed."

She dismissed that with a flick of the wrist. "That has nothing to do with you, with us."

He stopped pacing and turned to face her. His expression was a mixture of confusion and impatience. "It has everything to do with me, with us. It's why you're scared, right? That the same thing is going to happen again? With me?" He waved a disparaging hand in the air and continued his rant, "It's part of why I'm terrified. That maybe unconsciously you're on the rebound. He's moved on and now so are you. And once you get that out of your system, it'll be over for us. Or worse, maybe he'll change his ways and want you back. Then I'm really screwed."

Laurel shook her head from side to side in disbelief. They had the same problem, were in the same place, but for different reasons and were coming at it from different angles. Still naked, she rose and went to him. She grabbed the sides of his face and kissed him. Deeply, possessively, affectingly. Unlike herself he responded in kind, folding her into his arms. When the kiss was over, she leaned her head back, but kept her hands on his face. "I'm not on the rebound and there's nothing I need to get out of my system. And if Grant walked in the door today and begged me for forgiveness, tried to woo me, convince me to give him another chance, I would say no. But not because of you." Gov stiffened at that, but Laurel kept going, "I would have said no before I met you and I would say no now, not because of you, but because I don't love him. The only difference is now, because of you, I know that I never really loved him. Because of you, I know why I never really loved him. Because now I know the difference between love and infatuation, between love and lust, between being in love with someone and truly loving them. Because of you."

She stopped and let out a shallow breath as Gov stared at her, wide-eyed and gape-mouthed. Her heart was beating at Herculean speed, her stomach was churning and her breaths were coming out in sharp spurts. She was admitting all that to herself as much as to him. Finally, after a long moment, his eyes started to shine and with a mischievous smile he said, "No lust?"

She threw her arms around his neck and fell into him as he held her tight, lifting her off the ground and swinging her back and forth. "I love the way you hold me and kiss me and make me feel inside. I love that you care enough about me to not rush me and enough to be scared because you want to. I could hurt you and you could hurt me. But we'll never know unless we try," she told him as tears welled in her eyes. "And I'm willing to try if you are."

"I'm in," he told her, setting her down. He pulled back a little and used his thumbs to wipe away her tears. "Now it's my turn. I've never loved anyone the way I love you, didn't think it was possible. I've never spent more than a few consecutive nights with a woman I wasn't related to. I've never contemplated moving in with a woman, let alone conceived of a future with her. But I want all of that with you, to whatever degree you're willing, in whatever time frame feels right to you."

Elation and relief flowed through her. "And I've never realized all that, let alone told anyone all that, before. So I guess we're even."

"Well, not exactly," he replied with a grimace.

Laurel sent him a nonplussed look, feeling her nerves start to rattle again. "What do you mean?"

"We're not even. You still owe me, from last night. The bet."

"Oh…right," she said, reading his mind and matching his tone, rich in innuendo. "The bet, of course. Well, come back to bed. I'm ready to settle."

# CHAPTER NINE

CARLI HARPER HAD it all. Two healthy kids and one on the way, married to the love of her life, a house in the suburbs, the ability to stay home to raise her children and a college degree no one could take away from her. She knew she could dust it off at anytime and get a job, even if she had to start at the bottom again working weekends at the mall like she did in high school and college. To anyone on the outside looking in, even her best friend, she was living the dream.

But things are not always what they seem.

Carli was pretty sure her husband was interested in the new singer in his band. And she was positive she was interested in him. But she didn't think he'd done anything about it. Not yet anyway. She hadn't lied to Laurel when she said she wouldn't change a thing; that much was true. But that didn't mean everything was perfect all the time.

She and Zack met on the first day of school sophomore year of high school. He'd transferred from another school after freshman year when his parents got divorced. He'd wanted to live with his mom full-time and the house she'd rented wasn't in a great school district, so he'd guilted his father into paying private school tuition. That and the fact that the school had a renowned music program and was equidistant between his parents' houses had sealed the deal.

They fell hard and fast for each other. They had three classes together that year, two of them with Laurel, as well as the same lunch period. He asked her to Homecoming a month after they met and became the first boy she ever kissed. It was her first kiss and last first kiss all in one. He asked her to be his girlfriend that night.

Then he wrote a song about it.

In his yearbook senior year, she wrote of that first day of school and how it felt like the first day of the rest of her life. And he wrote a song about that too. His band performed it at their Prom. What had started out as puppy love had grown into the real thing. And had lasted. She went to college and he went on tour, opening for garage bands in small venues up and down the California coast. And it lasted. Everyone, especially Ronnie, expressed their concern about what life on the road would be like for Zack, about how Carli was letting some of her best years pass her by, committed to someone living a rock and roll lifestyle. And it lasted. Carli lived at home and commuted to school, living vicariously through Laurel's dorm and apartment life, roommate dramas and bar crawls. And it lasted.

Carli finished college in three years, working part-time and meeting Zack at gigs whenever she could, often with Laurel in tow. There would also be long stretches of Zack and the band being home, working on new songs, recording, rehearsing. He worked part-time at a guitar store and lived with his mom and she worked at Macy's and lived with her parents, so privacy was hard to come by. Then the band got their first recording contract. Zack got an apartment with a bandmate and put down a deposit on a ring. They got married eight years to the day after they met. His buddy moved out of the apartment and Carli moved in.

And still it lasted.

So why now, after surviving the turbulence of adolescence, navigating all the twists and turns of coming of age and maintaining a long-distance relationship as unique as they come, would she be concerned about some fly-by-night backup singer coming between them? Carli wasn't sure, she thought, as Laurel's name popped up on the screen, but she didn't really need a reason. She had a feeling and she didn't like it. She hit the button on the steering wheel to answer the call. "Hey."

"Hey." Laurel's voice sounded thin, harried, a little strung out. "Is this a good time?"

"Yeah. I'm driving to my parents' house to pick up the boys. What's wrong?"

"What makes you think something is wrong?"

"Because your voice is high enough to shatter glass and your tone sounds as frayed as a scratched record."

"God, you're good. Those kids aren't going to be able to get away with anything when they're teenagers."

"Like either one of us did. Ronnie watched both of us like a hawk."

"Actually, I think your parents were in cahoots with her. They were just more discreet about it."

"Yeah, if there's one thing Ronnie wasn't, it was discrete. But that's not why you called."

"No. I have a dilemma. Gov wants me to meet his parents."

"Great! So what's the dilemma?"

"It's only been a few weeks. Don't you think that's rushing it?"

Carli felt a smile coming on. "Cut the crap, Laurel. You're being a scaredy-cat."

"I am not! I'm just—"

"Scared," Carli finished for her. "Of what? Going out to dinner? You've done that all your life."

"It's not going out to dinner, it's a cookout," Laurel corrected loftily. "His parents just got back from Palm Springs where they spend the winter. Anyway, he's seeing them on Memorial Day and he wants me to go with him."

"Even better."

"No, not even better!" Laurel contended. "It's at their house in Reno. Where he grew up. It would just be the four of us. And I bet his mother doesn't even know he asked me to come."

Sometimes Laurel could be so much work. This was an exercise in futility. She already knew she was going. She and Gov had spent most nights and much of their free time together for the last three weeks. What she was really looking for was someone to talk it through with. And as usual, that would be her. "So what would you do on Memorial Day instead?" Carli asked with a sigh, turning onto her childhood street.

Laurel had to think about that. "I don't know. I guess the same thing I've been doing for the last month. Work on my book, research, explore Tahoe."

"My God Laurel, your life is already so entwined with his that you can't even think of your day without him. And you have to eat either way. You're going, we both know it. Ask him what you can bring to contribute to the meal. He won't know, so if he hasn't told his mother you're coming, that will force him to. You were raised right, you know to bring wine, a hostess gift, your best manners. Wear a pair of dressy shorts, no denim, a flowy top and sandals. And relax. They'll love you. After all, even I manage to," she teased.

There was silence on the other end of the line for a long moment. Carli visualized Laurel biting her bottom lip and pacing around what Carli assumed was the back deck of the house where she did most of her writing. "Fine. I don't know why I'm so nervous. It's ridiculous."

"Because you might really love this guy," Carli reminded her gently, pulling into her parents' driveway. "And that's a good thing."

"I think I may. But there are so many things we have to figure out..."

"Then you will, in due time. Don't get ahead of yourself."

"Thanks. What would I do without you?"

"We've been over that. And you might not have to for much longer. Barring the unforeseen, the boys and I are coming up for the Fourth."

"Yay! No Zack?"

"He has a gig up north," Carli told her, hearing her voice drop a notch. Fortunately, Laurel didn't seem to notice.

"More girl time for us."

"Right. I have to go. I'm here," she informed Laurel as the boys came running out of the house to greet her. She felt her heart swell in her chest and a smile narrow her eyes. She'd only been gone for a few hours but you'd think it'd been weeks. She bid Laurel good-bye, stepped out of the car and bent down to take her boys in her arms. She hugged each of them a little longer than usual, kissing the top of their heads, as her baby moved inside her. After a moment she looked up to meet her mother's eyes. Like hers, they were brimming with tears.

She'd been wrong. She really did have it all.

~~~

Laurel woke up on Memorial Day feeling a little better about things. After her chat with Carli, she'd asked Gov what she could bring to his parents' house. He said they had it covered, but there could never be enough wine. When she'd asked red or white, he'd said either. So Laurel got both. She'd also bought something for Gov's mom at one of the home stores in town.

Despite the holiday, Gov had gone over to a job site to check on a few things since the building inspection was scheduled for first thing in the morning. His plan was to stop by his place to change and then be back to pick her up at four. She'd taken most of Carli's fashion advice, but instead of shorts and a top, she'd chosen a romper. It would be lightweight against the heat of the day, but still dressy. The calendar might denote Memorial Day as being the official start of summer, but it had been warm in Tahoe and Reno would be even more so.

Gov arrived right on time dressed in khaki shorts and a golf shirt. He greeted her with a kiss. "You look nice, but you may be a little overdressed. My folks are pretty laid back. My dad will man the grill and my mom will handle everything else. We'll have a couple of drinks and visit, then eat and call it a night. They turn in early these days. And my dad has to work in the morning. He has a part-time job at a golf course during the summer."

"I'll be fine and that sounds great," she told him as he stepped inside. "Where's Boot?"

"At home. The heat gets to him and my parents don't have a fenced-in yard. He'd want to be outside with us and I'd have to watch him every second since he hasn't been there in a while." He pulled her to him. "And I want this to be about you, us. No distractions from a curious, wandering dog teetering on heatstroke."

For some reason, that made Laurel nervous again. His tone was lighthearted, but his expression had turned serious. Obviously his parents' opinion meant a lot to him. She gave him her best smile. "Got it. I need to grab the wine and the hostess gift," she said, stepping out of his embrace and heading for the kitchen.

"Hostess gift?" Gov asked, following her.

"Yeah. For your mom."

He gave her a puzzled look. "She gets a present? You already got her wine and I'm bringing beer."

Men, she thought with a sad shake of the head. "Yes, but it's the first time I'll be a guest in her home. It's like a thank you for having me," Laurel explained matter-of-factly.

That still didn't seem to make sense to him, but he shook it off and picked up the gift bag and the wine. Then he looked at her expectantly. "Ready?"

"Yeah." She grabbed her purse and they walked out through the garage. The day was clear and bright and the breeze carried the vroom of boat engines and the scent of grills firing up. They got situated in the truck and headed down the mountain. Laurel tried to calm herself by making small talk and looking out the window. They were stopped at a light at the base of Mount Rose when Gov laid a hand on hers and said, "Relax, they don't bite. But remember, my mother was a teacher. She can smell fear."

Laurel turned to face him with a scowl. "Very funny."

"What are you so worried about anyway?"

"I don't know exactly," Laurel replied, shifting in the leather seat. "It's been about ten years since I've done this. What if they don't like me?"

Gov started driving again. "Of course they'll like you. What's not to like?"

Laurel laughed without opening her mouth. "Let's see, I'm recently divorced, unemployed, come from a storied show business family. Oh, and you've known me for less than a month. And we're obviously already sleeping together."

He took exception to that one. "How are we *obviously* already sleeping together?"

"Please," Laurel drawled, rolling her eyes. "Your mother will take one look at us and know. A blind man could see."

"So what? We're both consenting adults. This isn't my first rodeo either, Laurel. How you make a living is none of their concern. And my mom had nothing but nice things to say about your family, remember?"

He had a point there. "I know. But I'm still nervous."

With a perplexed shake of the head, Gov turned into a residential area flanked by oak trees and garden ponds. He pulled up to a guard shack and a swing gate immediately opened. "It's just for show," he informed her, driving down the main thoroughfare of the community. Laurel saw a clubhouse with a pool and tennis courts, busy on a hot day. He drove on as the road curved and twisted, eventually revealing the valley below. He headed down the next street on the left, then took an immediate right before pulling up to two-story house at the end of a cul-de-sac. The craftsman-style home sat on a large lot with a manicured yard bursting with flowering bushes and pots of geraniums. Shoving the truck into park, he turned to face her, then lifted her chin with his index finger to level their eyes. "I love you and they will too. They love Matt and he took their only daughter and grandchildren halfway across the world to live. Twice. Any issues you may have pale in comparison to that." He kissed her softly. "Okay?"

She nodded as her eyes welled up with tears. "Yeah."

"Good. Let's do this. I'll grab the booze and you get the present."

"Hostess gift."

"Right. There's a difference somehow."

Laughing, Laurel got out of the car and met him on the driveway. With an upward nod, he directed her to the walkway leading to the front door. Opening it without knocking, he announced, "Lucy, I'm home," and ushered her inside. "The kitchen is straight back. I'll be right behind you."

Supporting the gift bag from the bottom with both hands, Laurel walked down the hallway, passing the living room and a home office. A petite, blonde-haired woman wearing a floral sundress and a bright smile met her halfway to the kitchen. "Just in time. I was about to open some wine. Please come in."

Laurel followed her. The hallway opened up to a large, modern kitchen. White cabinets and quartz countertops complemented gray-washed oak floors and stainless steel appliances shone in the afternoon sunlight. It was immaculate, functional and inviting at the same time. "Thank you for having me, Mrs. Scott."

"Sheryl." Gov's mother waved the formality away, then dried her hands on a dish towel. "And it's our pleasure."

"Hi, mom." Gov set the beer and wine on the peninsula island, then hugged his mother and planted a kiss on her cheek.

"Hi, honey." She held her son for a moment longer, then eased back a step, put her hands in his and took him in. "You certainly look no worse for wear since Christmas. In fact, you've got a bit of a sparkle in your eye." She winked at Laurel. "I can't imagine why."

Gov gave her a look of mocked annoyance saying, "Mom, this is Laurel Reynolds. Laurel, my mother, Sheryl Scott."

Sheryl turned to Laurel, looking at her with the same sublime brown eyes that graced her son's face. "Welcome, Laurel. I've been looking so forward to meeting you. Now, put down what I have a feeling is a gratuitous gift for me so I can give you a proper greeting."

Laurel set the bag on the island and the other woman took her into a warm embrace. "That's better," Sheryl said, pulling back with a wide grin. "My husband just ran out for propane. We're still not fully restocked from the winter away. He'll be back shortly." She turned and addressed her son, "McGovern, open whichever wine Laurel prefers; I'll drink either. And there's plenty of cold beer in the garage fridge. Laurel and I will get the hostess gift formality out of the way while you do that."

Gov, shaking his head in defeat, did as he was instructed.

"Oh, Home Tahoe," Sheryl delighted, noting the logo on the bag. "One of my favorite stores. May I?"

"Please." Laurel looked on as Sheryl removed the layers of tissue paper from the bag and slid the oblong dish out on the counter. "It's a chip and dip," she explained. "You can accessorize it based on the occasion." She gestured to the small box sitting inside the larger cavity of the dish. "This is just a starter set, but there are all kinds to choose from. I went with the basic holidays."

"What a wonderful gift!" Sheryl gushed, opening the box. Inside were three colorfully painted ceramic picks—a flag, a pumpkin and a turkey. "I don't have anything like this. And the white stoneware goes with everything." She took Laurel into another embrace. " I love it. Thank you."

"Of course." Relaxing a little, Laurel returned the heartfelt hug. She looked up to find Gov watching them. He nodded subtly and gave her a measured smile.

"There he is! My pride and joy!" A sonorous voice filled the kitchen.

Gov crossed the room to greet his father, relieving him of the propane tank he carried and giving him a hug. "That's Kenzie, Dad."

"Well, she's not here, is she?" Gov's father replied with a chuckle, slapping Gov on the back. "Good to see you, son. Who do we have here?" he asked, turning his attention to Laurel.

Gov set the tank on the floor. "Dad, this is Laurel Reynolds. Laurel, my father, Jay Scott."

The older, grayer version of Gov offered his hand and a warm smile. "Nice to meet you, Laurel." His crystal blue eyes held hers for a long moment and Laurel could see him mentally turning back time. And trying not to be obvious about it.

"Likewise. Thanks for having me to your lovely home."

"That's all Sheryl. She does all the work I just play golf these days."

"*These* days?" Sheryl teased. "Honestly, Jay, you're not fooling anybody." She directed her ensuing words at Laurel. "Let's get this out of the way. Jay and I, like everyone born in this century other than our son, knew of your grandmother. I was so sorry to hear she passed away. You know you resemble her, I know you resemble her and my husband clearly knows you resemble her. Still, I apologize for his lack of discretion. He can't help it; he loved her madly from afar for years. But we are thrilled to meet you and look forward to getting to know you. Not because of your grandmother, but because you are obviously very important to our son." She shifted her gaze to Gov. "Who was supposed to be pouring us some wine."

"Guilty as charged," Jay laughed, big and boisterous, dissolving any tension that might have formed in the air. "While he does that, I'll fire up the grill," he announced, picking up the tank. "McGovern, grab me a beer when you come out."

"Will do," Gov said returning to the task at hand.

"Thank you," Laurel told Sheryl after Jay took his leave. "But no need to apologize. I consider the family resemblance a compliment. And I'm used to the double-takes. An old friend of my grandmother's only did a marginally better job of hiding his reaction a few weeks ago."

"Mac," Gov elaborated, handing both his mother and Laurel a healthy glass of wine.

Sheryl nodded in acknowledgment as Laurel continued, "And I'm looking forward to getting to know you, too. Because your son is also very important to me." She looked up at Gov with a satisfied smirk. "Thanks, McGovern."

With an audible sigh, Gov grabbed two beers and went out the sliding glass door to the backyard.

The next two hours consisted of plenty of wine, food and conversation. Laurel learned more about Gov in that time than she would have gotten out of him in two years. She lapped it up like a cat does milk.

"He was a late bloomer," Sheryl explained as they loaded the dishwasher. "Especially compared to his sister. I know you're not supposed to compare your children, but it's impossible not to. Kenzie was born a social butterfly and took to athletics at an early age. She was the leader of the pack in elementary school, always a contender for the superlative vote in middle school and Homecoming and Prom Queens in high school. McGovern always had buddies to hang with, but he was more of a homebody. He liked the competition of sports more than the camaraderie of them, even as a young boy. And he was small for his age. Until one summer a switch flipped. I swear he grew an inch a week. Ate me out of house and home. Then he made the varsity baseball team as an underclassman and really started to come out of his shell. Everything changed after that. I was so relieved."

"I told you he was fine," Jay weighted in, setting a platter of leftover hamburgers and chicken breasts down on the counter. "She can be such a worrywart," he told Laurel, grabbing plastic wrap out of a drawer.

"I guess he just needed some extra time to mature," Sheryl went on, ignoring her husband. "And being an educator, I was reading all sorts of books about adolescence and what was age-appropriate. I was overthinking it."

"No, you were underthinking it. As an educator, you should have known the one surefire thing that gets a preteen boy to come out of his shell." Jay wrapped up the platter and opened the refrigerator, exchanged it for two beers and closed the door. "Girls."

The three of them burst into laughter just as Gov walked in from outside.

"What?"

"Nothing, McGovern," Sheryl answered, trying to regain her composure. "We were just telling Laurel about you making the baseball team as a freshman."

"I was a sophomore and you know it," Gov replied skeptically.

"Were you? I'd forgotten," Sheryl said, closing the dishwasher door. "Laurel, let's walk off our dinner a bit before we serve dessert. Top off our wine and we'll take a stroll around the block. I'll show you where the kids went to elementary school—it's right up the street. In exchange for which you'll have to indulge me by letting me give you a tour of my backyard gardens. My retirement project."

"That'd be great," Laurel agreed readily, grabbing the wine off the counter and dividing the rest of the bottle between their two glasses.

"We can recycle that on the way out," Sheryl said as if the matter had been settled.

"Whoa, whoa, whoa," Gov said, his voice laced with panic. "She's not going anywhere with you. You two are up to something."

"Don't be ridiculous, McGovern. Laurel is perfectly capable of making her own decisions. Isn't that right, Laurel?"

"Yep. And I'm in the mood for a walk around the block and a tour of your gardens."

"Wonderful. We'll finish this up later."

Laurel gave Gov a big smile and an air kiss and followed Sheryl out of the kitchen. She heard Jay snicker and mumble something under his breath as they made their way to the door. She imagined Gov standing there, stunned and alone in the kitchen, wondering what had just happened. She couldn't help but laugh.

Sheryl must have been thinking the same thing because she said, "I hope I didn't go too far."

Laurel went with her gut and replied, "No, you don't."

"You're right, I don't," she chortled and took a sip of wine.

They walked for a few minutes, then came to the house on the corner. "This was where Kenzie's best friend lived. Her family has long since moved, but in retrospect, I think she was the first girl McGovern had a crush on." Sheryl hesitated a moment, then turned to Laurel and met her eyes. "And I think you might be the last. If you don't mind my saying so," she added.

Laurel found herself not minding one bit. "I don't. Do you? Mind?" she clarified. "If I am?"

"Not at all, but it wouldn't matter if I did."

"Oh, I think it would. I can tell how important you are to Gov. That's part of why I was so nervous about coming here today."

"And now? Are you still nervous?"

"No, actually. I'm not," Laurel realized out loud. "In fact, I stopped being nervous after about the first ten minutes."

"Good," Sheryl said, giving Laurel's arm a supportive squeeze. "I have a confession to make. I was nervous too."

That had Laurel stopping dead in her tracks. Sheryl followed suit. "You were?"

"Uh-huh. My son hasn't brought a girl around, let alone home for dinner, in years. Like close to a decade. Oh, I know he's had women in his life. We've met dates here and there; someone he brought to a wedding or a family function, a mention of someone in his weekend plans. But home? Just the four of us? No one."

"That's nice to hear," Laurel said and meant it. "It's all happening a little fast. And as I'm sure you know, I've been down this road before."

Sheryl started walking again. "Actually, I don't know. I don't know anything about you aside from what McGovern has told me, which is very little. I mean, I know of your family, of course. And he said you're in Tahoe to write a book. That's very exciting and I'd like to hear more about it."

Laurel found herself wanting to tell her, but first things first. "I was married, I've been divorced for about two years. I thought you might find that, among other things, off-putting."

Sheryl waved that away. "Half the world is divorced, Laurel. And half of the other half probably should be. Marriage is not for the faint of heart. And if by other things mean your famous pedigree, I already told McGovern how much I admire your family. Show business

142

is not for the faint of heart either. You guys beat the odds."

"I know that. It's nice that you do too."

"Even if I didn't, it's not fair to you to be judged by them. We are who we are. Who we become because of it, or in spite of it, is up to us. You did good. You all did."

Laurel thought about that, the simplicity of it, for a moment. "Thank you. And I'm proud to by judged by them. My mother in particular. I know it wasn't always easy for her."

"Anyone who expects life to be easy all the time has a big wake-up call coming. Deservedly so. And you should be proud to be of them. I'm sure they're proud of you."

Laurel nodded. "They are." They were in front of the house now, having circled the block twice.

"Shall we go in, put McGovern out of his misery?"

As much as Laurel knew they should, she was enjoying herself. "What about your gardens? I didn't really get a look at the backyard beyond the patio area."

"That's good because there isn't much to see. I was looking for an excuse for us to talk alone. I owe Jay one for not calling me out."

"Had me fooled," Laurel told her with a grin.

"Once a teacher, always a teacher. Let's—"

She was interrupted by the sound of the front door swinging open. Gov stood there, dwarfing the frame. He eyed them suspiciously for a long moment, then began walking toward them with long, purposeful steps.

"God, he reminds me so much of his father, save the eyes. Those long legs and broad shoulders. No wonder he was such a versatile baseball player," Sheryl commented. "He'll take the walk in five easy strides."

He did it in four. "What are you guys doing?" he asked Laurel more than his mother.

"Talking," Laurel said, sending Sheryl a conspiratorial look.

"About what?"

"This and that," Laurel replied, suddenly noticing his eyebrow was twitching. She had never seen it do that before. She reached up and touched it. "What's going on here?"

Sheryl snorted and turned her head away.

He grazed a fingertip over the spot Laurel had touched. "Nothing. I thought you guys were just walking around the block."

"We did."

"You must have been taking baby steps."

"I saw no reason to hurry. Did you, Sheryl?"

"None at all. Thanks for the walk, Laurel. I'm going to head inside to get dessert out and put on some coffee. Take your time."

"Dad and I finished up in the kitchen, Mom."

"Even better."

Gov watched his mother walk up the driveway, then turned back to Laurel. "For someone who was nervous about coming to dinner, you sure did settle in quickly."

She tilted her head to the side. "Isn't that a good thing?"

He closed the small space between them and laid his hands on her shoulders. "Yeah. But I think she likes you better than me now."

"I think you're safe there," Laurel replied around a laugh, then sobered. "What's going on with you?"

"I've hardly seen or talked to you all night. I don't like it." He ran an agitated hand through his hair. "I don't like that I can't touch you whenever I want to. I don't like that I have to share you. And I especially don't like not knowing what you're wearing under that dress."

"It's a romper."

"Whatever," he replied dismissively. "Do you realize this is the first time we've been out together with other people? We've mostly just been hanging at your place."

She hadn't thought of that. He had a point. And could he get any cuter? "Wow. We really need to get out more."

"Very funny. I guess I'm just not used to it."

She studied him for a long moment through slitted eyes, then said, "I think the real problem is that you're feeling vulnerable. And you're not used to that. But that's part of being in a relationship. One that matters, anyway. So I'll take it as a compliment."

He drew her to him and rubbed his hands up and down her back, then buried his face in her hair and said, "God, you feel so good. I can't wait to get you home. I can't wait to find out what's under that…romper."

Laurel felt that twitching between her legs, that flip in her stomach. Suddenly she couldn't wait either. She wanted to touch him until he couldn't take one more breath without being inside her. She wanted him on top of her, straddling her as she arched beneath him, driving him deeper and deeper. She wanted them to climax together, hard and fast, sweet and slow and everything in between. But mindful of where she was, she reeled herself in and whispered in his ear, "It's a thong. Red. Lace in the front, a thin string in the back." She felt him stiffen, then move his pelvis forward a little. She pulled on his earlobe with her teeth and finished in a sultry voice, "And it's a size too small."

She heard him whimper, take a few short gasps, then tighten his grip around her waist, pressing her to him. "Can you feel that?"

"Yeah," she breathed.

"That's what you do to me just by telling me what you have for me, what you're willing to give me. When I get it, I'm going to grab it with everything I've got and then some. I'm going to take you places you've never been, like you do to me every time you touch me. Once, twice. Then, just when you think it's too much, that you can't take any more, I'm going to stop holding back and we're going to come together. And you're not going to be wearing that thong. Or anything else."

Laurel needed a moment, took it. Then she eased back and looked into Gov's eyes. They were fierce, almost warrior-like and swimming with urgency. But something more subdued rimmed them. The edges held tenderness, respect, love. She wondered what he saw in hers.

"Okay?" Gov was asking.

She shook off the melancholy and nodded.

"Good." He kissed her forehead. "Now, as much as I'd like to bail on dessert, my mother's Key lime pie is not to be missed. The limes are apparently in season early this year. And since she's your new best friend, you'd hate to upset her. "

"Well, we can't have that," Laurel laughed as he took her hand and led her toward the house.

"So what were you guys really talking about?"

"Girl stuff. Your name came up."

"Shocker."

"You were right about her being intuitive. She doesn't miss a trick."

"Tell me about it."

No, Laurel thought as they reached the door, not that he was really asking. She'd keep that to herself, for the time being at least.

# CHAPTER TEN

MAY FOLDED INTO June and Lake Tahoe was replete with summer. Bright, crisp mornings gave way to long, hot days that segued into cool, clear nights. The beaches were punctuated with colorful umbrellas, the docks were bustling with boats and jet skis and the local businesses were printing money.

And Laurel couldn't stop writing.

She'd been waiting for the click, for the dam to break and the words to flow out like a busted water main with a faulty shutoff valve. And then one perfect, cloudless day in June it did. Suddenly, it was all there for the taking. She almost couldn't get the words out fast enough.

"Scott" and Whitney had known each other as kids—their families had vacationed in Tahoe by happenstance for years—but had lost touch as adults. There had been some stolen kisses here and there during the teenage years, an occasional phone call or email during the school year. Their mothers kept in touch and passed on relevant family information. Graduations, marriages, babies. Divorces.

"Scott" and his brother had inherited the multi-generational family business. But after a falling out, "Scott's" brother had bought him out. Family and business don't always mix, after all. He'd been going through a divorce at the time, further complicating things. Down on his luck both professionally and personally, he wanted a fresh start. The first place that popped into his head was Tahoe.

Laurel decided to ignore the coincidence.

Whitney hadn't been back to Tahoe since college. She'd bounced around professionally, dabbling in real estate, doing a little modeling, even submitting a treatment for consideration to a couple of networks. She was newly and unexpectedly single, after having lived with her significant other for five years. She supplemented her capricious income with her trust fund, a detail she kept to herself. She saw no better time than the present to turn her yet to be acquired screenplay into a book. And no better place to do it than Tahoe.

Again, the commonalities were not lost on Laurel. But write what you know.

So how would they reconnect? Social media seemed trite as did looking each other up at their mothers' collective urging. Walking on the beach? Too saccharine. She sells him a house? Too cliché. Maybe they don't recognize each other at first; it's been nearly twenty years after all. Maybe they keep running into each other and eventually connect the dots. But what's the goal here? Neither of them is looking to go another round right now. So what's their motivation? Sex? Does something that starts out as strictly physical turn into something more? And the conflict becomes what to do about it? But who becomes conflicted and why? How does that get them to happily ever after? Laurel was firmly committed to that.

She also chose to disregard that parallel.

She was still mulling that over when Don Henley's flawless voice filled the air. "Good morning."

"I didn't wake you, did I?"

"Hardly. I've been up for hours. It's light here by five."

"God."

"I know. But I'm getting used to it. What's up?" It was too early for a social call from her mother.

"I'm thinking about crashing your little party up there. I have a few free days and I want to see you and meet this guy you've been talking about."

She really hadn't told her mother all that much about Gov. Which only meant one thing. "Run into Carli, Mom?"

"Inadvertently. Rosa and I had a late lunch at The Roof Garden yesterday. We ended up back at her house because she wanted to show me the kitchen remodel and one thing led to another. Zack is on the road and Carli and the boys were coming over for dinner, so I waited until they got there and we had a drink. They're growing like weeds."

Laurel put a hand on her head and rubbed her temple. For some reason, she was exhausted all of a sudden.

"Would that be okay?" Veronica was asking.

"Yes, of course," Laurel replied and meant it— mostly. Later it would occur to her that the reason she wasn't thrilled to have her mother visit had everything to do with herself and nothing to do with Veronica. She wasn't ready to acknowledge her feelings for Gov, let alone be held accountable for them. And it would be blatantly obvious to her mother the moment she laid eyes on the two of them. Veronica Reynolds and Sheryl Scott had a lot in common.

"Great. I'll book a flight. Maybe Thursday? First thing?"

"That's fine. I'll pick you up. We can stop for lunch on the way up."

"Sounds good. And I'll stay out of your way. I have work to bring and it's not like I don't know my way around the North Shore."

"Actually, I could use your help. I'm making progress but would like another set of eyes on my manuscript. You always helped me with my papers in high school and college."

"I don't know how much help I was. I think you just needed someone to talk it through with. But I'm glad to read it over. I used to help Ronnie when she'd get stuck."

Laurel sat up a little straighter in the deck chair. "You did?"

"A bridge here and there, substituting one word for another, finding ways to convey like meaning without being repetitive."

"I never knew that."

"Mom would drive herself, and me, crazy if she couldn't finish a verse or if the lyrics and the notes didn't mesh. She'd get frustrated, obsessed and then unbearable. I had to do something."

Laurel shook her head in wonder. Her mother was probably the most underestimated and resourceful person she knew. "Do you remember which songs you helped her with?"

Veronica thought about that for a moment. ""Jasmine Blue" sticks out in my mind. The part about waking up at sunset. Mom couldn't find the right words for the second line of the chorus at the end. *Seems like I'm always behind, waking up as the sun goes down.* But the song is about doing things your own way, not about conforming to social norms. The title refers to the color of the sky just after sunset, the blue hour. When things really started happening in Ronnie's world. She wasn't behind on today, she was ahead on tomorrow. So I said to change the chorus up. Let the lyrics evolve with the song. *I come alive as the sun goes down. Jasmine Blue is my time to shine*. I guess it worked."

"I think it was one of her number one hits."

"I think it was. I can't remember off which album, though. I'd have to look on the office wall, which would require me to get up and I'm still enjoying my coffee in my pajamas."

"Honestly Mom, you never cease to amaze me. Just when I think I know all there is to know about you, I learn something new."

"Likewise. I'll forward you my flight information. I'll come home on Sunday so Mark doesn't miss me too much."

Suddenly, Laurel couldn't wait. "Sounds good. He's welcome to tag along."

"I know that and so does he. But we'll keep it tight this time."

They exchanged good-byes and Laurel turned her attention back to the task at hand. The talk of songwriting reminded her of Ronnie's forgotten lyrics. *Once Tahoe got hold of my heart she never let go, like a lover from long ago, who keeps comin' back around, making sure nothing keeps me down*. Should the story take place over years' time, told in part with flashbacks? She'd have to explore the personal connection both of her characters felt to Tahoe and how it pulled them each back in times of uncertainty. And why.

It also made her wonder again about Ronnie having a lover in Tahoe. There was something about the way Mac spoke of her, the moony flash in his eyes, that stayed with Laurel. Almost as if he was reliving a cherished memory long-buried. He was younger than Ronnie, probably by at least a decade, which of course mattered little. Friends with benefits long before friends was benefits was a thing. Maybe that's how "Scott" and Whitney would start out. Two people seeking comfort and companionship more for the body than the soul. Falling in love was the last thing either of them wanted.

Another similarity she'd choose to ignore.

What she could not ignore was that Gov crossed her mind multiple times a day, at seemingly random and often inconvenient moments. She'd been in Tahoe for six weeks, four of which she'd been sharing a bed with him several nights a week. She'd never thought of herself as libidinous, but she found herself looking forward to their sexual encounters, even disappointed when life got in the way of them. She'd enjoyed sex with Grant, as any consenting, heterosexual woman would. He'd prided himself on pleasuring her, but in retrospect only if he could bring her to peak before his own climax. After that, he'd just roll over, sometimes leaving her high and dry. And despite what she considered to be an active sex life, he was getting even more on the side.

Gov, on the other hand, not only made a conscious effort to hold off as long as he could, but pushed on after his own orgasm, wanting her to follow. And unlike Grant, Gov seemed genuinely invested in her pleasure. She'd never had such a generous, selfless lover. But could it last? Surely most people, like the couple she'd seen on the beach, didn't have heart-stopping sex every night for decades on end. Even the strongest flame burns out eventually. And she was only here for a few months. Alternately, his life was here, both professionally and personally.

The ping of an incoming text brought Laurel back to reality.

*I assumed she knew. You usually tell her everything.*
*Not this time.*
*Why?*
*Idk*

That'll do it, Laurel thought. She counted backwards from 5. She got to 2.

"Sorry if I started something," Carli said by way of greeting.

"You didn't, not really. She's coming."

"She's curious."

"Among other things."

"She's allowed. When?"

"Thursday."

"Part of you is looking forward to that."

"Actually, most of me is. That's why I'm so confused."

"Laurel, your mother knows you're not a virgin."

"I know. I told her the day after the night I stopped being one. She didn't even freak out, quite an accomplishment considering our family history."

"She put you on the Pill before you went away to college to avoid repeating your family history. She didn't freak out because she trusted you. Now it's your turn to trust her."

"She's going to take one look at us and know we're having crazy monkey sex."

"So? Weren't you afraid of that with Gov's mother? And that was fine."

"Gov's mom likely assumed we are sleeping together. My mom will know the extent of such. It's hard to explain, but it's like a snap in the air, an energy between us."

"And you two walk around town like this, sizzling and crackling?"

"Of course not." Laurel felt a smile curve her lips. "We don't go out that much."

"Seriously."

"It's not something just anyone would pick up on."

"I think you're being paranoid, but we'll put it to the test in a few weeks. What else am I missing here?"

Damn Carli anyway. She was too smart for her own good. "Once she sees us together, she's going to start asking questions."

"Questions you're not ready to answer."

"Right."

"Because you don't know the answers or because you're not ready to accept the answers?"

"Maybe a little bit of both."

"Then wait. Let the answers come to you. They will. Even a force of nature like your mother can't pull them out of thin air."

Just then the breeze picked up, quaking the Aspens and fluttering their heart-shaped leaves. And the wind chimes in the corner.

"No, but maybe another force of nature can," Laurel muttered under her breath.

"What?"

"Nothing. Enough about me. What's going on with you? Mom said the boys are growing like weeds. I can't wait to see them."

"Nick more than Ollie. No preschool in the summer, but I'm trying to make sure Nick is ready for kindergarten in August. He's young for his grade. Flashcards, puzzles, crafts. And I'm putting Ollie in preschool every morning in the fall with the baby coming."

"Zack's been on the road?"

"Yeah. They're booked solid all summer." Carli paused, then added,"Which is great."

"Is it?" Laurel asked the hesitation in her friend's voice.

"Sure. We need the money, especially considering the last couple of years."

"Mm-hmm."

"I knew what I was getting into, Laurel. I'm used to it."

"I know. You sure that's all there is to it?"

"Yes," she dragged out the word.

"If you say so."

"I do," Carli justified in an even tone. "Let it go. I'll talk to you later."

"Okay." For now, Laurel added to herself after they hung up. She'd let it go for now.

~~~

"Thanks for coming in." Jack Brody stood up from behind his desk and extended his hand. The two men had a good working relationship, bordering on a friendship. They were both from Reno and had gone to the same high school, but Jack was three years younger so they never had any classes together or ran in the same circles. He was married with three children and had taken over the family business earlier than planned due to his father's sudden death. He had strawberry blonde hair to Moira's coal-black and hazel eyes to her emerald green. They barely looked enough alike to be siblings, let alone twins. "Have a seat," he offered, gesturing to the pair of chairs at Gov's back. "Coffee? I think Moira made a second pot."

"No, thanks," Gov declined, obliging. "I'm all coffeed out for today."

"No such thing," Jack disputed good-naturedly and sat back down.

"I run hot enough without it. A cup or two first thing is all I need. But then again, I don't have a new baby at home. How's everybody doing?"

Jack's face broke out into a wall-to-wall grin. "Great. Emily makes it look so easy, having three kinds under four. But she's got both our moms at her beck and call and I try to make it home by bath time. Which brings me to the reason I asked you to meet with me. I have a proposition for you."

Gov couldn't imagine what it could be. "Okay. Shoot."

"Let me preface this by saying this has been in the back of my mind ever since I hired you. But recent events, both personal and professional, have accelerated any timeline I might have had." He leaned back in his chair and made a steeple with his fingers, then rubbed his hands together a few times. "I'd like to offer you a minority partnership in Brody and Sons. I need more than a right-hand man and a foreman. I need a collaborator, a confidant, an ally, someone who has some skin in the game."

Gov was floored. And flattered. And he didn't try to hide it. "Jack, I'm honored. But you don't have to make me a partner for that."

"I know; you've demonstrated that over and over again. But I'm talking about some high-level responsibilities. Decision-making, financial matters, goal-setting and direction there of. Moira has every intention of returning to work full-time after the baby. But there's no guarantee that's going to work for her, especially in the long run. She's likely going to have more than one child. Her husband has an architectural firm of his own; he's as busy as I am. It may eventually serve them better as a family for her to take a step back here or help him in his business instead." He took a breath, then finished, "I can hire another employee or two, but I need more than that. I need a wingman. Someone with drive, perspective and vision. Someone like you."

"Neither of your brothers is interested?"

"No," Jack reiterated with a shake of the head. "They never have been. We've already begun the buyout process with them anyway. Let's just say my father was a little optimistic when he named the place. Moira doesn't care enough about titles for us to rebrand."

"And Paul Webster?"

"I won't pretend I didn't discuss this with him first. He was like a brother to me, in some ways more than my own, long before he married my sister. But he's got his own shop and a merger wouldn't solve my problem, only create another one."

Gov started running through scenarios in his head. He was happy and fulfilled with things at present, but had to think of the future. He liked the way Jack did things, the way Moira ran things, the industry itself. And the market was certainly cooperating, at least right now. But owning a business, even as a minority partner, meant putting down roots. Permanently. Here. For the first time in his life he had someone else to consider. Someone who lived in L.A.

"I just wanted to throw the idea out there, test the waters. If you're interested, I can have our attorney draw something up, key discussion points and a business model, a profit sharing matrix. If not, no hard feelings and it's business as usual."

"I'm interested," Gov heard himself say. "And extremely flattered."

"Likewise. I'm open to any ideas you may have as well. And I'd like to keep this between us for now. I've only discussed it with Moira and Paul. And of course Emily."

How nice to have someone at home to run things by. Someone you trusted explicitly, who had your best interests at heart, a stake in things. A partner of a different sort. A life partner. Gov had his father, but that was different. "Of course. And I'll jot a few things down that I can bring to the table as well."

"Great," Jack said. "I think we could really divide and conquer, especially with you living up at the lake. How's that going, by the way? Are you bored to death yet?"

Hardly, Gov thought. "I love it, even in the winter. Once prices stabilize, I might buy something, but probably not in Incline. It's a little out of my league. Maybe Crystal Bay or Kings Beach. I miss having a yard for Boot and some privacy. But the condo works for now."

"Let me know when you're ready. I'll try to convince old man Baker to sell. He hasn't gone up there in years, has no kids or grandkids to leave the place to. I've thought about buying it myself, as an investment property and weekend place, but we'll be out of our first house before I know it. It's as close to the lake as you're going to get for under a million dollars anymore. And near shopping, restaurants, etc. without being smack-dab in the middle of things. It's been meticulously maintained and updated, even as a rental, and despite having an interior lot, has a lot of privacy. It's a hidden gem."

Gov couldn't agree more. "Thanks, I will."

"No news is good news when it comes to the tenant, right? Moira said you did an exterior inspection, didn't find anything major that needed to be addressed."

"Right. I've also been inside and everything seems copasetic." Should he have mentioned to Jack and Moira that he was seeing Laurel? It wasn't a conflict of interest but still.

"I didn't realize you'd given the inside a once-over as well. Even better. One less thing for us to worry about for a while."

"It was more by chance and not really an inspection. I'm actually seeing the woman who's renting the house."

Jack gave him a startled look, prompting Gov to ask, "That's not a problem is it?"

"No, of course not. Your personal life is none of my business. But thanks for letting me know. It's convenient if nothing else."

"If I come across anything, I'll take care of it and let you know."

"Sounds good," Jack said. "I'll give the attorney the go-ahead on the preliminary proposal. Maybe we can get together one day the week after next?"

"Sure. You know where to find me."

"That I do," Jack replied, rising to signal the end of the meeting. "I'll walk you out."

Gov stood and the two men walked out into the open-air office. "It's still kind of weird for me to be in there." Jack threw a thumb over his shoulder. "Instead of out here in the trenches. But such is the life of being the boss, despite how it came to be."

"Luckily for you, everyone knows that Moira is really the one in charge," Gov teased, returning the parting wave she gave him from her desk, phone to her ear. "So no harm done."

"True enough," Jack returned in kind. "Just out of curiosity, how long did it take you to figure that out?"

"I think it was about halfway through the second interview," Gov told him with a grin.

"Slower than most, then."

They shook hands and parted ways. Gov got in his truck and headed up the mountain. The route was familiar and the traffic light, allowing him to turn Jack's proposal over in his mind. He was short on specifics, so he started with what he knew.

He enjoyed working for the Brodys. The pay was competitive, the work rewarding and he was good at the job. He had plenty of responsibility and autonomy, but he wouldn't mind more. He and Jack made a good team.

He liked being back in Reno and Tahoe. He liked seeing his family whenever he wanted to while still having his own life. He liked the lifestyle and the people, the familiarity of the area, the seasons and the scenery. He could see himself here in the long-term.

He was in love with Laurel. Like all the way in love. He'd known there was something special about her the second he saw her, but it was mostly superficial at that point. She was breathtakingly beautiful, of course. But he felt like he fell in love with her over and over again. Every time he unpeeled another layer, he discovered something else to love about her. Her sense of humor, her resilience, her ambition and of course her passion. She was so generous, so responsive, so genuine. He'd never met anyone like her. And he didn't want to lose her at the end of the year. Or, he admitted to himself for the first time, ever.

He passed the Mt. Rose Ski Resort, the halfway point to Incline Village. He had a few projects to check on and by the time he was done, it would be after five. He could swing by home and take Boot out, give him dinner and then pick up something to eat for he and Laurel. Or maybe she'd like to get out of the house tonight. Italian sounded good. He hadn't talked to her today and he'd had a meeting last night, so they hadn't seen each other for a few days. He decided to add missing her to the list of things he knew.

"Call Laurel," he commanded, activating his Bluetooth.

She answered on the first ring. "Hey."

"Hey. How's it going?"

"Good. Actually, better than good."

"Great. I'm heading back from Reno. How about dinner?"

"Sure."

"In or out?"

"In," she replied after a moment. "I have an idea."

"Okay. Will six-thirty work?"

"Aren't you going to ask me what my idea is?"

"I will if you want me to."

"On second thought, I think I'll wait until you get here."

"You'll have my undivided attention."

"I'm counting on it."

Gov heard the suggestiveness in her voice and was already contemplating postponing his stops when she added, "But I'll give you a hint." She made a puckering sound with her mouth. "It's for research."

His throat went dry, a contradictory sensation since his mouth was starting to water. He swallowed hard and said, "In that case, I'll rearrange my schedule and be there in thirty minutes."

"Perfect. Come find me," she said and hung up.

Gov made it to town in record time. When he got to the house, he went with his gut and let himself in through the garage. There were no signs of life in the kitchen or on the deck, but Laurel's laptop and notes were sitting on the table in a neat pile. He could hear the shower running in the near distance.

He had to stop himself from sprinting down the hall.

Through the open bathroom door he saw two folded towels sitting on the edge of the vanity. The room was lit by only the late afternoon sunlight coming through the frosted glass window and a few candles. The mirror over the sink was hazy and the hook next to the shower held a black robe. A short satin one.

He was unbuttoning his shirt when Laurel pulled back the shower curtain. Her hair was piled on top of her head and her body was glistening with water droplets, some of which were dripping off her turgid nipples. It was the most sensual, erotic thing Gov had ever seen.

"That was fast."

"You have no idea," he said, kicking off his boots, then his jeans. He joined her in the shower and drew her to him. "But the ticket would have been worth it."

"We can pretend you got one," she purred, as he began to kiss her neck. "So I have to make it up to you."

"We can pretend anything you want as long as I get to have you in this shower. You are so sexy wet. Why haven't we done this before?"

She made a guttural sound from deep in her throat and slanted her head back as his hands slid up and down her torso. "I don't know. So let's make it worth the wait."

He took her mouth in a long, lazy kiss as his hands settled on her slick breasts and the water beat down all around them. He felt himself begin to swell even before she took him in her hands. "God, that feels so good," he muttered. "You feel so good." He glided his hands down to her waist and hips, then cupped her buttocks and pressed her pelvis to his. Their bodies were flush now, with his erection resting against her triangle. "You shaved."

She met his eyes. Hers were ablaze and full of the devil. "I did. Do you like it?"

"I love it." He moved one of his hands forward and laid it on her center. "I want it. Even more than last time. Which I thought was impossible."

"I've been thinking about you all day, wanting you, wanting this." She took his mouth in hers, showing a new kind of initiative, wielding a new kind of power with tongue and lips, driving him up.

He'd never seen her like this. He was putty in her hands, completely at her mercy. He tried to move his hand down to touch her folds, but her thumb was making tiny circles on the tip of him now, effectively incapacitating him. He wanted his fingers inside her, to arouse her the way she was him, but his mind was blank, his equilibrium skewed, his hands inept. He would surely go insane for the want.

She was like a goddess of the sea, as if the steam gave her some kind of mystic reign over him. Damp auburn tendrils were framing her face now and her bewitching eyes hung on his as she propelled him faster and faster, taking him higher and higher, harder and harder. He had never felt so helpless, so starved and so gluttonous all at once. But he didn't want to come like this. In one desperate move, he grabbed her by the waist and spun her around. He pressed the palms of her hands against the wall for purchase and entered her from behind.

She cried out as he tunneled into her, finding her wet and warm and tight. She threw her head back against his neck as he found his rhythm began to move. God, he loved being inside her. It was like every time was the first time, every time brought a new sensation, a higher level of ecstasy. His hands pumped at her hips and she rose to meet him, contracting around him as he thrusted deeper and deeper. It took every ounce of willpower he had to hold back when she howled into the misty air as waves of orgasm rolled through her and superlatives escaped her lips. She was still catching her breath when he knew he couldn't hang on any longer. "I can't wait one more second. Not one more second to come inside you," he ground out just as she shuddered and fell with him one more time.

# CHAPTER ELEVEN

VERONICA REYNOLDS MIGHT favor her father in appearance, but she commanded a room like only Ronnie Reynolds could. Standing in baggage claim, Laurel watched her mother's long, purposeful strides eat up the carpeting of the terminal breezeway. If her brunette hair had a touch of red in it and her olive skin was a shade or two lighter, she could pass for Ronnie in a heartbeat. Her gait, her posture, her tempo was all Ronnie. She wore white jeans and a short gold jacket over a blue top. Unassuming Hermès tote flung over her shoulder and coordinating Birkin hanging from the crook of her arm, she sent Laurel an air kiss and a beaming smile.

And Laurel realized how much she'd missed her mother.

A siren wailed over Laurel's shoulder, warning passengers that the baggage belt was about to start. A peek at the monitor told her it was for a San Francisco flight. As efficient as the Reno-Tahoe airpot was, it was no match for her mother. Laurel met her at the halfway point between them and stepped silently into her arms. Veronica's signature Chanel filled the air and her shoulder-length waves skimmed Laurel's cheek as she hugged her as tight she had the morning after her first sleepover away from home.

"My baby girl!" Veronica eased back and blinked away the tears that had amassed in her ocean blue eyes. "Let me look at you." She took Laurel's hands in hers. "As beautiful as ever. And I like to see the sparkle back in your eyes," she finished with raised eyebrows and an impish grin.

Laurel made a mental note to tell Carli I told you so. "Right back at you. Except for the sparkle," she added with a laugh. "You always seem to have that."

"I come by it honestly." She pushed up her jacket sleeve, displaying a column of multi-colored bracelets. "In fact, I brought a little Ronnie sparkle with me."

"You're wearing hers now too?"

"Only on special occasions. And this qualifies." She slipped an arm through Laurel's and steered them toward the baggage carousel. "Let's get my bag and grab some lunch. Do you remember Rosie's?"

"In Tahoe City? Vaguely. But that's fine. I've been wanting to get over to that side of the lake anyway."

"If you can spare the time, we can shop around a bit afterward, take the scenic route back to Incline."

"I can. It's good for research too." As soon as the words left her mouth, a smile of remembrance curved her lips.

"What?" Veronica asked with a nonplussed look.

"Nothing." Laurel shook off the memory and changed the subject. "What bag did you bring?" she asked, turning as the belt started moving again, announcing the LAX cargo.

"My champagne weekender."

Forty minutes later they were on Highway 89 approaching Tahoe City. "It's a bluebird Tahoe day," Veronica remarked, looking out the window. "Not so much as a whisper of a cloud in the sky and the lake so blinding a blue it almost breaks your heart."

"It's been like that most days since I've been here. Not a drop of rain."

"And the snowpack can only do so much on its own," Veronica said with a sad shake of the head. "We'll see what the Fanny Bridge has to say about the water level of the lake. I bet it's at or below the rim."

"I remember going there as a kid. We'd get ice cream and walk across the bridge to the dam over the Truckee."

"Ronnie wrote a song about the rushing river, comparing it to the rush of falling in love. How it feels in the beginning, when you first fall. The quickening in your chest, the flutter in your stomach." Glancing over at Laurel, she paused for effect. "The sparkle in your eyes."

Laurel met her mother's measured look head-on. "Mom, I've known him for six weeks."

"More like seven. Didn't you meet him the night you got here?"

"Do you remember everything?" she asked, turning her attention back to the road.

"About you? Yes."

Laurel, approaching the roundabout into town, slowed down. "Well, I'm going to give you another memory tomorrow night. We're having dinner with him."

"What a wonderful idea!" Veronica exclaimed.

"As if you didn't have the same one. I made a reservation at Hues of Blue. I told Mac you'd likely be up at some point and he wanted to see you."

"Even better. My old stomping ground."

"Yes, that's what he said when I called. He also said you already had a dinner reservation for Saturday night. He wanted to know if you were going to grace him with your presence two nights in a row."

Veronica shrugged and gazed back out the window. "I wasn't sure of your plans for the weekend. I didn't want to be underfoot."

"Nice try. Your reservation was also for three."

"It's high season," Veronica contested inadequately. "They're busy."

"They're always busy. And we both know you could have gotten in anyway."

"Why chance it? I want to spend some time with my daughter and get to know the man she's seeing at one of my favorite places. So shoot me."

Laurel shook her head from side to side. Part of her didn't blame her mother and part of her was irritated with herself because she should have seen this coming. She wondered what else she had up her sleeve.

"Look, there's a spot," Veronica said, gesturing with a tip of the head. "And there are some cute shops around here for after lunch."

Laurel navigated into the parking place and they made their way into the heart of Tahoe City, busy with the lunchtime crowd. Quaint shops and restaurants lined the main street of the quintessential mountain town with the lake serving as an omnipresent backdrop.

"Well, you haven't lost your touch," Laurel commented smugly when Veronica managed to finagle a table outside.

"It's not me, it's Tahoe. Everybody is so happy. No incentive necessary."

They settled in with glasses of Chardonnay. "So what have I missed at home?" Laurel asked.

"Not much. It's been hot, but no fires, at least not yet. I'm working on a fundraiser at the Hollywood Bowl over Labor Day weekend."

"Talk about old stomping ground."

"That's exactly what I was thinking." Veronica wagged an index finger in the air for emphasis. "What could be more nostalgic than where Ronnie started out as a backup singer? Mark helped me put together some talent—a few cover bands and some veteran musicians—and I'm focusing on the vendors. T-shirts, hats, etc. They already have phenomenal food and drink options there."

"If it were anyone else, I'd ask how you were able to secure the Hollywood Bowl for a charity event over a long holiday weekend."

Veronica brushed that off with a flick of the wrist. "Ronnie did a lot for the artistic community over the years. It sold itself out overnight."

Laurel found herself sorry she'd miss it. "I'm sure it'll be awesome, Mom."

"I think so. Zack is headlining. He's working it in around Burning Man. I thought it might be too much and tried to talk him out of it, but he wouldn't take no for an answer."

"He still thinks he owes his success to Ronnie because she gave him a start, an in, a push. But he's a natural talent. And he earned it. He put in the work, made the sacrifices, survived the lean years."

Veronica nodded in agreement. "And so did Carli. She always believed in him."

"She and the boys are coming up for the Fourth. But you probably already knew that."

"She mentioned it."

"Among other things." Laurel sent her mother a knowing look as their food arrived.

After the waitress left, Veronica elaborated, "We had a nice visit. But I wanted to see for myself. Tell me about the book, Gov, what else you've been up to."

Over Greek salads and wine, Laurel told her mother about the progress of the book, her routine and lastly, Gov. "We apparently have an old acquaintance in common."

"Oh?" Veronica interjected around a bite.

"His boss. She's about my age. She had a picture of Carli and me, herself and a friend playing on the beach here. I was probably about seven. I'll show it to you."

"There were always tons of kids playing on the beach. Some were only in town for a week or two, some all summer like us, some were locals."

"I guess the other girl's family had a home down the beach from ours. She still owns it."

"Do you know her name?"

"No. But Gov works for Brody and Sons Construction. His boss' maiden name was Brody."

Veronica squinted a bit, as if mentally rewinding time. "Brody doesn't sound familiar off the top of my head. Maybe the picture will ring a bell. Either way, what a small world."

"It gets even smaller. Gov's family used to rent a condo on that beach. His mom remembers seeing us around town."

"That sounds more like fate than a small world to me," Veronica put in.

Laurel couldn't deny having the same thought. But she only said, "Or we both just happened to spend our summers in Tahoe."

"Ah-ha."

They finished lunch and spent the next few hours walking off their meal and browsing through the vintage shops and unique boutiques of Tahoe City. A visit to the Fanny Bridge confirmed Veronica's fears that the lake level was below the natural rim. Another year or two of drought would expose the river's sandbars and start to affect wildlife migration. Laurel could almost see the wheels start to turn in her mother's head.

"Thinking of taking on another cause?"

"Maybe. But I'm not sure how much of a dent I could make in this one."

Laurel put an arm around her mother's shoulders. "If anyone can make a difference it's you."

Smiling, Veronica tapped the side of her head to her daughter's. "Thanks, honey. It certainly would be a cause close to my heart. We have so many fond memories of Tahoe. I can't imagine it not being here for generations to come."

They walked back to the car and started toward home, taking the long way around the lake. "Did you end up incorporating Emerald Bay into your book?" Veronica wanted to know as they passed the overlook and the line of cars parked along the side of the road.

Laurel had forgotten all about that. "No, actually. Turns out my main characters knew each other as kids and are reconnecting after a series of unexpected life events. I didn't use Emerald Bay as a meet-cute after all."

"Like an in another life type of thing?"

Laurel thought about that. "More of a life got in the way type of thing."

"Got it," Veronica said with a nod as they approached Stateline. Chalet-style resorts and mom-and-pop shops gave way to multi-towered hotels and lively casinos. "God, I haven't played blackjack in ages. Maybe I'll go over to the casino one day, try my luck."

"You should. You always had card sense."

"Not like Ronnie. Do you remember when you were too young to go into the casino, she and I would take turns sitting with you in the restaurant?"

"Yeah. I'd get about a hundred Cokes between the two of you."

"I'd get frustrated and give up, but Mom would keep going, determined to at least break even."

"Typical Ronnie behavior."

"I think half the time she'd use you as an excuse to go home and just say she won."

"She loved the cards."

"She grew up in it. As a girl she'd go with her grandfather to play cards in the backroom of some corner store. The pot was whatever change they all had in their pockets. The price for her silence was half of his winnings."

"Simpler times."

"I'll say," Veronica agreed. "But those are the things that shape us. The simple things."

"Thank you, Mom," Laurel said after a long moment.

"For what?" Veronica asked, turning to face her.

Laurel laid a hand on her mother's. "For all the simple things. Sometimes I forget how it could have been."

"Not on my watch," Veronica replied in a watery voice. "That was a hand I couldn't risk losing."

They rode the rest of the way in companionable silence. When they got to the house, Laurel gave her mother the ten-cent tour. "Each room is more charming than the last!" Veronica proclaimed, turning in a circle once they were back in the kitchen. "I love it. Especially the stacked molding on the fireplace. They don't build them like that anymore."

Laurel hadn't really noticed. "I want to show you the backyard and the deck where I write. I'll get us some wine."

"While you do that, I'll settle in," she said, grabbing her bag and heading down the hallway toward the bedrooms.

Laurel uncorked the wine and let it breathe. Once Mac heard that her mother was visiting, he'd insisted on putting a bottle of Barbera aside for her. When she'd dropped by to get it, she'd found two bottles marked paid in full waiting for her.

It was a warm day but the deck was shaded and the afternoon breeze would be kicking up soon. When Veronica returned, she'd thrown her hair up in a clip and ditched her shoes. Laurel had two glasses of wine and her manuscript sitting on the patio table.

"It's beautiful back here," Veronica commented, taking the seat next to Laurel and rubbing the palms of her hands together in anticipation. "So this is it? Your masterpiece?"

"Masterpiece is strong. It's the first five chapters of my *manuscript*."

"Call it what you want and I'll do the same." She lifted her glass in the air between them. "To my daughter, the author, as she starts a new chapter of her life."

Laurel clinked her glass against her mother's. "To my mother, philanthropist extraordinaire. Thank you for helping me write every chapter, past, present and future. And without whom I would be completely and totally lost."

After a sip and an utterance of approval Veronica added, "I could say the same. And to Ronnie. For starting it all."

"To Ronnie." They each took another sip and Laurel slid her manuscript across the table to her mother. Veronica got her cheaters out of her pocket and removed the binder clip and red pen attached to the stack of papers. She started reading the first page and then glanced up at Laurel. "You're not going watch me, are you?"

"I was thinking about it."

Veronica waved her hand in the air. "Think again. Be gone with you."

"Fine. I'll go check my email."

"Perfect."

Laurel picked up her wine and retreated to the kitchen table. Through the open deck door she could see her mother's profile as she pored over the pages. Occasionally she'd make a notation, but for the most part she seemed to be genuinely engrossed. My first beta reader, Laurel thought with a nervous chuckle. She opened her laptop and tried to focus on checking emails, but couldn't stop her mind from wandering. Finally she got up and grabbing the bottle, went outside on the pretense of topping off her mother's wine.

Without sparing Laurel a glance, Veronica laid her hand over the top of the glass. "Not yet. I'll be singing and I want you to believe me when I tell you how good this is."

Laurel didn't try to hide her excitement. "Really?"

"Really," Veronica confirmed, meeting Laurel's gaze. "I love it already."

"Where are you?" Laurel asked, sitting down next to her and setting the wine bottle on the table.

"Just finished chapter two," Veronica answered, taking off her glasses. "Their inadvertent and I have a feeling fateful second encounter."

"Bingo."

"I'm already cheering for them, especially him. But I'm having a little trouble connecting the name and the face. Scott doesn't mesh in my mind."

God, she was good. "Scott is just a placeholder name, like a working title for a song."

Veronica nodded, then tapped an index finger over her top lip. After a pensive moment she went on, "You need something bold, but not too long. Something unique, noteworthy, commanding. Maybe a stalwart family name or something usually thought of as a last name."

Like McGovern, Laurel thought, but only cleared her throat and asked, "What do you think of Whitney?"

"I like her, but not as much as I like him. I don't sympathize with her as much. At least not yet."

"I can work on that. But do you sense the tension between them? The internal conflict they're both struggling with?"

"His, yes. Hers, no. Maybe I need to give it more time."

"Anything else?"

"She's not vulnerable enough. I don't feel invested in her happiness."

"Great insight. I'll work on that, too."

"But I love that she's independent and strong without compromising her femininity. Don't change that about her, but soften her up a bit. Maybe expand on her backstory, particularly the breakup and how it shapes her decisions now."

"Got it," Laurel said, standing. "Thanks, Mom." She hugged her mother from behind. "I'll get started on that while you read the rest."

Veronica patted her daughter's arm. "My pleasure." She handed Laurel the hardcopy of the first two chapters. "I made a few notes, highlighted a couple of other things you might want to look at."

Laurel nodded and was starting to walk away when Veronica grabbed her hand. She turned back to her mother.

"Don't let her give up on love too easily, Laurel. Don't let her past determine her future. "

"I won't," Laurel replied, noting the benevolent insinuation in her mother's voice.

"Give Whitney the guts to take a chance and the strength to persevere if it turns out to be a chance not worth taking. Courage and survival aren't mutually exclusive."

"I know, Mom."

Veronica started to respond, but before she could get the words out the breeze picked up, stirring the wind chimes. The two women shared a moment of inertia as the uncanny coincidence passed between them. Then, with a subtle nod and a deliberate smile, Veronica turned her attention back to the manuscript and Laurel went inside to save Whitney from herself.

~~~

Gov had spent the much of the week dealing with one snafu after another so Friday couldn't come soon enough. To add to the anticipation, Laurel's mother was visiting for the weekend. Laurel had made dinner reservations for them for Friday night. He'd been looking forward to meeting Veronica Reynolds, but he had no idea it would turn out to be one of the most interesting evenings of his life.

They'd gotten the formalities out of the way straight off when Gov picked the women up. To cover all his bases, he'd brought wine and flowers and worn a sport coat despite the warmth of the night. He greeted Laurel with only a hug and a brush across the lips. Over a drink, he found Veronica to be warm, funny and affable. He was immediately comfortable in her company. But the real fun started when they got to the restaurant.

His first surprise came in the form of a table for four in the much-coveted atrium at Hues of Blue. Laurel had mentioned her mother had a long-term boyfriend but not that he'd made the trip.

He hadn't.

The next surprise came in the form of Mac. Not bar manager Mac. Not therapist Mac. Not even matchmaker Mac. This was Mac as Gov had never seen him. This was Mac as... Mac.

And he was joining them for dinner.

They had no sooner gotten to their table when Mac appeared, wearing an animated grin and navy blue pants with a checkered dress shirt. It was the first time Gov had ever seen him in something other than solid white or black or a combination thereof. His eyes lit up like sparklers as Veronica jumped into his outstretched arms. Gov watched his friend lift Laurel's mother off the ground and swing her around in a circle a few times before setting her down with equal flourish.

But that was just the beginning.

Veronica's whoops of joy echoed through the restaurant with Mac's belly laugh close behind. After a lengthy hug and lingering kisses on both cheeks, Mac pulled out a chair for Veronica, then greeted Laurel and did the same. Laurel, seemingly unfazed by the whole thing, thanked Mac and sat. Then Mac turned to Gov.

"You're next," he teased, taking Gov into a half-hug. "Hey, Gov. How ya doing tonight?"

Before Gov could respond, Veronica patted the chair next to hers and announced, "He's mine tonight. We have a lot to catch-up on."

Still processing what was happening, Gov slowly took a seat between Laurel and Mac. "They're old friends," Laurel explained, setting a hand on his thigh.

"Yeah, I'm getting that."

The next thing Gov knew, wine was being uncorked and appetizers were being served. Mac, of course, stuck with his typical club soda. "So where did you find it?" Mac asked Veronica.

"Find what?" she asked after an appreciative sip.

"The fountain of youth."

Veronica squeezed Mac's jowls. "It's in the genes. But thank you."

Dinner was ordered and served, the wine kept flowing and Gov learned more about Laurel's family in a couple of hours than he could have in days of scouring the Internet. Veronica and Mac seemed to be in their own little world. Telling stories, cracking jokes, reminiscing. Gov couldn't get enough of it.

"Sometimes I still can't believe she's gone," Veronica told Mac in a weepy voice as dinner was wrapping up. "I find myself wanting to tell her something or run an idea by her. Especially when it comes to troubleshooting. She was always good at that—coming up with a plan B, or even C or D on a moment's notice."

"Like when there was a fire at that club on the West Shore the morning of her show. She just told them to move the whole thing outside. The show must go on, after all," Mac interjected.

"I remember that! She actually started a trend—indoor/outdoor concerts. Sell more tickets, entertain more people, enjoy being outdoors with all the conveniences of the indoors. Everybody wins."

"Did she really show up here after closing sometimes? To try out a new song or just stretch her legs?" Gov couldn't help but ask.

Veronica glanced over at Gov, then shifted her gaze back to Mac. "I'll let you take that one."

Mac looked off into the near distance, as if conjuring up the memory. "God, I haven't thought about that in years. Ronnie'd waltz in, unannounced of course, usually just as I was counting the drawer. I'd conveniently forget to turn off the taps and secure the open bottles and we'd all kick back and enjoy the show. Sometimes she'd do a whole set. I can see her now, sitting at the piano in front of the window with the moonlight bouncing off the water. We'd turn down the lights and it would feel like we were in a different world. She was positively mesmerizing."

Veronica leaned toward Mac, touching her shoulder to his. He put a strong arm around her as both of their eyes filled. Gov looked over at Laurel just as tears began rolling down her cheeks. And felt like a complete ass. "I'm sorry. I didn't mean to bring everybody down."

"You didn't," Veronica insisted, dabbing the inner corners of her eyes with her napkin. "Those are good memories and it's wonderful to share them. And I'm being rude, talking so much about the past. Gov, tell me more about yourself and your family, your work."

Gov gave Veronica the condensed version of his life story and then flipped the conversation to Laurel. "Tell me about Laurel growing up."

Laurel swore under her breath and emptied her wine glass.

"She was a joy to raise," Veronica began with a proud smile. "And the love of my mother's life. She saved Ronnie from herself, forced me to grow up and completed both of our lives. I'll let her give you all the details, fill in the blanks. She is the best person I know and deserves the best life has to offer." She let that simmer for a long moment and then affixed her gaze to Gov's. "And the best person to complete hers."

Gov acknowledged the thinly veiled intimation with a nod and held Veronica's steady gaze. He wanted to be that person and had no intention of being shy about it. "I couldn't agree more."

"That's my mother's subtle way of saying that I haven't always made the best choices in the," she made air quotes with her fingers, "person to complete my life department."

"*Your* choices were not the problem," Veronica gently corrected, placing a hand over her daughter's.

Just then the waitress arrived and presented their coffee and dessert options. After she left Laurel excused herself to go to the ladies room and coincidently, Mac had to check on something at the bar despite it being his night off.

The second they were both out of earshot, Veronica slipped over and filled Mac's chair. "Thanks for indulging me tonight. I'm sorry if our walk down memory lane got a little out of hand."

"No need to apologize," Gov said and meant it. "I love hearing all those stories. It's part of what makes Laurel so special. And it's the stuff of legend. My mother is going to be so jealous."

"Well, I'm glad we could accommodate you," Veronica said around a laugh. "But I really do want to hear more about you. That's one of the reasons I came. To meet you."

"Meet me or check me out?"

"Maybe a little bit of both."

He couldn't blame her. "And?"

"You pass with flying colors. But I knew you would. Laurel has excellent judgement when it comes to people. With one unfortunate exception," she qualified with a wry grimace.

"So I've heard. What did you think of him?"

"Grant? I liked him because she loved him. He came from good stock, had a bright future. He treated her well for the most part. But he was superficial, selfish, impulsive. He was used to getting what he wanted when he wanted it. And when he didn't want it anymore, moving on to something else."

"A malcontent."

Veronica chewed on that around a sip of wine. "I suppose, of a different stripe. I saw Laurel overlook a lot of things with him over the years. I was relieved that she didn't overlook such an abject indiscretion."

"She'd never find herself in that position with me, Veronica."

"I believe you. And in the interest of full disclosure, Mac told me that about you."

So she really had checked him out. "What else did he tell you?"

"He told me he served you your first legal beer," she replied after a moment of consideration.

"Legal being the operative word. Anything else?"

"He told me you're the best guy he knows. And I believe him, too. Because it takes one to know one," she finished with a wink and returned to her seat just as Laurel came back to the table.

"What have you two been up to?" she asked warily, slicing her gaze between the two of them.

"We were just chatting," Veronica maintained, throwing Gov a furtive glance. "Getting to know one another."

"Yeah," Gov concurred. "Turns out we have a lot in common."

"Such as?"

"You, for starters. And Mac. Look, he's back," he pointed out as Mac approached the table, saving the day once again.

# Chapter Twelve

THE CLOSER CARLI got to Tahoe, the more anxious she became. The boys had fallen asleep around Modesto, so she couldn't blame it on them. She felt fine and the trip had been uneventful. Neither her parents nor Zack had been crazy about the idea of her driving to Tahoe alone, but she had a new SUV that practically drove itself, plenty of things to keep the kids occupied and had promised to leave her location tracker on for the duration of the trip. On several occasions lately she'd considered asking Zack to do the same, but had always thought better of it.

The reason for her rising anxiety had nothing to do with the drive and everything to do with Laurel. The second Laurel saw her, she'd know something was wrong. She was already suspicious, Carli could hear it in her voice. And the irony of that was not lost on her. They couldn't hide anything from each other if they tried and Carli was tired of trying. Being a hypocrite seemed less exhausting. But for some reason, putting this whole thing with Zack into words terrified her. It was as if saying it out loud somehow made it all true.

That aside, she'd been looking forward to the weekend. Hanging out with Laurel and seeing her new life, meeting Gov and getting away from the everyday. Although, she thought, glancing in the rearview mirror, she'd brought the everyday with her. Literally and Figuratively. Still, nowhere knocked the worry out of you quite like Tahoe.

She'd been giving Tahoe a lot of thought lately, remembering those lightsome summer days when she came up with Laurel. She'd stay for a week or two, then Veronica would drive her to Stockton to meet up with her parents. Sometimes the three of them would stop at one of the coastal towns for a night or spend a day in San Francisco on the way home. Carli looked forward to doing those kinds of things with her children as they got older and a long weekend in Tahoe was a good place to start.

Entering a construction zone, Carli slowed her pace and mentally returned to the matter at hand. She'd gotten a full debrief from Veronica, of course. Gold seal of approval for Gov, Laurel more like herself than she'd seen her since the divorce. And the book? Interesting was all Carli could get out of her. Veronica didn't want to ruin it for her, after all. But if Laurel didn't offer, Veronica had said more than once, Carli should ask to read it one night after the kids went to bed. Preferably before she met Gov. She hadn't thought much about the time-related qualification at first, but now that she'd had a couple hours of quiet with nothing but highway to look at, she realized there had to be more to it. She couldn't imagine why it would matter when she read Laurel's book.

Interesting.

But lots of things were interesting these days. Like Zack coming home for forty-eight hours at the beginning of the week and napping or playing with the boys most of the time. And choosing sleep over sex for the first time in her memory. Granted, she didn't feel very sexy these days, but she still would have been a willing partner. Not to mention his phone, uncharacteristically facedown on the nightstand, buzzing with notifications all night.

Interesting.

One thing at a time, she told herself, entering Truckee. She remembered being here not only as a girl, but with Zack when he was starting out. Truckee hosted a lot of outdoor concerts in the summer and Harper & Company had played here dozens of times. He'd get a room for them at the hotel on main street; she drew the line at sleeping on the tour bus with the band. They usually hadn't seem each other for a few weeks and would have sex like rabbits for most of the night. The first summer the band had started selling merchandise he'd gotten her a personalized t-shirt that said "I'm with the band." She still had it. The other guys didn't have girlfriends back then, so she knew he'd taken some ribbing for it. But he never seemed to care, she remembered as tears gathered in her eyes.

A stirring in the back seat brought her back to the present.

"Are we almost there?" Nick asked in a sleepy voice.

"Almost," Carli answered as they crossed into Nevada. "Look how blue the lake is. Isn't it pretty?"

"Yeah. But we have a lake at home."

"We have an ocean at home. There's a difference. I'll show you in your new book when we get there."

"Okay. Hey! Look at the signs! They're big and squiggly!"

"Those are hotels and casinos. And you're right. The signs are really tall and skinny," she told her son of the vintage steel icons.

Just then Ollie woke up and joined the party with an audible yawn. Carli couldn't help but peek in the rear-view mirror. He was always so cute after a nap. His little fists rubbing his heavy eyes, his honey blond hair disheveled, his voice but a murmur.

"There's my other sleepyhead."

All she got in return was a grunt.

After being on the road for eight hours, the boys would be wild men when they got to Laurel's. She'd have to earn bedtime tonight. And peeing would be first order of business. They'd only stopped once.

"What are we gonna do at Aunt Laurel's?" Nick asked.

"Go to the beach, watch the fireworks, explore the mountains."

"Can we get ice cream?"

"Yeah."

"With sprinkles?" Ollie wanted to know.

"Sure."

"I bet they have red, white and blue sprinkles for the fireworks."

"Maybe."

"Is Daddy going to come here too?" Ollie's voice was hopeful.

"No," Carli told him. "Not this time."

"But I want him to."

"I know. Me too."

"He has to sing," Nick chimed in. "It's his job right, Mommy?"

"Right."

"See," Nick informed his brother knowingly. "Daddy has to work on the days we don't go to school. Tyler's daddy works on the days we do go to school. But when you sing at night you can't do it that way."

Carli didn't know whether to laugh or cry. Kids were so literal, so candid, so authentic. The choice was taken away from her because the GPS announced Laurel's street. "Okay, here we are!"

"Yay!" Nick exclaimed. "Aunt Laurel always buys us candy and presents."

"Nicholas," Carli reminded him gently. "We're here to see Aunt Laurel and enjoy the lake, not for candy and presents. And it's not like she's at home. There aren't as many stores around here."

"I bet she got us those big suckers again," Nick went on, undaunted.

"Yeah!" Ollie blurted out, excitedly kicking his legs in his car seat. "The ones with all the swirly colors!"

"But remember, we can't eat all of it on the first day. 'Cause we'll get sick."

"Yeah," Ollie replied.

Now Carli couldn't help but laugh. "Okay, this is it!" She put the car in park and got out, shaking off the drive as she opened the backdoor. Nick was halfway up the driveway before she could unbuckle Ollie. "Wait for me," she told him.

He obeyed and they walked up to the front door together. Before Carli could knock, the door flew open and Laurel appeared. "Hi!" she exclaimed in delight, squatting down to take the boys into a bear hug. "Look at you two! You look like teenagers!"

"I'm five," Nick reminded her, holding up a hand to demonstrate.

"I know, silly," Laurel said ruffling his brown waves. "I just meant you're getting so big."

Ollie, after a bit of struggle, displayed three fingers for Laurel. "I don't have as many."

"That's okay, you'll catch up one of these days. Go straight back," she told them. "Surprises in the kitchen."

"Walk," Carli called as they ran whooping and hollering inside. Then she turned to Laurel and took her voice down a few notches. "Hi."

"Hi," Laurel returned in kind. The two woman shared a heartfelt embrace. "You're getting big too, lovey."

"Thanks. I think."

"That's a good thing. Come on in."

They started down the hall just as Nick cried out, "Wow! Suckers *and* candy *and* presents!"

"Really?" Carli mocked annoyance. "As if they're not already jacked up enough."

Laurel waved that off. "You can ration out the candy to last the weekend. And it's just some beach toys and Hot Wheels."

"What do you guys say to Aunt Laurel?" Carli asked her sons as they joined them in the kitchen.

"Thank you!" they collectively chanted, starting to unwrap the suckers.

"You're welcome. Are you guys hungry?"

"Whoa, whoa, whoa. First things first. Everybody needs to go potty and wash their hands. Then Aunt Laurel can show us around and we'll get our bags out of the car. Then we'll have a healthy snack. *Then* we'll open the suckers."

"Okay," Nick grumbled, laying his sucker down on the table. Ollie followed suit.

"This way," Laurel directed as they guided the boys down the hall. "And *then* maybe Mommy will tell me what's really going on with her," she said under her breath, throwing Carli a sidelong look.

Carli, knowing she wouldn't have a choice, didn't even waste her breath arguing.

~~~

"You're literally insane you know that, right?" Laurel told Carli a few hours later. They'd gotten the boys to sleep and were sitting on the deck enjoying the cool, quiet night. "You must have a girl cooking in there because you were completely lucid with your other pregnancies."

Carli didn't move a muscle, just stared at Laurel, her black eyes owl-like and unblinking. Laurel felt her breath catch in her throat. So she was serious. Laurel stretched her arm across the table and laid her hand on her friend's. "Start at the beginning," she said, as dread and disbelief wound into a tight braid in her gut.

"I'm not sure where the beginning is."

"Maybe because there isn't one."

"There is."

"Then start in the middle. That's the surest way to find the beginning."

Carli let out a ragged breath. "Last year, before things really started opening up again, Zack was taking any job they could get. Small clubs with an outdoor space, beach stages, even mall parking lots."

"That sounds familiar," Laurel commented, remembering when Zack was struggling to make a name for himself.

"Right. Anyway, remember how Alex and Cody got married during lockdown?"

Laurel nodded. Cody was the other founding member of the band and Alex booked shows for them and managed their social media and logistical arrangements. She could sing backup well enough, but couldn't hit the high notes consistently. She was a marketing genius, meticulously organized and had the metabolism of the Energizer Bunny. She was the granddaughter of Ronnie's former business manager. She and Cody had been involved for a while.

"They decided that her being on the business end of things was better for their relationship than working, living and touring together twenty-four seven. One of Zack's goals had always been for them to form their own company for marketing, bookings, travel, etc. and not be slaves to a record label. He was just about there when the pandemic hit. Alex was slated to be a big part of that, so they put out feelers for a backup singer. Someone who would travel with them, get a piece of the pie, not just be paid by the night or the week, but be a true member of the band." Carli stopped to take a sip of water, prompting Laurel to do the same with her wine.

"They had plenty of time for auditions and interviews during lockdown and they found a girl from Pasadena who fit the bill. She was waitressing and modeling, still living at home and ready not to be. She'd been singing since she was a kid and had danced competitively. She'd made it to final cuts as a Rams cheerleader and was taking some college courses online. You get the picture."

Laurel nodded, trying to keep up without drawing any premature conclusions. She knew Carli needed to lay it all out, establish a timeline and was putting the pieces of the puzzle together as she went. She also knew she was likely verbalizing the whole thing for the first time after ruminating over it thousands of times. It was cathartic, but more importantly, it was productive. Laurel hoped by doing so her friend would see how paranoid and ridiculous she was being.

"So they hired her, started rehearsals. Alex got a schedule together, mostly shows within a few hours drive, to test the waters, see if the world was as ready to get back to life as they all were. Turns out it was."

"Which was good."

"Absolutely," Carli agreed, pushing her fingers through her long brown hair. Her tight spiral curls reminded Laurel of their younger years. Carli had worn her hair straight for the last decade other than when she was pregnant. "We'd been living on savings and Zack had lost a guitarist and most of the roadies to other jobs. Everybody had to do what they had to do. But things were coming back, looking up. So they got a tour together and Alex organized a kickoff party." Carli's voice trailed off and she looked out into the yard, as if asking the towering trees and night sky for permission to continue. She turned back to Laurel with a gulp. "And that night I just knew."

"Knew what?"

"That she was trouble."

In Laurel's mind this proved nothing. "Because she's young, presumably hot and can sing?"

"Yes. And before you say I'm stereotyping, which I know I am, there's more to it. There was something about the way she looked at Zack, acted around him, chose her words, her movements. It was different than with the other people at the party, even the other men."

"And you're basing this whole thing on one encounter a year ago?'

"It wasn't the only encounter and it wasn't a year ago. And before you start doing the mental math, I wasn't pregnant yet."

"But you weren't trying not to be," Laurel reminded her.

"My hormones have nothing to do with this." She turned away, but even in the dim light coming through the kitchen window, Laurel could see tears sliding down her friend's cheeks. She instantly felt sick inside. Carli was the least dramatic person she knew, a rock in times of trouble, never one to worry about things until there was something to worry about. Which meant there was something to worry about. Laurel immediately went to her.

"Car, I don't know what to say." She took her in her arms and hugged her tight. She smelled like bubble bath and fruity gum. "I'm so sorry. But there has to be more to the story. Tell me the rest so I can help you made sense of it. There has to be an explanation."

Carli snuggled against Laurel, laying her head against her shoulder. She dried her cheeks with one hand and rested the other on her baby bump. Laurel laid her hand on top of it with a supportive squeeze. "When Zack went back out on the road in the fall, we were still on the fence about having another baby. So we decided to let nature take its course. He'd been home for over a year, which had never happened before in our marriage. Since we didn't know it was going to be such a long abeyance going in, neither one of us had thought much about it at the time. We, he, adjusted pretty well. And he got a much better sense of what my life is like. Routine, structured, mundane compared to his. I think he came to appreciate our home life and what it takes to run a house, take care of two kids and stay sane. But as time went on, I could tell he was getting restless. Every time he saw the light at the end of the tunnel, something happened. A new variant of the virus, more restrictions, people moving on. And the next thing we knew, another summer was going by. Even with living lean, it was getting scary. And I just couldn't bring myself to go back to work yet, even if we could work out the logistics."

"So hiring the singer and Zack going back on the road was a positive thing at this point." Laurel released Carli and scooted her chair back a little, sitting at an angle to face her more directly.

"Yeah."

"So then what happened?"

"They started doing shows around L.A., up and down the Central Coast. Corporate events and weddings weren't back yet, but fall festivals were happening and there was a lot of pent-up need to get out and about, especially to hear live music. To economize, the guys were sleeping on the tour bus again, which hadn't happened in years. But Leah was getting her own room since she was the only woman."

"Leah is the new singer?"

"Yeah," Carli affirmed. "Zack would only be gone for a night or two at a time at first because a lot of the shows were close to home. He'd gotten used to tucking the boys in at night and he'd FaceTime them before bedtime whenever he could. I swear she was in every frame, always just happened to be around. She'd only met us once by then, but she'd wave and talk to the kids like we were all old friends. And there was something in her eyes that just gnawed at me, like she was saying, 'Watch out, I'm coming for him.' That was often the only chance Zack and I would get to talk rather than text. But instead of excusing herself, she'd hang around in the background, as if listening to our conversation. Zack never seemed to notice. Once or twice I texted him, asked him to step away, but he'd say he had to get off anyway. He was oblivious."

"That's the least surprising thing you've said all night."

That eked a smile out of Carli. "Yeah, that's part of the problem. Typical male boneheadedness."

"That's something we haven't talked about yet. Zack. Aren't you underestimating him?"

"I'll get to that." She stopped short, tilted her head toward the house and knitted her brow.

"What?"

"Nothing. I thought I heard something. I don't want Ollie to wake up and not remember where he is. But it looks like it was just one of them rolling around."

Laurel's eyes went to the monitor sitting on the sill of the open kitchen window. She hadn't heard a thing. "How the hell did you hear that?"

"It's a mother thing. At home I have the camera synched to my phone. This is my old monitor."

"Anyway," Laurel said, drawing out the word. "You were getting to Zack's part in all this nonsense."

Carli began again with a shallow breath, "It was Christmas before I brought it up. They'd booked a few shows at some small venues in Vegas, which was more open than California at the time, leading up to the holidays. I missed his call one night and when I called him back, she answered his phone." She paused, sending Laurel a pleading look. "I mean, come on."

"Okay, I have to admit that breaks girl code. But, we're talking about him, not her, right now. I'm sure there was a perfectly logical explanation."

"Oh, there was. The gig included lodging since were so many available rooms in Vegas at the time. They were all hanging out in his room and he went to the bathroom or something. And he didn't call me back until after the show because he didn't realize that I'd called until then. Because *she* never told him."

"Which was not his fault," Laurel pointed out.

"No, but it does speak to my position the next day in our follow-up… conversation."

"Which I assume was not pleasant."

"You could say that. I know I should have waited until he got home. I know I should have discussed it with him in person. And I know it just added fuel to the fire that he was traveling with her, but I couldn't hold it in for one more minute, let alone one more day."

"And how did that go over?'

"Like a lead balloon. He thought I was being crazy, paranoid. He had the *nerve* to suggest I take a pregnancy test!"

"Okay, that's shitty and I see your frustration there. He didn't validate your feelings, no matter how far-fetched they may have seemed to him. And we've established that we don't like Leah and she's not in the girlfriend club. But I think you're forgetting that Zack is the best guy we know. He loves you, Car. He would never jeopardize you and his kids, his life, for a roll in the hay. He's probably had numerous opportunities over the years to do that and he never did. Why start now?"

"I don't know." Carli shook her head from side to side. "This is different somehow. I can't quite put my finger on it."

Laurel decided continuing to indulge her friend in her flight of lunacy was the only way to bring this thing full circle. "So what happened after he got home from that trip?"

"We talked about it. He apologized for being insensitive. He said he'd try to be more aware around her, pay more attention to make sure he wasn't giving off any signals she was misinterpreting. But I could tell he was just placating me; he still didn't get it. He was home for Christmas and it got lost in the shuffle of the holidays. They played locally on New Year's Eve and he didn't go back out on the road until the end of January. I got pregnant somewhere in between."

Laurel sent her a smug smile. "Well, things were obviously fine between you then."

"We've never had trouble in that department, you know that."

"So what's the problem now?" And why is this the first I'm hearing about it, Laurel added to herself.

"It seems like she finds ways to constantly insert herself in his life. She sends him random texts, only him, not group texts. She'll post things on social media and tag him. She even brought by Easter baskets for the boys. They don't even know her. And Alex has noticed it too. She said something to Cody and he looked at her like she had two heads."

"What does Alex think?"

"She doesn't like her much. Leah has apparently made no effort to get to know the other members of the band or the road crew. She's laser-focused on Zack. Manages to sit by him, talk to him, pull him aside for one reason or another. It's a tough spot for Alex to be in because she's a good fit for the band overall."

"Alex brought it up to you?"

"Yeah. She mentioned it at Ollie's birthday party. And in Zack's defense, she prefaced the conversation by saying that he is completely clueless and innocent. But she still wanted to give me a heads-up."

"I've always liked her. She's definitely in the girl-friend club."

"For sure. And all the guys listen to her. She told me all I have to do is give her the word and Leah'll be gone. But that's not the way I handle things."

"I'm sorry, Car. I feel terrible that you've been struggling with this. For months now. And that I've been too caught up in my own world to notice."

"You did notice. Which is why we're sitting out here at ten o'clock at night talking about it."

"You know what I mean. I feel like I let you down."

"That would be a first. And I'm still pretty sure nothing has happened. I can read Zack like a book. He's going to be home for a few weeks when the baby comes, but after that it's back to business as usual. We sometimes go for a month without having sex because of his schedule. With the boys it's not like I can just pick up and go meet him wherever. And frankly, I don't want to anymore. But's he's a man and it's somehow different for them. Plus, I'll be out of commission after the baby is born for the rest of the time he's home. And we'll both be exhausted."

"I think you need to talk to him again—before the baby comes. This is weighing heavily on your mind and that's not good for you or the baby."

"I know. I keep thinking the next time something happens, I'm going to revisit it, use the new incident as an example. But it always hits me out of left field and then something else gets in the way. Alex volunteered to be my eyes and ears, but I'd like to leave her out of it."

"Where are they this weekend?"

"Redding. Then Eureka, Medford, Salem and Portland."

"Gotta make hay while the sun shines."

Nodding, Carli said, "I can't fault him there. Speaking of making hay, when do I get to read your masterpiece?"

"I don't know why everybody keeps calling it a masterpiece. It's a first draft of a manuscript at best."

"I don't know who everybody is, but I can call it whatever I want."

"You can read it anytime. I have either electronic or hardcopy versions for your perusing pleasure."

Before Carli could make her preference known, her phone went off. "That's still your ringtone? Hasn't he recorded like a hundred songs since then?"

"Not for me."

You're wrong about that, Laurel thought, getting up to give her some privacy. They're all for you. And Laurel decided she was going to make sure Carli remembered that before the weekend was over.

# CHAPTER THIRTEEN

CARLI HAD FORGOTTEN how nice it was to have help. She was sitting on the beach, chair dug into the sand, flipping through a magazine while Laurel played with the boys at the shore. They were both strong swimmers, but she'd put Ollie in his life jacket just in case. A lake was different than a pool and let's face it, she wasn't super light on her feet these days.

She was looking at decorating ideas for the nursery. She suspected it was a girl this time, but didn't want to jinx it, so she was holding off on purchasing anything. They'd painted the nursery a soft green when she was pregnant with Nick and hadn't changed anything when Ollie came along. She'd planned ahead for the boys to share a room and had bought bunkbeds and a large dresser for Nick's room when she found out she was pregnant again. They'd moved Ollie in there a few months ago, but had kept him in a toddler bed since Nick wasn't ready to sleep up top yet. The nursery furniture was white and she had decided to change out the bedding and curtains and add a pink and green wallpaper border if it was a girl. Which she was pretty sure it was, she reminded herself with cautious excitement.

She looked up from the magazine and took in the view of the lake and the mountains in the distance. It was as if an ultramarine haze had settled over the basin.

How could she have forgotten the timeless beauty of Tahoe? And how it heeled the soul as much as the mind and the body? Speaking of the body, she'd fallen asleep last night reading Laurel's manuscript and had woken up with it resting on her stomach. It was a good story, with rich, layered characters who had some baggage but weren't overly tortured. And it was definitely sexy and likely getting sexier.

Her mind drifted to Zack and their conversation last night. He'd sounded tired, a little hoarse and had apologized for not being able to talk to the kids before bed. He'd been troubleshooting some acoustical issues at the venue. He was good at that stuff, reminiscent of the days when he and Cody had to do everything themselves. He could rewire an amp in his sleep and devise a new rigging plan in the blink of an eye. It was among the many things Carli loved about him.

He'd clearly been alone, not so much as a pin dropping in the background, not even the TV. He'd mentioned that they'd gotten pizza delivered after the show, which he immediately qualified by saying that *he, Alex and Cody* had gotten pizza delivered after the show. He and Cody had some paperwork to go over and Alex was along for the ride on this leg of the tour. Carli already knew that as Alex usually kept her in the loop about her schedule. Occasionally, Carli had to send them something when they were on the road or facilitate something in town. He'd ended the call by telling her how much he loved her. She believed him; that wasn't the issue. But it had been nearly two decades for them and they hadn't known any other love but each another. It made her wonder if he ever thought about testing the waters, seeing what else was out there. Ronnie used to say one of the greatest gifts our parents can give us is to be born content. She had somehow given that to Veronica despite not enjoying the proclivity herself. Rosa had passed it on to Carli, as Ronnie had often reminded her. But Zack, in Carli's estimation, was in the Ronnie camp. It was a double-edged sword. It drove you and cursed you.

Carli was still mulling that over when Laurel brought the boys back. "I think we've had enough beach for today. Nick is hungry, Ollie has to pee and my fair complexion is screaming for shade. Want to head back to the house for a bit? We can take them out to do something later."

Well, that had been nice while it lasted. "Sure. Even my olive complexion is getting a workout. And their hybrid ones." She smiled at her sons, touching each of their arms. "You guys are starting to look a little pink. Let's go in and have some quiet time."

"Can we have more of our suckers now?" Nick wanted know.

"Sure."

"Yay!" They cried in unison.

"Everybody grab your towel and help carry something," Carli directed, rising from the chair with a little assistance from Laurel.

They packed up the beach bag and Laurel hoisted the two chairs on her back. Each holding a boy's hand, they walked up the beach and across the street, then down the few blocks to the house. Once Carli got the boys dressed and settled in front of the TV for a little quiet time, she went looking for Laurel. She found her sitting at the deck table with her laptop.

"Everybody good?"

"Yeah," Carli replied, plopping down in the chair next to Laurel. "They might fall asleep for a bit, which at home might be a problem come bedtime, but the sun here takes so much out of them."

"I can relate. I could use a nap myself. I can't imagine how you must feel."

"I've never been able to sleep during the day. Even with a newborn."

"I remember. Do you want to take them out for pizza and ice cream tonight? That place we used to go to is still open if you can believe it."

"That'd be nice. What are you doing?"

"Editing what I wrote yesterday before you got here."

"Maybe I'll go read for a bit then. Have a little quiet time of my own. It's weird not to have something to do."

"How far did you get last night?" Laurel asked, easing back in the chair.

"I remember starting chapter three, but not much about it. So I guess the first two chapters."

"And?"

"It's good, Laurel. I really like the storyline and how the characters are endearing, but not pathetic. Especially Scott."

"I hear a but."

"No but, *but* I want to like Whitney more than I do. Like a sister-friend thing. I think he might be too good for her."

"That's what my mom said. I'm working on it."

Interesting. There was that word again, Carli thought. "I'll go check on the boys and see if I can settle in for a bit, read a chapter or two more before we go out to dinner."

"Okay. Oh, wait," she added as Carli stood and started to walk away. "This is the picture I told you about."

Carli took the snapshot from Laurel's outstretched hand and examined it. "Where did you get this again?"

"Gov's boss Moira Brody gave it to him. She's the dark-haired girl. I think it was the summer before second grade."

Carli nodded in agreement. "I remember the bathing suit. Yours and mine."

"Do you remember either one of those girls? Or even the name?"

"No, but I wasn't up here nearly as much as you were. That could have been the only time I saw them. You don't?"

"No," Laurel said with a shake of the head. "My mom couldn't place them either."

"Who took the picture?"

"Moira didn't know, but she had it, so likely her mom or dad."

"Humph," Carli said with a smirk.

"What?"

"Seems like it's one coincidence after another, doesn't it? Actually, I think we're moving past coincidence and on to fate," Carli said, handing the picture back to her.

"You sound like my mother."

"I'll take that as a compliment. Now, I have children to check on and a masterpiece to read." With that, she left Laurel to her editing.

Carli found both boys asleep on the couch. She turned off the TV and covered them with a blanket. Then she went to her room and grabbed Laurel's manuscript from the nightstand. She snuggled into the oversized chair in the corner and started chapter three. Yes, she remembered this now. Scott and Whitney had just seen each other again and the palpability of their connection was not lost on either one of them this time. He was picking up some odd jobs to keep himself from going crazy and she was considering investing in a lakeside property. He was doing an inspection for another potential buyer when she stopped by to check the place out. He couldn't take his eyes off of her and she couldn't hide her attraction to him. Carli was just getting into the heart of things when her phone vibrated. She pushed down the disappointment that it was Veronica instead of Zack. She had yet to hear from him today.

*Hope you're enjoying your visit. Have you had a chance to read the manuscript yet?*

*Reading chapter three as we speak.*

*And?*

*I love it! But apparently you and I had similar thoughts about Whitney. Laurel is being too hard on her.*

*Yes!*

*How do you think she is overall?*

*Laurel or Whitney? :)*

*I think Laurel is doing great!* But, Carli silently added, we've mostly talked about me. She needed to remedy that. *More like her old self like you said.*

*Good to hear. Let me know what you think of the rest. Try to get through chapter four tonight.*

*Will do.*

Carli put her phone down and repositioned herself in the chair. It didn't surprise her that she and Veronica had similar impressions of Whitney. Veronica was like a second mother to her and Ronnie had been like the grandmother she'd never had since her grandparents were in Mexico. But Veronica seemed overly-invested in her feedback, specifically the timing of it. And she obviously knew of their plans to see Gov tomorrow.

Interesting.

She went back to the story. The sexual tension was escalating between Scott and Whitney. Their initial encounters, then ending up at the same grab-and-go case at the grocery store and now the same blackjack table at the casino. He brings her a decent glass of wine from the bar, not settling for the basic offerings the waitress brings around, and they end up talking for the rest of the night at a cozy table in the corner. They connect the childhood dots, he offers to see her home, she refuses. It's clear that he's sincere and just being a gentleman. It's also clear from Whitney's knee-jerk refusal that she prefers to and is perfectly capable of taking care of herself. To a fault. But the attraction is growing on both sides as is the struggle not to get involved. Carli had a feeling they were going to end up in bed, have mind-blowing sex and then think they could just move on. And be wrong.

She couldn't remember the last time she and Zack had mind-blowing sex. They'd had plenty of it over the years; different places, different positions, different desires. He was her only sexual partner and she his. They'd been sixteen and clumsy and it had practically been over before it began. But she'd loved him so and he'd been so sweet with her. She couldn't imagine being touched by anyone else, she thought, rubbing her belly as their baby kicked inside her. And the thought of Zack touching another woman made her sick to her stomach.

She also couldn't remember the last time she'd read a romance novel. Or a book that didn't have something to do with babies, parenting or cooking. During the day on top of it. She refocused on the story and started chapter four. Laurel was doing a good job of describing the physical connection, but she was rushing the romance. This was supposed to be new love, a slow burn, maybe even the love of each of their lives. It deserved a little time, a little care and some attention to detail, she thought as her eyes grew heavy. Carli drifted off to sleep and dreamed of young love, mind-blowing sex and a daddy who sings at night.

~~~

If Tahoe had a high season, it was July. And no time was more celebrated and festive than the week of the Fourth. The beaches were packed, the restaurants slammed and the hotels overbooked. Innovation and technology were blending with tradition this year with a state-of-the-art drone firework display. This might be Gov's first Fourth of July living in Tahoe, but it was far from his first at the lake. He'd seen the fireworks explode over the water countless times. But this year would be different. This year he'd be spending it with Laurel.

They hadn't seen each other in a few days and he found himself missing her, especially at night. Not just for the sex; they spent some nights together just sleeping. But he longed for her company, looked forward to seeing her at the end of the day, missed waking up beside her. Her smile, her laugh, her disposition soothed him. She'd become such an integral part of his life in such a short amount of time.

Today he was going to meet the legendary Carli. Every guy knows how important the best friend is.

Especially a lifelong one. So he intended to shine. He'd won Veronica over so he should be able to handle Carli. Plus he liked kids and didn't get to see his niece and nephew that much. It would be fun to throw a ball around with someone other than Boot.

He'd picked up some wine for Laurel and flowers for Carli. He'd also bought a T-ball set for the boys. Laurel had mentioned that neither one of them had expressed an interest in music yet, but the older boy played T-ball and his brother wanted to do whatever he did. There wasn't anything like that at the rental and Gov knew from his sister that stuff like that was a pain to bring on trips.

Laurel said to come around four and that he'd be in charge of the grill and she and Carli would handle the rest. When Gov walked up to the front door, he had the T-ball stand under his arm, the wine in one hand and the flowers in the other. Boot announced their arrival with two resounding barks and Laurel met him at the door.

"Hi! Here, let me help."

"Just take the wine. It's probably better if I keep walking."

Laurel obliged and followed him to the kitchen. She set the wine on the counter and gave Boot a rub, then turned to Gov. "What have you got there?"

"Flowers for Carli and a T-ball set for the kids," he answered, laying the flowers on the island and letting the stand drop to the floor.

"How thoughtful." She walked over to him and put her arms around his neck. "Anything for me?" she asked with a mischievous smile.

There it was again, Gov thought. That whirlwind of emotion he felt every time she touched him. It was like his heart tripped in his chest and then fell to his stomach, swirling around like a recalcitrant dust devil. He drew her to him and laid his lips on hers, intending to make it short and sweet. But she slid her hands up and cupped his face, covering his mouth with hers. The next thing he knew, his tongue was searching for hers and his hands were on her buttocks. She wrapped her calf around his ankles, pressing him against her. He felt himself begin to grow.

"Oh, I've got something for you," he huffed out. "But I don't think this is the right time to give it to you,"

"Mmm," she cooed. "Yeah, I can feel that. I'm going to hold you to it."

"Deal."

Just then Boot, who'd made a beeline for the backyard, returned to the kitchen. He brought with him two little boys and a pregnant woman. Laurel stepped out of Gov's embrace and turned to them. "I see you guys have met Boot. This is my friend Gov." She moved behind the taller boy and put her hands on his shoulders. "This is Nick." She sidestepped and did the same with the other one. "And this is Ollie. "

Gov closed the small space between them and stuck out his hand. "Hi, Nick, it's nice to meet you." Nick shook it politely. "You too, Ollie," Gov addressed the younger boy.

Ollie did the same, a little more enthusiastically. "My real name is Oliver. But only teachers call me that."

"Well, since I'm not a teacher, I guess I'll stick with Ollie," Gov said, suppressing a laugh. Then he turned to the woman. "You must be Carli. I've heard so much about you."

"Likewise," Carli replied. "It's great to finally meet you." Waving away his outstretched hand, she took Gov into a warm hug. "I think we're past that."

Just as the hug was ending, the boys eyed the T-ball stand. "Cool! I have one of those at home!" Nick exclaimed.

Carli gave Gov a knowing look. "Thank you. You didn't have to do that."

"My pleasure. It's fun for me too. Brings back a lot of good memories."

"Carli, Gov brought us flowers and wine," Laurel announced.

"How nice. Thanks again."

"I'll go grab the bat and ball from the car. I bought a helmet too."

"Wow," Carli said, clearly impressed. "You covered all the bases, so to speak."

"I have a niece and nephew, so I know the drill." Gov went back out and retrieved the bag from the sporting goods store along with Boot's food and toys. Laurel kept a bed here for him but Gov didn't plan on staying over with the kids in the house. But after that kiss, he might reconsider.

Carli was nothing like he'd pictured. She was the polar opposite of Laurel in coloring, height and for obvious reasons, weight. The boys were adorable and well-mannered; Nick seemed to favor his mother and Ollie looked more like the pictures he'd seen of Zack Harper. When Laurel had told him Carli's husband was a musician, he hadn't thought much of it. But Harper and Company was a tried-and-true rock band with a solid following. It made Gov appreciate their music even more to learn that Zack was as good a person as he was a musician, especially since Carli meant so much to Laurel.

Gov spent the next two hours in the backyard supervising T-ball and tending to the burgers and hot dogs. He was sitting at the table after dinner, watching the kids play with Boot, when Carli came out and joined him.

"Thanks for keeping an eye on them. They love the T-ball set and the dog."

"No problem. I offered to help with cleanup but Laurel refused."

"Me too. She told me if I didn't sit down for a little bit, she wasn't going to let me go watch the fireworks. Because she knows I'll fall asleep halfway through."

"She's one to talk."

Carli smiled in understanding, then cocked her head to the side and gave him an appraising look. "Truth be told, I only agreed so you and I could talk. Get to know each other a little."

More grilling, Gov thought but kept it to himself. He'd been expecting this. "I figured you already know all there is to know about me," he half-joked.

"That may be. But I like to draw my own conclusions."

"And?"

"So far you pass with flying colors."

"Then I'm two for two. That's what Veronica said."

Carli's eyes began to twinkle. "I know."

"Of course you do. Laurel said Veronica is like a second mother to you."

Carli affirmed with a nod. "And Ronnie was like a grandmother."

"You called her Ronnie too?"

"Well, she certainly wouldn't answer to Mrs. Reynolds!" Carli's eyes filled with melancholy and her tone turned wistful. "And I basically grew up in her house."

"That must have been interesting."

"It was. And wonderful. A completely different world from the one I knew, the one I went home to every night."

"Tell me about it," Gov heard himself say.

Carli started to protest; this conversation was supposed to be about him, after all. But after a moment of hesitation she began on a sigh, "I'm a first generation American. My parents got married at nineteen, immigrated at twenty on a work visa sponsored by a company who placed domestics. Being a couple was advantageous because it only required one room for housing for two employees. My dad did maintenance and gardening and my mom housekeeping. After a few years, they became citizens of their own accord. When my mom got pregnant with me, they went out on their own, got their own place. My dad started his own landscaping company and my mom took in sewing and cleaned offices at night. My dad was actually the one who started working for Ronnie. One day she mentioned she couldn't get a housekeeper to stay for more than a few months to save her life. He said his wife was looking for something because their daughter was going to kindergarten. The rest is history."

"The epitome of the American Dream. Think big, work hard and you'll be rewarded."

"Yes, my parents are certainly poster children for that. And Ronnie was a big part of the reward."

"Laurel said you guys are part of the family."

"Ronnie used to say only children make their own family. I'm a beneficiary of that."

"It sounds like you miss her too."

"Some people we miss, some leave a void. Ronnie checks both boxes."

Gov thought about that for a long moment. Then he said, "Do you think that's part of the reason Laurel is here? To try to fill that void?"

"No? Yes? Maybe?" Carli finished with a noncommittal shrug. "And I've thought about it a lot. It's out of character for her to do something like this. But you've probably already figured that out."

He had. "Then why?" He was afraid the answer was going to be the divorce, but he had to ask. Laurel categorically denied it, but the notion still lingered between them. And if anyone would know, it would be Carli.

"Laurel had a rough couple of years between the divorce, the potential fallout from it at work and Ronnie's death. She'd talked about writing and at first I didn't understand why she couldn't just do that in L.A. Rent a place on the beach if you want to get away. But she needed a change of scenery, literally and figuratively, to get out of her own head. And for some reason, her gut kept screaming Tahoe. Now that I'm back here again, I can see why."

"So it wasn't because of Grant?" Gov bit off the name like a bitter pill.

Carli started on a long breath, "He must have something to do with it, whether she's willing to admit it or not. I mean infidelity is one thing, but to have it thrown in your face like that? Publicly? And for him to be so audacious about it? Even I was surprised he was that blasé."

"Sounds like you weren't a big fan."

"Of Grant? He was okay. Fine, actually, for the most part. I was there the day she met him and I was there the day she left him. So I've come full circle with the whole thing. He made her happy in the now but I never saw it going the distance. I think when we're young we don't always think in those terms. He didn't seem to grasp the enormity of marriage, take the long view into consideration, think about the consequences of his actions and how far-reaching they might be. I was never prouder of her than I was on the day she left him. I think he was shocked."

Gov found that inconceivable, not only that Grant would treat Laurel and his marriage so cavalierly, but that he thought she would put up with it.

The boys running up on the deck prevented Gov from verbalizing that. "Mommy, when are the fireworks?" Nick wanted to know.

Carli looked at her watch. "We're leaving in about twenty minutes to get a spot at the park."

"Can Boot come?" Ollie asked Gov.

"Not this time. Dogs aren't allowed at the park tonight," Gov said. "Plus you guys are wearing him out. He'll need a nap."

"Okay," Nick said begrudgingly. "Can he come to our house sometime? We have a yard too."

"I don't think so, buddy."

"But if you come to see Aunt Laurel, Boot could come with you. She's going to come back after her book is done. And Aunt Veronica has a really big house with a yard and a pool even bigger than my grandma's. With a diving board!"

Gov was processing that, trying to come up with a response that would appease Nick as much as himself when Carli came to the rescue."Okay, guys. Why don't you go inside and fill-up Boot's water dish? He looks thirsty. And see if Aunt Laurel needs any help in the kitchen."

After the boys ran off with Boot, Carli said, "Sorry."

"Don't be. They're great. And I have a feeling a dog is in your future. So I should be the one apologizing."

"It was inevitable. If ever two little boys needed a dog, it's them."

There was a long moment of silence as Nick's comment hung in the air between them. Finally, Gov took the plunge. "Do you think this timeline of Laurel's is determinate?"

Carli stared over his shoulder in contemplation for a few seconds, then met his steady gaze. "I think she thinks it is."

"What do you think?"

She turned her head to the side and looked into the house, confirming that Laurel was in the kitchen with the boys and out of earshot. "For the second time in six months, I don't know what to think. When she told me about this whole thing, I thought it was a whim, a flight of fancy and that it would pass. Then she did it. And she actually stayed here. And is writing. And it's good. Have you read it?"

"No. She hasn't offered."

Carli gave him an upward nod, as if that made sense. She started to say something, then reconsidered and changed gears. "By nature, Laurel is a planner, predictable, self-disciplined, focused. She's basically Veronica in a different body. Except for this one little part.

There's a little piece of Ronnie in there, a sliver really, that rears its head every once in a while. Like with Grant. When she met him and let herself get caught up. And when she cut her losses and left him because she was fed up, done. That's all Ronnie. Impulsive, decisive, strong. When Laurel decided she was going to move to Tahoe to write this book, she was in Ronnie-mode. But she calculated her savings, projected her expenses, planned accordingly. Seven months, give or take. Veronica to a tee. She had these characters, ideas, concepts floating around in her head and suddenly if she didn't harness them, write them down and get them out, she was going to go crazy. Ronnie all week long and twice on Sunday. I threw her a working title just so she could get past that and move on to actually writing the book."

"She told me that much. *Christmas in Tahoe*. But it's not a Christmas book."

"Who cares? At that point she didn't know what it was. But in her mind you can't have one without two or A without B. Back to Veronica-mode."

"Order, structure, planning."

"Right. The practical, methodical, proper Laurel is Veronica. You can't start writing a book without a title, right? That's the majority of her. But that creative sliver, the risk-taker, the pantser is Ronnie bleeding through, not willing to be forgotten. You don't need a title yet. You can change the title of a book until it goes to print, right? It should be fluid, flow with the story, name itself. Like a song does."

"So the Laurel I know is only a small part of her?" Or maybe he didn't really know her at all, Gov thought as trepidation and disappointment formed an icy ball in his gut.

Apparently his face was falling along with his stomach because Carli began again with a sympathetic smile, "Maybe. But for your sake I hope not, judging from your visceral reaction. And remember, we're flip-flopping here."

Gov didn't know what that had to with anything. "Flip-flopping?"

"Between the Veronica part of Laurel that has always kept her grounded and that little spark of Ronnie that brought her here. The Laurel you know, the Laurel who is fulfilling a dream, the Laurel who is—"

"On a tight schedule," he reminded her keenly.

"The Laurel who is growing," Carli barreled over him. "The Laurel who is as happy as I've seen her in a long time. Maybe the reason for that has less to do the book she's writing and more to do with who she's really writing the book about."

Gov shook his head from side to side, struggling keep up. "You lost me at flip-flop."

"Maybe the Laurel you know is the best of both. Maybe Laurel's best self is a little less Veronica and a little more Ronnie. And maybe this was the only way she was ever going to unlock that part. By coming up here and writing a book and…" She started to say something else, but swallowed it.

"And?" Gov had to know.

Carli looked away, then back at him again. She let out a contemplative breath and then asked, "Do you know how we find our best selves, Gov?"

Gov knew she wasn't really asking, so he just waited for her to elaborate.

"Not in ourselves, in other people. I could say something cliché like I found my best self in my husband and he in me and while there's some truth to that, I find my best self in my kids and Zack finds his best self in his music. But neither one of us could do those things without each other. I wouldn't have the capacity to be the mother I am without loving him and he wouldn't have the courage to be the musician he is without loving me. Because we have different strengths and different things to offer each other. We complement each other."

Gov instantly thought of his parents. "Teamwork."

"That comes later. Balance, wholeness, fate." Carli settled on the word. "Laurel is supposed to write this book and she is supposed to be here to do it. And I think you're supposed to be a part of that. In so doing, she'll discover her best self. But eventually she'll have to find a happy medium between the Veronica Laurel and the Ronnie Laurel or she'll never be content. She's searching for that middle ground, that happy medium, she just doesn't know it yet."

"How can I help her find it, this middle ground you say she needs?"

"She has to find it herself. In the book."

"But I have no idea what the book is about." Gov's voice reflected his mounting frustration.

"Neither does she. Not yet, anyway. And you don't have to. You just have to wait."

"Waiting is helping?"

"Yeah. And sometimes the waiting really is the hardest part." She stood and gave his shoulder a squeeze. "I have to round up the boys."

"Carli." Gov grabbed her wrist. "All I wanted to know was if you think Laurel will go back to L.A. at the end of the year."

"I know."

"That's not an answer."

"It's the only one I have. But you're not really asking if Laurel will go back to L.A. at the end of the year. You're asking if you're going to lose her if she goes back to L.A. at the end of the year."

"Am I? Or is that in the book too?" His tone was more clipped than he'd intended for it to be.

A satisfied smile curved Carli's lips. "It just might be. Along with Laurel's best self. And maybe yours too." She bent down, kissed him on the cheek and walked inside.

Gov could only stare at her retreating back for a long moment as the cacophony in the kitchen became a dull roar. Then standing, he grabbed his beer bottle and went inside. He found Laurel in the kitchen adjusting the lights.

"Ready?"

He shook off the reverie. "Yeah. Where is everybody?"

"Carli took the boys for a potty break and to get their jackets. Can you move your truck? It'd be easier to take Carli's car because of the car seats."

"Sure." He threw his bottle in the trash and went to her. He put his arms around her waist and looked deeply into her eyes. "I love you, Laurel."

Her face broke into a broad grin and her eyes began to shine. "I love you, too." She patted down the tufts of hair on his forehead like she had that first night in the kitchen. "Where did that come from?"

"I can't tell you that I love you?"

"Of course you can." Her hands moved down and fanned his neck. "I'm sorry. I was just taken off guard."

He leaned in and kissed her with everything he felt in his heart. So much more than love. Commitment, fidelity, promise. And to his amazement, it evoked no physical reaction below the belt. It was a steady crescendo instead of a hurried flash, sweet instead of sensual, warm instead of hot. He couldn't put his feelings into words, not yet at least, so he was counting on the kiss to do the talking. He was all-in for the first time in his life. He wanted her, this, them, for the long haul. He wondered if she sensed it because when he pulled away, she swallowed hard and gave him a shaky smile.

There was no time for debate because Carli and the boys instantaneously appeared. Laurel got Boot situated while Carli loaded up the kids and Gov moved his car to the street. They piled into the SUV with Gov at the wheel since he knew the area best. He found a parking space in a residents only lot and hung his placard from Carli's rearview mirror. He grabbed the blankets and chairs and the women each took a boy's hand and off they went. The park was already packed, but Gov found a spot and they set up camp. Soon the music swelled and the show began. It was definitely different this year, Gov thought as the drones lit up the night sky with depictions of skiers, flags and vignettes of the lake. The boys were mesmerized and no one seemed to miss the traditional fireworks. Ollie fell asleep on the way home and Gov carried him to bed for Carli. He was just about to leave when she returned from putting Nick to bed.

"Thanks, guys. That was really fun," she said around a yawn. "See you in the morning."

"Actually, I was just leaving," Gov said, gathering up Boot's toys.

"You're not staying over?"

"No. With the boys here I thought I'd go home."

"Don't be silly. They're out like a lights. And even if they weren't, they're too young to think a thing of it."

"That's what I told him," Laurel chimed in.

"I think they'd be disappointed if Boot wasn't here in the morning, but that's up to you. Thanks again. Good night." She turned on her heel and started back the way she'd come. After a few paces, she stopped short and turned around. "Laurel can attest to the fact that I sleep like a rock. I have selective hearing; I only hear my kids." With a loaded wink, she resumed her stride.

"Good night, Car," Laurel called after her. Once Carli was out of sight, she turned to Gov. "You'd hate to disappoint the kids," she said with a flirty smile. "I mean, unless you were looking forward to going home and sleeping in your own bed." She paused and licked her bottom lip, then bit on it. "Alone."

Gov hooked her by the waist and brought her to him. "That's the last thing I was looking forward to. I was trying to be a gentleman."

Laurel tucked her hands into the back pockets of his jeans. "I think I've had enough gentleman Gov for tonight."

"Have you?"

"Mm-hmm. Earlier you said you had something for me. Where is it?"

Gov reached around and grabbed one of her hands. He brought it up front. "Right here."

"Oh, yeah. That's more like it." She started to rub him through the denim. "Do you still want to go home?"

Gov had to close his eyes for second, take a breath to stop himself from coming undone. "I never wanted to go home. And you know it."

She all but bit the air in front of his face. "Prove it."

"Laurel," he murmured on a curse, laying a hand on her busy one. "I won't be able to if you keep doing that out here."

She stilled her hand, then leaned in and kissed him full on the mouth, pulling away with a nip. "You check the locks and get Boot—we'll have to shut my bedroom door tonight. I'll turn off the lights and make sure Carli's all tucked in. She'll be sleeping with one eye open until Zack calls. I'll meet you in my room."

He obliged her in that and everything else she asked of him for the next hour. And when he woke in the night and turned to her, she gave herself to him again in the predawn light. It wasn't *like* a dream, it *was* a dream. His dream from the night before their first date. Laurel was on top of him, moving over him with the agile motions of a feline in heat. He was clutching her at the waist as she slinked up and down over him, fluid as water, while he stiffened to a steel rod inside her. Head flung back, hair disheveled and sweat beading on her skin, she was clenching her teeth, trying to suppress the cries of pleasure threatening to escape her throat. She was vibrating all around him, on the verge of coming, as he filled his mouth with her breast. Arching her back, she pushed herself forward and brought him even deeper. It somehow made it even more potent that they had to be quiet, as if they were breaking some medieval law by bringing each other to climax. He couldn't get enough of her, wanted it to last forever, but he knew his clock was ticking. He slid his hand around to her center and finding her her wet, fleshy core, started moving his thumb circuitously.

She froze on a detached breath. Righting her head, she met his eyes and let out a series of short gasps. "Gov…Oh God, Gov." She was unraveling now, as if her body wasn't hers to control, floating above him as the orgasm took hold. "Yes…oh…yesss…faster, faster, ooh, yesss!" she ground out, her voice barely above a whisper. He kept going, kept rubbing, indulging in the feeling of being inside her as she spasmed around him. Hands cupping her breasts, she looked skyward as the second orgasm began rolling through her, suspended her and then slowly let her fall. And just as she tumbled down those last few glorious pegs, he growled her name and unleashed all he had into her.

# CHAPTER FOURTEEN

LATE SUMMER IN Tahoe hit different, Laurel thought as she drove home from Gov's one September morning. The mornings were a little cooler, the days a little shorter, the nights a little crisper. She rarely stayed at his place, but last night he'd been working late so she went over to take Boot out and give him dinner. He'd brought back takeout and she'd crashed there after having more wine than usual. It had been unplanned and a little inconvenient come morning, but spending some time alone there had given her new perspective.

She'd known from the other times she'd been over that Gov was neat and clean, especially for a guy who lived alone, and that he had decent taste when it came to home decor. No paintings on the walls, but a high-quality black leather sofa and chair, a flat screen TV that any sports fan could appreciate and even coordinating towels and accessories in the bathroom. He also had a scattering of family pictures around the living room and matching dishes in the kitchen, complete with linens. Laurel figured Sheryl had something to do with that.

She knew he liked living at the lake, but it was obvious that he wasn't planning to stay in the condo in the long-term. His bedroom closet was full of unpacked boxes and the kitchen pantry was minimally stocked at best. Her time there at loose ends had forced her to think about her own plans. She could probably extend her lease if she wanted to. She was behind schedule on the book and more than a little surprised that it didn't bother her as much as she would have expected. And while she and Gov had yet to discuss the future, there seemed to be a mutual understanding that they had one. She was pulling into the driveway, contemplating that, when Zack's ringtone filled the air. Her stomach dropped. The baby. She answered on the first ring.

"Everything's fine." Zack's voice was raw, scratchy and a little on edge. He'd just come off Burning Man and the fundraiser at the Hollywood Bowl. He was home for a couple of days.

Laurel let out a breath she didn't know she'd been holding. "You scared the shit out of me. Why are you even up this early?"

"Because I haven't been to bed yet. Do you have a minute?"

"Sure." Laurel pulled into the garage and killed the engine, sending the call to her phone. She grabbed it and her purse and went inside. Coffee was the first order of business. It was the one area where Gov fell short, she thought, scooping her special blend into the filter and filling the canister with water. Plus she doubted he had any dark chocolate in the house.

"I need you to tell me what's going on with Carli."

Laurel knew where this was headed, had expected it at some point, but Zack was going to have to earn her counsel. "Well, she's about eight months pregnant and wishes she were nine."

"That I know. Now tell me something I don't know."

"You're going to have to be a little more specific, Zack."

"She's obviously mad at me about something that has nothing to do with being eight months pregnant. She's polite but distant, almost to the point of being business-like and seems to be carrying the weight of the world in her eyes every time she looks at me."

"Here's an idea. How about asking *her* what's going on?" Laurel snarked, recalling her conversation with Carli over the Fourth. She'd said if the opportunity presented itself, she'd reiterate her concerns about Leah. If Zack confronted her, she'd have the perfect segue. And no more excuses.

"I've tried! Several times! She won't talk to me. I'm done screwing around here, Laurel. I've never seen her like this. I'm going back on the road in a few days ahead of the baby coming. I need to know she and I are okay when I do."

Laurel was stuck between a rock and a hard place, torn between her loyalty to Carli and her faith in Zack, in them. Best-case scenario was this whole thing got resolved with a ten-minute conversation. Worst-case was it opened up Pandora's box.

"Laurel, please. I'm going crazy here."

"Where is she now?"

"She took the boys to school and was going to run a few errands afterward."

Laurel closed her eyes and inhaled the rich, nutty aroma of the dark roast brewing in an attempt to clear her head. Then she went for it. "Zack, there's no delicate way to say this. And since I love you almost as much as I love Carli and consider your kids like my own, I'm going to betray the confidence of someone who is an extension of myself. Are you sleeping with your new singer?"

"No." Zack didn't hesitate, but he also didn't sound shocked.

"That was quick."

"The truth doesn't require much thought."

"Touché."

He ignored the snappish remark. "Does she really believe that?"

"No… I don't know. Maybe. I think she thinks it's a possibility."

"She's wrong."

"For the record, that was my initial reaction. But she gave me a few scenarios, some instances she pointed out to you that you didn't take seriously, some things that don't add up."

Zack blew out a conspicuous breath. Laurel imagined him running his hand through his thick blond hair, pacing in the galley kitchen of their house, likely wearing only his briefs. "Laurel, I never touched her. But yes, she came on to me. It was after Car brought it up. I was trying to be more cognizant of it, keep my distance, avoid finding myself alone with her. She approached me in the hall of the hotel one night and asked me in for a nightcap and insinuated more. I told her no. Firmly. Repeatedly."

"Did you tell Carli?" Laurel asked, already knowing the answer.

"No," he answered after a moment. "I thought about it. But why? It wouldn't change anything."

"Because Zack, then Carli would know that she isn't crazy and that you are trustworthy. And that you guys are still on the same page. Has it happened again?"

"Not really."

"That's qualified."

Zack began on a sigh, "Not as brazenly. I sometimes find her staring at me. She's made…" He paused, chose his words carefully. "She's made it clear that she's interested, nonverbally, let's say."

Laurel shook her head from side to side and swore under her breath. This is the kind of bitch who gives all of us a bad name. "Did you reiterate your commitment to your wife, your family. Jesus, Zack, she knows Carli's pregnant, doesn't she?"

"Yes, of course she does! She has no reason to doubt my commitment or my priorities. None of us are like that; it's not the seventies for Christ's sake. You of all people should get that. This has never happened to me before."

"And you think ignoring it is going to make it go away?"

"No, of course not. And to add insult to injury, I also run the risk of being massacred in the court of public opinion if Leah makes up a story to retaliate for me turning down her advances. I have to tread lightly. Cody has been sticking to me like glue in case I need a witness. With his phone at the ready."

Laurel got out the half and half and put a splash in her cup along with a packet of sugar. "Anything else?"

"She texts me sometimes. I delete them without reading them."

"You should have told Carli, Zack. You have to. Today."

"What if she gets upset? The baby…I would never forgive myself."

"She's already upset! And she knows your phone is pinging at night and why. She's not an idiot."

"Jesus, Laurel. Why didn't you tell me? You've known me, us, forever. Do you know how many opportunities I've had over the years to go out on her? Countless. I love her. I don't want anyone else. Not then, not now, not ever."

Laurel's eyes filled with tears. "Then tell her that, just like that. Remind her of all you've been through, all you've built together. Don't let her bring this baby into the world until you do."

Zack didn't reply at first. Finally, he said, "I will. But Laurel—"

"I won't say anything," she said, reading his mind. "But do it before you go back out on the road."

They ended the call there, without exchanging goodbyes. That was often their way, like a sibling relationship. An understanding had been reached and both of them knew the other would hold up their end of the bargain. They were united in purpose, shared the same goal, loved the same people.

One problem solved for the time being, Laurel finally took a sip of coffee. As the liquid gold did its magic, her thoughts went back to Zack's reference to the seventies. She wondered how Ronnie had navigated the perils of show business and the demands of motherhood while managing to have any semblance of a love life. If she had one, had Mac been a part of it? And why did it seem it matter so much? Because of the unfinished song about Tahoe? And how she could personally relate to it?

Speaking of which, *Christmas in Tahoe* wasn't going to finish itself. Laurel couldn't believe how fast time was going. She almost felt like life here was lived in a bubble, as if the periphery of the lake somehow insulated her from the outside world. She hardly even went on social media anymore. She picked up her phone, tapped on Instagram and started scrolling. A couple more of her sorority sisters had babies, several of them were on their second or third kids like Carli. A former colleague had gotten a hefty promotion, another was switching careers and going to grad school. And here she sat in Tahoe, in a short-term rental, all but unemployed, writing a book that only her mother and best friend had read. She was in love with a man completely different from the man she'd thought she'd spend the rest of her life with. A man to whom she would have to answer to before much longer about the future. A man's whose life was rooted as deeply here as hers was in L.A.

Wasn't it?

She looked forward to seeing Gov at the end of the day, had fallen into a routine with him. One that wouldn't work in her real life, the life she was presumably going back to. But she was starting to realize that she didn't really want her job back, even if it was still waiting for her. Early morning meetings, designer suits and business dinners had nothing on being woken up by the birds, writing on the deck as the breeze whistled through the trees and sipping wine as the alpenglow bathed the mountains in soft, vermillion light.

Taking in the backyard as it greeted the day, she reminded herself that she'd come here, to a place she'd loved as child, to seek sanctuary as an adult. She'd found so much more than that, so much more than she'd expected, so much more than she'd wanted. She'd based her story here, created her characters accordingly and started strong. But she still couldn't come up with a suitable name for her hero, let alone endear the reader to her heroine. She'd spent much of August stuck in the sagging middle of a novel that had no direction, no purpose, no goal. She couldn't move the story along, couldn't define the conflict, couldn't forge a path to a happy ending. Whitney and "Scott" weren't running away and hiding in the Sierra, they'd simply found themselves there. And then they'd found each other. But what were they really looking for? And how would they find it in one another? Had it been missing all of their lives or just in their previous partners? Sexual chemistry was one thing, but that alone doesn't make happily ever after. There had to be more.

Speaking of sexual chemistry, she and Gov certainly had that. She'd put the shower scene in the book; he hadn't minded being her muse that night. The way she felt when she was with him was completely different than with Grant. She felt whole, protected, free. She loved knowing when he was about to come, loved watching him teeter on the edge, then yield to her. He'd whimper her name as if it was the first time, cradle her face in his hands and kiss her, then let go. And she'd never orgasmed so frequently, so consistently, so fully before, as if each individual cell in her body experienced the sweeping pleasure every time. Then he'd hold her, still joined, until it was no longer feasible, as if not wanting the union to end. The memory of it made her breath catch and her pulse quicken. She wondered if he ever thought about her, about them, that way.

She forced her mind back to the matter at hand. The only reason she even had a working title was because Carli had indulged her, knowing she couldn't move forward without one. But soon she'd need to have a cover made, secure formatting, decide whether or not to self-edit. She poured another cup of coffee and sat down at the table. She opened her laptop, pulled up the file and ran a word count. Thirty-thousand. She'd thought she'd be at almost twice that by now.

She could hear her creative writing professor's voice in her head, reminding her that frustration and self-doubt were part of the process and that giving up was not. Maybe she needed to do something else for a while, put her head to rights. Obviously her morning routine had been altered today, so in an attempt to get back on track, she decided to go for a walk.

She changed out of yesterday's jeans and t-shirt into leggings and a pullover, laced up her running shoes, filled her water bottle and grabbed her sunglasses out of the car. She headed toward the lake, finding it much less crowded this morning than it had been for the last few months. She'd walked many mornings since she'd been here, often ending up at the beach, but had yet to see the older couple again. She wondered if they'd been leaving Tahoe that spring day instead of arriving.

The morning was invigorating and bright. A few boats dotted the lake and about a dozen people milled about at the shore. An elderly woman with a metal detector walked slowly up and down the sand. Laurel had seen her every time she came to the beach, especially in this area by the boat launch. She had to laugh. According to Mac, she was loaded.

Then, as if telepathic, Mac appeared in her peripheral vision, forcing Laurel to do a double take. He was standing at the shore with the water up to his ankles, pants rolled up to the knees, wearing a tan fishing vest and a bucket hat. She looked on as he attached a lure to the line and cast it into the lake with the precision of a professional angler. Laurel walked over to him. "Mac?"

He turned and with a look of surprise gave her an easy smile. "Laurel. Good morning. Fancy meeting you here."

"Good morning. I didn't realize you were a fisherman."

"Couldn't live in Tahoe for almost forty years and not be. I think there might even be a law against it. Excuse my back," he said, returning to the water.

"Excuse the interruption. Don't the fish usually bite earlier?"

"Yeah, but my old bones didn't want to get out of bed this morning. I closed again last night. And I'm not going to get anything this close to shore unless I walk out to the drop-off anyway."

"Do you fish a lot?"

"A couple of mornings a week. Usually off the dock behind the restaurant, but it's closed for repairs for a couple of days. And with Labor Day behind us, I figured it wouldn't be too busy here. Too late for the serious fisherman, too early for the tourists."

Laurel nodded and shifted her gaze to the lake, postcard-worthy this morning. The water glistened like a myriad of flashbulbs exploding under the boundless blue sky. The waves lapping the shore reminded her of skipping stones with Carli to see who could make the most bounces.

Suddenly the rod started to buzz and sway, then came to a halt. Mac held on tight, pointing it slightly skyward before slowly reeling it in.

Empty.

"Bastard got away," he grumbled with a disappointed shake of the head.

"Sorry. I probably scared him."

"Naw," he said, walking up to her. "If I were serious about catching something I'd have gotten up at the crack, gone to Cave Rock. But I find fishing more relaxing than anything. I'd rather be playing golf, but that's a rich man's sport. I've got to pace myself." Mac stowed the rod next to his tackle box in the sand and took a seat on the adjacent bench. "What are you up to?"

"Not writing," Laurel replied with a self-deprecating grimace, joining him.

Mac laughed without opening his mouth. "That's par for the course with you creative types."

"I don't think of myself as one of those," she made air quotes with her fingers, "creative types."

"Well, maybe you should. Then you'd be at home writing instead of here humoring an old man."

Laurel tapped her shoulder against Mac's. "I'm doing none of the sort. I'm visiting with a friend on a bluebird Tahoe morning."

Mac smiled at her, a hearty smile that brought out the deeply carved lines around his eyes. "A little writer's block, huh? It happens. It'll pass."

"Actually, maybe you can help me with it." She angled herself on the bench to face him. "My mom sent me a song of Ronnie's, one she never finished, as inspiration, a springboard. It was about Tahoe."

"That doesn't sound like Ronnie, not to finish it," Mac put in around a frown. "She was like a dog with a bone whenever she got on a tangent. Classic addict behavior. No gray area."

He'd known her in a different way, Laurel reminded herself. She still wondered just how intimately. "The gray area. That's what she called it, that period of time between starting a song and finishing it," she realized out loud.

"Life is best lived in the gray area, in moderation, in the space between the extremes," Mac said matter-of-factly. "Some of us realize that when we're twenty, some when we're fifty, some of us never do. But eventually most of us figure it out. When is a matter of how hardheaded you are."

"So maybe life, sobriety, age rounded out that part of her?" And me, Laurel added to herself.

"Maybe. Sobriety is a trade-off, the lesser of two evils in some ways. Some of the greatest creative minds in history were lunatics, alcoholics or addicts of one sort or another. And many met an early demise. But Ronnie still wrote songs, great songs, in her sober years. And her voice, so distinctive, so perfectly blended, only got better with age."

Laurel gave herself a moment to take that, and Mac, in. There was an ineffable shift in his demeanor when he spoke of Ronnie, a nuance she couldn't quite put her finger on. His eyes warmed and turned dreamy, his tone softened, grew reflective. Maybe Ronnie couldn't finish the song because she never found love again. Or maybe she had and it was unrequited. Or so she'd thought. Suddenly Laurel felt achingly sad for her. "Mac, do you want to see it?" she heard herself ask. "The song? It's just a few verses and a chorus with random lyrics, but maybe you could help make sense of it."

"Why?" Mac asked, turning to her. "How will that help with your writer's block?"

"I don't know, but you said how unlike Ronnie it was not to finish it. And you're right. I can't seem to move past this part of my manuscript, which is also out of character. And everyone, even you, says how much I remind them of her."

Mac didn't comment on that, just cocked his head to the side and narrowed his eyes. "Laurel, what's really going on here? Do you have something to say? Something you'd like to ask me?"

"No," she half-lied. "I'm just frustrated with myself. How can I finish the book if I can't even settle on a name for my hero?"

"You mean the protagonist?"

"Yeah."

Mac mulled that over with a tip of the head. "That is a pickle. I've never written a book, but that seems like the first order of business, naming the main characters. But I don't see what Ronnie's song has to do with it."

"You tell me," Laurel said, bringing up the picture from Veronica and passing him her phone. She looked on as Mac enlarged it and read the lyrics, then scanned it again. He gave the phone back to her with an even look.

"Well?"

"Ladies first."

She decided the time had come. "Are you the lover from long ago?"

"Does it matter?"

"Yeah, it matters."

"Why?"

Laurel didn't know, she just knew it did. "I'm not sure."

Mac looked out over the water for a long moment, then returning to her said, "If I were, would it change anything?"

"No. But it would make me feel better, knowing she had that, had you, that way."

"But it wouldn't help you finish the book, would it? Or name your hero?"

"It might, if I'm so much like her. Why couldn't she finish it, Mac? She wasn't one for loose ends, you said so yourself."

"I don't know. Or if it had anything to do with me. And I'm not one to tell tales out of school. But if Ronnie and I did have that kind of relationship, you're theorizing that because nothing ever came of it, she couldn't finish the song?"

"Not necessarily, but wouldn't you like to know if you meant that much to her? Because the feeling was clearly mutual. I can see it in your eyes every time her name comes up."

He smiled and the crow's-feet intensified again. "And I can see it in yours. Love comes in all shapes, sizes and degrees, Laurel. But Ronnie didn't belong to me, or to your mother or even to you. She belonged to the music, to the business, to the world. She was too big, too full of life and color not to. That's one of the reasons she loved Tahoe; here she only had to be my Ronnie or your Ronnie, not everyone's Ronnie."

*My* Ronnie, Laurel noted. "Then why did she stop coming here? If she was so comfortable here?"

"Your guess is as good as mine. Maybe because Tahoe would always be here, waiting for her. She would have gone crazy living here all the time; the pace wouldn't have been enough for her. It's sort of like knowing you have a sleeping pill in the house. You might never need it, but knowing it's there helps you sleep."

"The gray area."

Mac nodded. "Knowing you can come back is more important than leaving. Anyone can leave. It's the coming back that matters, that takes courage."

"And you were the lover who kept coming back around, making sure nothing kept her down."

Mac didn't confirm or deny, just raised his eyebrows and held her gaze as the corners of his mouth curved into a vulpine simper.

"And if she finished the song," Laurel connected the dots out loud, "it would become everyone's, belong to the world. But if she never recorded it, just had it in the house, it would be there in case she needed it."

"Ronnie came here to get away, to get sober, to save her daughter, to raise you. Not fall for an alcoholic who tends bar. But things don't always go according to plan."

Laurel took that in with a shiver of relevance as Mac shifted his gaze back to the water and continued, "And maybe you can't name your lead character, let alone finish your book, because you're not ready to leave after you do. Too much unfinished business. You came here to write, not anything else. But things didn't go according to plan and you need to come to terms with that. Once you do, you'll finish the book. Once you figure out what, or who, you need to keep in the house."

She gave that a moment, gave herself permission to let it sink in and resonate. "So maybe Ronnie didn't finish the song because you and she never gave it a real shot, but most of all, because she didn't want to. She wanted to keep it for herself, in case she needed it, needed Tahoe, needed you. And she knew you'd always be here if she did, in the house if she couldn't sleep. Because you understood."

Mac turned back to her. "Life is Tahoe is lived in kind of a parallel universe; it doesn't necessarily transfer to the real world. That's part of why I stayed. No temptations, no pressures, work to live, not live to work. At first, I didn't trust my sobriety enough to chance it. Then Tahoe became a part of me, like Ronnie did. And because of that, she knew I'd be here."

"Does my mother know?"

"Probably. She always was a smart cookie, despite some of the questionable choices of her youth." Mac laid a hand on Laurel's and gave it an avuncular squeeze. "But once she made her most important choice, everything else fell into place, for all of you. That's the power of love, in all its shapes, sizes and degrees."

"And you were okay with that. Being here, waiting?"

"There's no place else for me, nowhere else for me to go. I knew Ronnie wouldn't need me, or the idea of me, forever. But it was enough, what we had and knowing what could have been. No regrets."

Laurel felt her chest begin to swell, her eyes begin to fill. Ronnie had found love again and it hadn't been unrequited. And she'd known it. She placed her other hand on top of Mac's. "Thank you."

Mac dismissed that with a shake of the head. "What worked for me wouldn't work for most. And it shouldn't. We can always find excuses not to do things, just like we can find excuses to justify doing the things we shouldn't. Finish the book, Laurel. No song should go unsung. Don't not fulfill a dream because you're afraid that if you do you'll have to give up one you didn't know you had, one you didn't know could exist. All because of some myopic plan. Don't be afraid to leave, be afraid not to have the choice to come back. Be brave like your mother and grandmother."

Laurel leaned over and kissed him on the cheek. "And the old man I'm humoring this morning."

~~~

Carli had expected Zack to be asleep when she got home. Instead she found him showered and dressed in a spotless kitchen that had been far from that when she'd left. A bouquet of blue Hydrangeas, her favorite, were sitting in a vase on the island and the fruit basket on the counter had been restocked, both likely from the farmers market down the street she preferred over the grocery store when time permitted. She was pleasantly surprised and instantly suspicious at the same time.

"Hey," he greeted, getting up from the table where he sat with his laptop. He relieved her of the canvas bags she held. "Is there more?"

"No," she replied, setting her purse on the island. "I thought you'd be asleep."

"I wanted to talk to you before the boys got home."

Carli looked up from the flowers. Suspicion was usurping surprise now. "Okay."

Zack deposited the bags on the counter and approached her. He put his arms around her and drew her to him. He smelled shower-fresh and his chin-length hair was damp at the ends. She closed her eyes and indulged herself in his familiar scent. Sometimes it was masked by the smell of hotel soap, but when he was just out of the shower at home, he smelled like himself.

He didn't speak at first, just held her. Finally, he said, "I love you, Carli. So incredibly much."

"I love you, too," she mumbled into his neck, pulling back to meet his eyes, the same steel blue as Ollie's. They had turned stormy, full of despair and reservation. Her stomach dropped. It couldn't be. Her nightmare was coming true. "Zack, what is it? You're scaring me."

"That makes two of us. You're obviously upset with me. We've always been able to talk about things. Car, talk to me."

Carli knew she was at a crossroads. She couldn't go on living this way, letting it eat her up inside. But there was a strange hope and comfort in uncertainty. She didn't even know if she could actually say the words to him without breaking down. She was debating that, looking unseeingly out the kitchen window, when Zack took the choice away from her.

"That's what I mean. So if you're not going to talk to me, I'm going to talk to you." He cupped her face in his hands, forcing her attention back to him. "I don't know how to phrase this, so I'm just going to spit it out. I'm not having an affair with Leah. Not now. Not before. Not ever."

Carli could do nothing but stare at him as he looked pleadingly into her eyes.

"Part of me is pissed that you could really think that," Zack continued. "But a larger part of me understands why you could. Now, at least."

Carli let out an overdue breath. "You talked to Laurel."

"Yeah," he affirmed with a nod. "Don't be mad at her, she mostly just listened. And read me the riot act for not dealing with this sooner. Can we sit down? I want to clear the air, tell you about it. I need to know that you believe me."

Suddenly she realized how incredibly foolish she'd been. "I do."

Zack's brow crinkled and his eyes narrowed in confusion. "But we haven't talked about it yet. I haven't explained."

"I know," she said with building certainty. "Go ahead. I'm listening."

"Car..." He brought her face to his and kissed her like he hadn't in months, maybe even years. With all of him, his heart, his body, his soul. Relief, affection, vulnerability. It was like a lifetime of kisses bound together by an oath. She kissed him back with matching ardor, hoping he felt it too. When the kiss was over, he rested his forehead against hers. "How could you ever think anyone else could make me feel the way you do? No one could even come close."

She didn't reply, just fell into him and laid her head on his shoulder as the baby kicked inside her. Zack must have felt it too, because he shifted a hand to rest on her stomach. "Do you lay awake at night with our baby in your belly thinking about this? Worrying about it?" He stepped out of her embrace and began to pace, trudging a guilty hand through his hair. "God forbid, crying about it?"

"No," she answered extemporaneously, then backpedaled. "Maybe. But it doesn't matter now. "

"The hell it doesn't!" Returning to her, he laid his hands on her shoulders. "I'm so sorry."

She cradled his face, as he'd done earlier, knowing he truly was. "I'm sorry too. I should have had more faith in you, in us. I should talked to you about it."

"You tried. I wasn't receptive. It wasn't even on my radar then."

"Then?"

Brushing her lips with his, he grabbed her hands led her to the table. "Sit. Let's hash this out, once and for all."

She obliged, sitting in her usual chair at the table as he sat in his next to her. It felt odd to be sitting there like that without the boys. He nestled her hands in his and held her gaze. "I went through some of this on the phone with Laurel, so I've already collected my thoughts. When you first asked me about it, I thought you were crazy. I should have known better; you aren't one to overreact and be paranoid, pregnant or not. Anyway, it was a few weeks after that when Leah made her interest known. I politely refused, thought I made it clear I wasn't interested. But it happened again, more blatantly, one night when we were all heading back to our rooms after dinner."

Carli resisted the urge to ask for more details on the initial incident. "When?"

"Phoenix. I reiterated that my position wasn't going to change. Cody was walking ahead of us, overheard some of the conversation. Leah isn't one for subtlety. He pretended he forgot his phone in the restaurant and backtracked, asked me if I'd seen it on the table. I offered to go back with him to look for it. We took the elevator down for appearances and Leah had gone into her room by the time we came back up. I know I should have told you right away."

"Why didn't you?"

Zack looked into the near distance, then faced her again. "I don't know. I didn't want to start something, make something out of nothing, put ideas in your head. And a little part of me didn't want to admit that you were right from the beginning. You know how the road can be and that would worry anyone. But we've always been different, somehow above all that. Car, I swear on the boys' lives I never touched her, never gave her any reason to believe I was so inclined. I never led her on, not even a little."

"I believe you," she told him and meant it. "So it's still happening?"

Zack started on a recuperative breath, "Not as outwardly, but yes. She's made it clear she's still interested. No strings attached. It would be our little secret."

So Leah says and as she had suspected, Carli thought with a disgusted grunt. "So it's just sex? She doesn't really want you per se, just the idea of you? She likes the idea of having another woman's man in her bed and the satisfaction of knowing she can?"

"Yeah, I guess," he conceded with a shrug.

Zack could be so naive. And his ego was not going to come out of this unscathed. In a conciliatory gesture, she reached up and stroked his cheek."I mean she doesn't expect you to leave your pregnant wife and children and settle down with her? She's only interested in the physical?"

"I don't know and I don't care. I only care about you and what you think, what you know. I don't want to sleep with her, I only want to sleep with you. I've been making love to you you since I was sixteen years old, you and only you. We both know the opportunities the life I've chosen offer. I've never been tempted before and I'm not tempted now. And it wouldn't be worth it for those few minutes, even if I was."

At that, she shot him a questionable look. So he had thought about it.

"That's all it would be—a few minutes," he qualified hastily. "Meaningless sex. Not making love. I only make love with you. Do you really think I would call you at night with someone beside me? I only want you beside me. You and the boys and whoever else you have in there are my whole life. Forever. Period."

She squeezed his hand. "Me too. And it's the life we both chose. We knew it would have its challenges."

"This is different. This isn't some overeager fan making flirty eyes at me backstage or a toothsome girl lifting up shirt in the front row. Leah's texting me, posting pictures that make it look like we're alone together, and not even attempting to hide her intentions from me or the band. Laurel's right; this isn't going to go away on its own. I have to face it, deal with it."

Carli was smart enough to know what was a stake here for him, for them. "So what are we going to do?"

A grin spread across Zack's face, replacing the troubled look that had been etched there. "We. That's what I like to hear. I don't want anything to change that, ever. The band means nothing to me compared to you. Should I fire her?"

"My self-serving, knee-jerk reaction is yes. But she's a good singer."

"She is," Zack allowed. "But there are tens of thousands of other good singers out there who'd love a stab at it. I might even be doing her a favor. She could probably make it on her own, especially if she's willing to sleep her way in the door. But—"

"But then you'll need another singer," Carli finished for him. "And it could happen again."

"Yeah."

"What does Cody think?"

"He's nervous, sees the problem, the potential consequences. Apparently Alex brought it up to him a while ago and he blew it off too. He'll support me either way."

Of course Carli knew that, but she didn't fess up. It was a moot point now anyway.

"But whoever she is, she's not you, so I'm not interested. Got it?"

"Got it." She leaned over and laid her mouth on his, feeling lighter than she had in months. This kiss felt different, like the one at their wedding, so familiar yet somehow new. Overflowing with joy, so full of love and promise that she could taste the future in it. And that's when she realized just how foolish she'd been. Their kind of love didn't happen everyday, it didn't always last and that's what made it so precious. What they had was so much more than sex and kids and a mortgage. He was a part of her and she him. She'd been crazy to think otherwise. The kiss intensified and Zack pulled her onto his lap. He was running his fingers through her hair now, feasting on her earlobe. How long had it been since they'd had sex? A couple of weeks for sure. She found herself in the mood for the first time in months.

"Babe, when do we have to get Ollie?" he muttered, kissing her throat.

"Noon," she responded in a thready voice, linking her arms around his neck.

She felt him lift his arm behind her head, checking his watch. "How about a little Mommy-Daddy alone time? It's only ten-thirty."

"Well, you did bring me flowers," she moaned, tilting her head to the side to give him better access.

"Yes, I did," he agreed readily, encircling her legs to his waist and standing. "Because you're my girl. Always and forever, right?" He was looking down at her with lust swimming in his eyes and a roguish smile curving his lips.

The song he'd written for her all those years ago. "*Always and forever, I'm your girl.*"

"*There could never be anyone else for me,*" he sang, carrying her toward the bedroom. "*For always and forever.*"

"*Because always and forever is a long time. But not quite long enough,*" she finished the verse just as they got to the bedroom.

Zack lowered her to the bed, then laid next to her. "Forever and a day isn't long enough."

"I don't remember that part of the song."

"That's because I just made it up." He swept his fingertips over her chest, then seemed to take her in for the first time. "Is that a new dress?"

Having forgotten what she was wearing, Carli looked down before answering. "It's a romper and yeah, it's new. I bought it for Tahoe. Do you like it?"

"Yeah. But I'd like it better on the floor."

"Your wish is my command." Carli untied the knot at the back of her neck and shimmied out of the romper. They loved each other slowly and sweetly and when they finally came together, like they had so many times before, it meant more than ever before. Because it was for always and forever.

# CHAPTER FIFTEEN

AUTUMN ARRIVED IN the Sierra as if overnight, tinting the aspen groves in yellows and golds and setting the red maples ablaze against the cerulean blue of the sky. The mornings were cold, the afternoons brisk and the nights chilly. The grocery store was bursting with pumpkins and gourds and smelled like cinnamon and anise. And with every passing day Laurel found herself feeling more at home here. She'd come across a fall wreath in the garage and hung it on the front door. She'd put fresh batteries in the jack-o'-lanterns she'd found in the laundry room closet and displayed them on the porch. She'd pushed through two more chapters, although she'd be the first to admit it wasn't her best work.

Gov had been busier than usual, trying to wrap up as many exterior projects as possible before winter set in and organize interior ones for the colder months. He was spending a couple of days a week in the office in Reno, often wearing business attire as opposed to his usual jeans and casual shirt. He also seemed a little preoccupied, something with which Laurel could relate. She wondered if he too saw the calendar as a stark reminder of the approaching inevitable. He rarely asked her about the book's progress anymore, as if he didn't want to hear she was almost finished. Which, despite

Mac's sage advice, she wasn't. And that still didn't bother her as much as it should.

Carli was ready to pop and Laurel was contemplating going to L.A. for a couple of days when the baby was born. She was torn between knowing she should stay here and stay focused and wanting to be there for Carli and see the baby. She and Zack were in a better place, after having cleared the air about Leah. The problem had solved itself because she had decided to leave the band after this tour was over, which it almost was. Alex would pinch-hit until they figured something out. Zack had a few more shows and then he'd be home for a month to help with the baby.

When Laurel heard a knock at the front door, she assumed it was Gov calling it an early day. Later she would kick herself for not knowing better. He usually called or texted when he was on his way and came in through the garage. Opening the door without looking through the peephole, she began on a smile, "Hey, you're ear—" then stopped short. Standing there in the backwash of the late afternoon light was Grant. He was wearing deeply pressed jeans and a starched linen shirt. His hair was darker and short; it was the first time she'd ever seen it shaved above his ears. His tan had faded considerably, making his blue eyes much less prominent. He had a timorous smile on his face and a bouquet of flowers in his hand.

"Hey, Laurie."

"Grant," she stammered, feeling her face fall. "What are you doing here?"

"I wanted to talk to you." He extended his arm and offered her the flowers. "The florist was fresh out of pink tulips, so I went with the autumn mix." Laurel lowered her gaze to the flowers, then met his eyes again. She could do nothing but gawk at him as he continued, "I've been doing a lot of thinking and I—" he interrupted himself. "Actually, can I come in?"

Laurel let out a shallow breath and tried to shake off the shock. "Umm. Sure." She stepped aside, allowing him to enter.

"Cute place," Grant remarked, looking around appraisingly.

"Grant, how the hell did you find me?" Laurel astounded as she closed the door.

He gave her a sheepish grin and an indifferent shrug.

"Right," Laurel said with a discerning nod, directing him back to the kitchen. He was the heir to an empire. Then, remembering her manners, she offered, "Can I get you something? Water, iced tea, wine, a beer?"

"No thanks," he refused with a shake of the head. "But feel free if you'd like something. I'm sure I gave you quite a shock."

"That you did. You can set those on the island for now," she said of the flowers. Then she grabbed a wine glass from the cabinet and poured herself half a glass from the bottle on the counter.

"Thank you for seeing me," Grant said, putting down the bouquet and sticking his hands in his front pockets.

"Since you showed up at my door unannounced, I didn't have much choice," Laurel returned pointedly.

"Yes, you did. You could have slammed the door in my face."

Squinting, Laurel cocked her head to the side. "But you knew I wouldn't do that, didn't you?"

Grant nodded. "Yeah, I knew you wouldn't do that." His eyes swept the kitchen, then landed on the table, "Can we sit down for a minute and talk?"

"Let's sit outside," she suggested, finally feeling like she had her wits about her. Grant followed her and took the seat next to her. She said nothing, simply stared at him expectantly as he took in the backyard.

"This is beautiful. I'd forgotten what a different world Tahoe is."

Laurel had had just about enough. "Grant, what do you want?"

"I told you. I want to talk to you."

"Then talk." She took a healthy sip of wine, then set the glass down on the table with a thud.

Grant took an emboldening breath, let it out. Then he turned to her and looked her straight in the eye. "I wanted to say that I'm sorry. Incredibly sorry for hurting you, for disrespecting our marriage vows and for being such an ass about it."

Laurel reminded herself not to take the bait. She hadn't thought this day would ever come and now that it had, she found herself surprisingly numb and extremely suspicious. She held his steady gaze. "And to what do I owe the pleasure of this sudden revelation?"

"I've been doing some thinking. A lot of thinking, actually. And reflecting. I've grown. I want to be a better person. And a better person apologizes for past indiscretions and doesn't keep making the same mistakes again and again. I'm starting with you."

"Starting?"

Grant glanced out into the distance, then met her gaze again. He set his jaw and gnawed on his bottom lip, something he did when he was nervous. "It's not working out between Cami and I. We're separated, have been for months. She filed for divorce last week."

Half of Laurel wasn't surprised and the other half didn't want to care in the least. But that was easier said than done. He'd been her husband and there was a child involved. "I'm sorry, Grant. I didn't realize that."

"Don't keep up with the rags since you've come north?"

"Not a bit."

"If you had, you'd not only know that I'm going to be one of those twice-divorced guys by thirty-five, but that it was predictable."

"I don't need to keep up with the rags to know that."

Oddly, that seemed to humble him, give him pause, instead of irritate him. "I deserved that."

"That's not up for debate. But it still doesn't explain why you're here."

"Like I said, I've been doing a lot of thinking, reflecting, soul-searching. And I've realized that the happiest I ever was in my life was when I was with you. I was wondering if you'd be open to giving us another chance."

The thought was so absurd that Laurel started laughing. Uncontrollably. To the point that her eyes filled with tears. After a moment, she collected herself and said, "You must be joking."

He was deadpanning her, pressing his lips tightly together and staring at her unwaveringly. She wondered if he was drawing breaths.

"Oh my God, you're serious," she realized out loud, running a fingertip under the outer corner of her eye to catch a stray tear.

He nodded. "Can we start with dinner? Tonight?"

"No, we cannot start with dinner. Tonight or any other night. Do you really think that after everything you could just waltz back in here as if nothing happened?" She waved an incredulous hand in the air. "And things would go back to the way they were?"

"No, of course not. I apologized. Sincerely. You were the best thing that ever happened to me, Laurie. I know that now. I was a fool to let you get away."

Laurel was beside herself. "I didn't get away, Grant," she retorted patronizingly. "I divorced you. You cheated on me. Flagrantly. Egregiously. Unapologetically. You fathered another woman's child during our marriage!"

"I know, I know. And I'd say I regret it, but then I wouldn't have my son. But I do regret my judgement. I'm not asking you to jump in with both feet. Not right away at least. We can ease back into it, take it slow. I'm just asking you to start by having dinner with me."

Laurel reminded herself that Grant was used to getting his way, how he wanted it, when he wanted it. Through a protracted sip of wine she also reminded herself that to a certain extent that wasn't his fault. She began on a tired breath, "Grant, I can't have dinner with you, tonight or any other night, let alone anything else. I'm sorry you are going through a hard time but I hope for the sake of your son that you guys part amicably. I'm sure you can find plenty of women to have dinner with."

Acknowledging that with a nod, he sat up a little straighter in the chair. "That's true, I can. But I don't want to. I only want to have dinner with you. I'm a screwup, Laurel. I always have been. I took advantage of my parents, phoned it at school, chased the caprice du jour. But my biggest mistake was losing you. I'm an entitled, egocentric narcissist who never grew up. Until now. I've come to realize what really matters to me and that's my kids and you."

"*Kids*?"

"Yeah, we have two now. Two boys. And I want them to be better men than I am. And that starts with me."

Laurel had never seen Grant like this, so vulnerable, so sincere, so humble. She looked at him, really looked at him, for the first time since he'd arrived. The years in the sun were starting to take their toll. He had coarse lines etched around his eyes, elongated parenthesis framing his mouth, even his arms were getting a little crepey. And there was something different about his eyes, they seemed more lucid, sharper. Maybe he had turned over a new leaf. Then she reminded herself that no one plays the middle quite like Grant. And that she had no desire to take a walk down memory lane with him, let alone relive their past.

"I'm working, really working, for the first time in my life," Grant was still talking. "I'm learning the business and enjoying it. I stopped smoking weed and only have an occasional beer or glass of wine with dinner. Most of my meals are takeout these days—I'm living in the Santa Monica house again since Cami kicked me out. That was a real wake-up call." He paused to take a breath and cleared the emotion from his throat before going on, "Not being able to see your kids whenever you want tends to do that to you."

Grant might be a screwup, but he wasn't a bad person. Laurel gave him a sympathetic smile. "I'm sorry, Grant. I really am. For the sake of your family, I hope you guys work things out one way or the other. But maybe your wife is the one you should be having this conversation with, not me."

"*You* are my wife, Laurie. It's always been you," he replied around a sad shake of the head. "I don't want to work things out with Cami and the feeling is mutual. She tricked me into the first pregnancy, I know she did. And I lost you as a result. We gave it a shot for the kid. We're not meant to be, even my parents can see that now."

So Grant's parents had played the money card. He suddenly looked so downtrodden she almost felt sorry for him. "Grant, I—"

She was interrupted by the sounds of entry from the house. "Laurel? Whose car is that?" Gov's advancing voice called from the kitchen. "Oh." He stopped short at the deck door. "I'm sorry. I didn't realize you had company."

Swearing under her breath, Laurel immediately jumped to her feet and went to him. "Neither did I. Gov, this is Grant Hurley. Grant, McGovern Scott. My...friend," she tripped over the word.

Grant pushed up from the chair and stood. He extended his hand in greeting. "Nice to meet you, Scott."

"Likewise. And it's McGovern," Gov corrected, shaking Grant's hand. "As in McGovern Scott. Not the other way around."

It was surreal to see them both standing there, the two great loves of her life, each so strikingly different from the other. Grant, of average height and build, with soft features and a light complexion. Gov, almost a foot taller with broad shoulders and dark hair and eyes. But their skin-deep attributes didn't begin to compare to their inherent differences. Grant, hubris from a lifetime of pretension and coddling and Gov, with his innate graciousness and aplomb were like two sides of the same coin. Even the way they shook each other's hand was telling. Gov's handshake, strong and firm while maintaining eye contact and Grant's weaker, more perfunctory attempt.

"Sorry, man. My bad."

"No problem. It happens all the time."

Laurel was thinking back to the night she met Gov and the irony of the name confusion when Grant put in, "Thanks for looking out for Laurel, seeing a strange car in the driveway and all. Are you a neighbor or something?"

It would never occur to Grant that she had met someone, moved on. He probably assumed she'd always be there waiting in the wings for him to come back and sweep her off her feet. And she bore some responsibility for that. It made Laurel realize how much she'd changed in the last two years, how much she'd learned about herself, how much stronger she'd become. Before she could correct him, Gov replied in an even voice, "Yeah, something like that."

"Well, Laurel and I were just heading out to dinner. I guess she'll catch up with you later," Grant said as if the matter had been settled.

"Actually, Grant." Laurel turned to Gov and took his hand in hers. "Gov is much more than a neighbor. And I never agreed to dinner and you know it."

Grant looked first at Gov, then to their joined hands, before resting his gaze on Laurel again. "I see. Well, I'd hoped we could talk some more, settle some things, tie up some loose ends."

"Whatever you have to say, you can say in front of Gov. And we actually do have dinner plans tonight."

"But, Laurie…" Grant contended unbelievably, as if suddenly at a loss for words.

Gov shifted his weight a little, then squeezed Laurel's hand and released his grasp. "I'm going to give you guys some privacy. No one hates loose ends more than me." He brushed his lips over Laurel's. Then he tipped his head at Grant as men do. "Nice to meet you."

"Yeah, you too."

Laurel watched Gov take his leave through the yard before turning back to Grant. He was staring at her, frozen in the inertia of disbelief, utterly dumbfounded.

She opened her mouth to speak, but before she could get any words out, the breeze picked up, tinkling the wind chimes. She couldn't deny the coincidence any more than she could agree to have dinner with Grant. "Give me a minute, Ronnie. I need to finish this once and for all," she mumbled to herself, giving the chimes an oblique glance. Then she refocused on Grant and with a cleansing breath said, "Now, where were we?"

~~~

Well, this totally sucks, Gov thought, pulling into a parking spot at Hues of Blue. He'd actually been having a decent day and was looking forward to spending a quiet evening with Laurel. But like he'd told Boot when he stopped at home, exes are like bad pennies; they have a way of showing up at the most inconvenient times. Boot had been more interested in doing his business and eating his dinner than hearing Gov bitch and moan, but there was always Mac. He actually got to paid to listen.

Gov hadn't bothered to change; it was Tahoe after all. His timeworn jeans and flannel shirt with the rolled up sleeves was more than sufficient for the bar. He didn't need to look like he'd just stepped out of a bandbox like some people, he inwardly scoffed. He aimed his gate for his favorite stool and took a seat. Mac greeted him with a smile and slapped a cocktail napkin and a roll-up down in front of him. He started to do the same with the adjacent spot, but Gov held up his hand.

"Eating alone tonight?"

"Who said anything about eating?" Gov shot back, throwing his phone down on the bar in a manner reflective of his mood.

"Ouch. I probably should have brought the beer before the napkin."

"Actually, I'll take a Macallan tonight. Neat," Gov decided on the fly. "And make it a double."

Surprise flashed across Mac's face, but he caught it just in time. "I'm going to go out on a limb and assume that your solitariness and choice of poison are related."

"No falling for you."

As Mac walked away shaking his head, Gov took stock in the events of the last hour. He'd wrapped things up at work early and texted Laurel to that effect. She hadn't replied, which wasn't unusual. She often showered in the late afternoon after a day of writing out back. He figured he'd stop by before going home so they could make a game plan for the evening. The late-model black convertible in the driveway was a bit of an outlier in the mountains, but not unheard of. A friend from L.A. visiting unexpectedly, someone considering the neighborhood with whom Laurel had struck up a conversation, a publishing colleague passing through town. But of all the scenarios Gov could have construed, ex-husband never entered his mind. In hindsight, he knew it should have. She shared a past with Grant, a big chunk of her life, including her seminal years. And she'd hinted that their love life had been her sexual awakening. He'd been naive to think all of that didn't still count for something.

"Double Macallan, neat," Mac announced, setting a lowball glass down in front of Gov and pulling him out of his thoughts. "I'll put that on the list of things I never thought I'd serve you. Want to talk about it?"

Gov knew he wouldn't be here if he didn't. But he wasn't sure where to start. So he just shrugged and took a nip of scotch.

"All right then, you know where to find me," Mac said mildly and turned on his heel.

Gov took a recuperative breath. "Laurel's ex-husband is in town. I just met him."

Mac processed that with a frown. "I didn't know she had one. I'm going to assume it didn't go well."

"It really didn't go at all. It was a less than five-minute conversation."

"So what's the problem?"

"I was blindsided for one thing. I walked in on them." At Mac's look of aporia, Gov hastily clarified, "They were sitting on the deck."

"So what?"

"I was thrown that's what! To see her with him, like that."

"Like what? What were they doing?"

"I don't know," Gov replied, suddenly defensive. "Talking, I guess."

"As one sometimes does with a former spouse. Not all of us ex-husbands are bad, Gov."

"You're the exception." He swirled his scotch around a bit, then took a meditative sip. Smooth as it was, he would never get used to the burn. "Plus hasn't it been like thirty-something years for you? They're on two."

Mac scanned the bar and finding everything under control, returned to Gov with a skeptical breath. "That's got you drinking two fingers of Macallan without dinner? An inadvertent, five-minute conversation with your girl's ex?"

"Among other things."

"Enlighten me as to the other things. Because I'm clearly missing something."

"Well, for starters he looks more like the corporate lawyer type instead of the deadbeat surfer type that Laurel made him out to be. And he all but sniffed the air in front of my face before thanking me for being a good neighbor and," Gov made air quotes with his fingers, "looking out for Laurel when I saw a strange car in the driveway." He went back to his drink, then finished with a snarl, "Right before he informed me they were on their way out to dinner."

Mac's eyes darted from side to side speculatively, as if putting two and two together. "Let me guess. Dark blond hair, fancy jeans and a pink linen shirt."

Gov jolted back in his seat. "How did you know that?"

"He was in here earlier. Had a couple of beers and a sandwich. Said he was from L.A."

"That's him."

"Paid in cash. I had to crack a hundred for him, which rarely happens over here. The casino restaurant usually gets that crowd."

"How the hell do you remember all this stuff?"

"For one thing, it's a Wednesday in October so we're not exactly slammed. He stuck out; alone in the middle of the day, not quite a businessman, not really a tourist. And he had a haughtiness about him. Didn't seem like Laurel's type."

"Well, she spent nearly a decade with him, so there had to be something there."

"Had refers to the past. Leave it there."

"He called her Laurie," Gov informed Mac with a disgusted scowl. "Like a pet name."

"Well, you called her Lauren at first, so maybe she does have a type."

"Very funny."

"Okay, what else is on your mind?"

Gov took a breath, let it out with borrowed conviction. "Jack Brody offered me a minority partnership in the business."

Mac nodded admirably. "Congratulations. Now, that does call for Macallan."

Gov didn't reply, only sent Mac a look from under his eyebrows that said maybe not.

"And this isn't cause for celebration because…"

"Because the end of the year, and Laurel's lease, is quickly approaching. And we haven't…"

"Gotten any further than that?"

Gov finished the last of his drink. "Right."

"And a partnership cements your life here."

"Well, it certainly isn't the kind of job that can be done remotely."

"What does Laurel think?"

"I haven't brought it up yet, but the clock's ticking. Jack and I have worked though the details and have a preliminary agreement. All he needs is a commitment from me and the lawyers will do the rest."

Mac studied him through narrowed eyes for a long moment. Then he began on a sigh, "I've known you for a long time. And I've never known you to shy away from anything, first and foremost commitment. Sometimes when we're on the verge of something life-changing, no matter how wonderful it may be, we pull back, put up our defenses. Maybe that's what you're doing. You're not sure how you feel about one thing, so you can't commit to the other."

"I'm confident in how I feel. Can't say the same for her."

"That's because you can't, or won't, see the way she looks at you. But I was talking about the partnership. See how one affects the other? What does your gut tell you to do?"

Gov didn't pretend he hadn't thought about this. He traced the rim of his glass with his index finger, then met Mac's eyes again. "To go for it. Even my attorney said the offer is a slam dunk. More than fair."

"Then talk to Laurel about it. Don't be too afraid of the answer to ask the question. Let the truth speak for itself."

"But first I have to figure out what the truth is."

Mac leaned an elbow against the bar, effectively pinning Gov down, preventing him from evading the issue. "No, you don't. You already know what the truth is in that hard head of yours. You need to let yourself believe the truth."

"I know, I know. Because not believing the truth doesn't make it any less true."

"Now we're getting somewhere." Mac straightened up. "And there's no time like the present to start," he said, sending his gaze over Gov's shoulder.

Gov turned to find Laurel approaching him. She gave him a shy smile and asked, "Is this seat taken?"

Gov swore his heart expanded in his chest and every cell in his body went on high alert. Maybe it was the scotch, but he actually felt giddy at the sight of her. She'd changed her clothes and her hair was free-flowing and wavy, not up in a clip like earlier. He found himself wanting to touch it, run his fingers through it, bury his face in it. And himself in her. But he managed a casual, "No, of course not." He started to stand but she waved him off.

She slid onto the stool with a friendly, "Hey, Mac."

"Laurel," Mac greeted in kind, putting a cocktail napkin down in front of her. "Glass of Barbera?"

"You know me too well. I'll switch it up tonight, have whatever Gov's having."

"I doubt that. It's two fingers of Macallan, neat. And if you have to ask what that is, you definitely don't want it."

Laurel reached over and picked up Gov's empty glass, then sniffed it. "That's Macallan all right. Single malt, sweet, fruity and exceptionally smooth." She handed Mac the tumbler. "I'll stick with the Barbera."

"And I'll have another," Gov told Mac.

Laurel and Mac exchanged a conspiratorial look, then Mac held out his palm saying, "That'll cost you your keys."

Gov started to protest, but instantly thought better of it. He reached into his pocket and begrudgingly obeyed. "Fine."

"Good man," Mac remarked, throwing the keys in a glass under the bar with a clang. "I'll bring some waters too."

"Thanks, Mac," Laurel said to his retreating back. Then she turned to Gov. "I've never seen you drink scotch, let alone Macallan."

"Well, it's not often I meet my girlfriend's husband."

"Ex-husband," she corrected sharply.

Gov didn't really know why he was in such a bad mood. Later he would figure it out, but right now either the booze or his pride was inhibiting his ability to think straight. "Laurel, what are you doing here?"

"Looking for you."

"I thought you had dinner plans."

"I do," she told him easily. "With you."

He knew she was trying to keep things light, but her mouth had become a tight horizontal line and her brow had furrowed. Maybe she was a little unnerved too. That made him feel better, although he wasn't proud of it. "You changed."

"I wanted to freshen up. I hadn't showered yet when Grant showed up."

Gov might be a little buzzed, but he hadn't lost track of time. "That's what you've been doing for the last hour? Getting ready?"

"Yes. What did you think I was doing?"

Gov didn't answer, just shrugged his shoulders and played with the corners of his napkin. Drowning his sorrows in scotch was one thing, but now he was being downright pathetic. What the hell was wrong with him?

Laurel scooted her stool closer and laid a hand on his forearm, forcing him to make eye contact with her again. "I'm sorry if you got the wrong impression earlier. I was just as blindsided as you. In fact, when I answered the door I assumed Grant *was* you."

Gov had to admit that made sense. But he only said, "You guys looked pretty cozy."

"The wine? That was his idea. I was surprised he didn't partake. He's usually the life of the party."

Deciding to bank what Mac had shared, Gov plowed on, "What did he want?"

Before Laurel could answer, Mac returned with their drinks, temporarily suspending the conversation. "Do you guys need menus?"

"Give us a few minutes," Laurel told him.

"You got it."

After he left, Laurel took a sip of wine, then picked up the conversation. "Me," she said matter-of-factly. "He wants me."

"That makes two of us," Gov grumbled around a swig of scotch. For some reason, it didn't taste as good as it did before.

Next to him, Laurel took exception to that with a resounding, "God, I hope not." She let that simmer for a moment, causing Gov to freeze mid-swallow and whip his head around to meet her gaze. "Because Grant just thinks he wants me," she explained. "What he really wants is the idea of me, the convenience of me. And I was hoping you wanted me for real, for me."

How could she think otherwise? Because he was being an immature prick, that's why. Gov set down his drink and let himself get lost in her eyes. They were filled with hurt and confusion and rimmed in apprehension.

Then he realized that was a reflection of his own. He wondered what she saw in his. He turned to face her and laid the palm of his hand on her cheek. He couldn't have stopped the words from spilling out if he'd wanted to. "I do. You're all I want."

She brought a hand up to cover his and gave him a tender look. "I know. It was written all over your face. Gov, you really couldn't have thought…I love you. You believe that don't you?"

"Yeah," he said, sounding more sure than he felt inside. "I know."

"Then why are you acting this way?" Laurel withdrew her hand, allowing him to do the same.

Gov looked unseeingly at the wall of bottles behind the bar. "I don't know. When I saw you there with him… I mean, I know you were married. I know you loved him, shared a life with him. I guess I don't like being reminded of it."

"That's ironic." Her voice was soft, tentative. "Because you're the one who's helping me forget."

He hadn't thought about it that way. "Do you want to? Forget?" He turned back to her.

She considered that with a slight tilt of the head. "No. Not entirely. Because it helped make me who I am today, who you fell in love with. But sometimes I think back to that Laurel and wonder if I would even recognize her. The Laurel who was so naive, so trusting, so oblivious. Part of the irony is that I could probably be that way with you and you wouldn't take advantage of me. I hope I have the chance to find out."

Gov's stomach fell and his chest went hollow. What was she saying? He swallowed hard and managed, "Why wouldn't you have the chance to find out?"

Laurel started on a sigh, "I didn't mean to fall in love with you, didn't want to, but I did. And I think that makes it even more special. Do you think I would jeopardize that to have dinner with the one person in the world who hurt me the most?"

Either he was sobering up or coming to his senses. Or both. "You didn't jeopardize anything, Laurel. I'm acting like a jerk."

"No, if you were a jerk you would have clocked Grant right then and there. And rightly so. He was being a pompous ass. But you didn't because you knew it would make things harder for me."

"I wanted to," Gov told her and meant it. "I still do."

"I know. You were all but clenching your fists when you walked out."

"I guess I was—"

"Jealous?" Laurel finished for him.

"Yeah," he admitted. "I guess that's what jealous feels like. I don't like it."

"I think it's kind of cute." She gave him a playful smile.

But Gov was not amused. He thought about what Carli had said about your soulmate bringing out the best version of yourself. Laurel had definitely not brought out the best in him tonight. "You like that side of me? Because I don't. Not my best self."

"Sure it was. You reeled yourself in. You staked your claim and left the rest to me."

"I barley touched you."

"It got the job done. I think the kiss really threw him."

"Talk about irony."

"I'll say." Laurel laughed. "In retrospect, I wasn't jealous when I found out Grant was cheating on me.

I was ashamed, mad, embarrassed, mostly with my-self. But putting myself in your place today, I probably would have been devastated. Maybe us knowing that is a good thing."

Gov nodded and took a long pull of water. Suddenly, he didn't want the scotch anymore. But he did want to know where she stood with Grant. "So where is he?"

Laurel turned over Gov's phone and noted the time. "Probably past Auburn by now. He drives like a bat out of hell when he's pissed and that Beamer can really pack a punch. Full disclosure, I walked him out to his car and gave him a parting hug. He had a packed duffle bag on the passenger seat. He'd obviously planned on staying with me tonight."

Gov took a twisted satisfaction in Grant's presumed disappointment. "So how did you leave it with him?"

Laurel's eyes began to dance and she gave him her first real smile of the night. "He said he didn't know or care who that guy was, but to let him know if it doesn't work out. And he made it clear he's of the opinion that it's more of a when as opposed to an if situation."

"Bastard has some balls. I underestimated him. What did you say?"

"I said I won't either way."

Gov wished she hadn't qualified that. Or initially in-troduced him as her friend. But he was coming out on top so he took the win. "How'd he take it?"

"Let's just say he was…" she paused and with that smile still firmly in place, settled on, "shocked and dis-mayed and leave it at that. But it's over now."

"No loose ends?"

She shook her head from side to side. "No loose ends." She leaned over and planted a kiss on his mouth.

"I was sure before. But now you are too. And that's just as important."

"Laurel, what are we going to do?"

She gave him a naughty look from under her lashes. "Nothing tonight if you keep drinking that scotch."

"I'm serious."

"So am I."

Gov knew eventually they'd have to discuss the elephant in the room, but maybe they'd had enough drama for one night. He was suddenly exhausted. The future would be there tomorrow for the taking. And he planned on taking it. With Laurel. One way or the other.

Just then Mac returned. "I took the liberty of ordering the special for each of you. I didn't want to interrupt and *somebody.*" He threw Gov a pointed look. "Needs something in their stomach to soak up all that alcohol."

"Thanks, Mac," Laurel said.

"If I eat my dinner can I have my keys back?"

"We'll see."

"Tell you what. We'll take our dinners to go," Laurel put forth brightly. "The truck will be fine here until morning." She turned to Gov. "My place or yours?"

"Boot will need to go out before bed, so either way we'll have to swing by my place."

"Your place it is. You settle up and I'll get the car."

Gov liked where this was heading. "Deal."

After Mac left to cash them out. Laurel started to get up, but Gov grabbed her arm. He couldn't resist. "He called you Laurie."

She let out a weary breath. "Yes. I never liked it."

"And you never said anything?"

"You got my name wrong the first time we met. I never said anything about that either."

"That was understandable, you said so yourself. But Laurie? Really? You don't look like a Laurie."

"Whatever a Laurie looks like."

She was right. The name had nothing to do with it. Gov just didn't like intimacy of the endearment.

Laurel must have read his mind. "I was young and madly in love. He could do no wrong."

Gov resisted the urge to roll his eyes. "And now?"

"Now I'm older and madly in love. And much too wise to let a man call me a name I don't like."

"So what can I call you?' he asked a prurient voice, brushing back a lock of hair that had fallen onto her face.

She cupped her hand under his chin and squeezed his jowls. "Anything but Laurie." With peck on the lips, she grabbed her purse and strolled out, leaving Gov speechless in Hues of Blue once again.

# CHAPTER SIXTEEN

JUST OVER A week later Laurel was awakened in the middle of the night by her mother's ringtone. "Mom?"

"Everything's fine, honey. I'm on my way to Carli's. Her water broke about an hour ago."

Laurel tried to will herself awake, caught between the dueling worlds of sleep and consciousness. She'd been having the strangest dream. It was Christmas morning and she was sitting on the living room floor of the rental house, under a Christmas tree twinkling with lights, surrounded by people whose faces she couldn't quite make out. It wasn't the tree her mom and Ronnie put up every year, but a real tree cut down from a forest in Tahoe. Yet all their family ornaments, including her childhood creations, adorned it. It was so tall that she couldn't see the top but somehow knew their heirloom angel crowned it. She was repeatedly opening a present, only to find another, smaller box inside. Finally, she came to a tiny box wrapped in silver paper topped with a red bow. She tried to untie it, but couldn't. It kept recoiling and retying. She felt confused and disoriented, but kept trying over and over again in vain.

"Rosa and Javier are going to meet them at the hospital with Zack's mom. I'm on babysitting duty," Veronica was saying.

Laurel sat up and shook her head from side to side in an attempt to rouse herself. Gov grunted something indistinct and rolled over on his side.

"Laurel? Are you there?"

"Yeah, Mom. I'm here," she answered through a yawn. "What time is it?"

"Four-thirty-five. We didn't want to wait to call you. Carli tends to deliver fast."

"Right. I'm glad you did. I'll text Zack," Laurel said as the cobwebs began to clear. She hopped up and grabbed her robe off the hook inside the closet. "He and Rosa can keep me in the loop."

"Sounds good. I'll be touch."

After disconnecting from her mother, Laurel made coffee, texted Zack that she was up and went looking for Boot. She found him in the living room under the picture window. He was sleeping like the dead, sprawled out on his back spread- eagle, exactly where the tree had been in her dream. It was too early for her to think any more about that and what underlying meaning it may have, so she tucked it away and focused on Carli. She knew this was going to be their last baby and she sent up a prayer that it was a girl.

"What's up?"

Laurel looked up to find Gov standing in the dim light of the hallway, wearing his briefs and a sleepy expression. His hair was going in a hundred different directions and his voice was sleepy and husky. She swore he got sexier every day.

"Carli's in labor. My mom is on her way over there now to stay with the boys. I'm sorry I woke you."

"No problem. That's a good reason to be woken up in the middle of the night. But I remember from my sister these things can take a while."

"Not with Carli. She goes fast. This one will probably slide out before they get her in a room."

"TMI." Gov yawned and scratched the side of his head. "Do I smell coffee?"

He was going to stay up with her, Laurel amazed. "Yeah. It should be done by now," she informed him as surprise and delight rippled through her.

"Cool," he mumbled and headed for the kitchen.

Laurel watched him ramble off, then turned her attention back to Boot. He'd stirred a bit at the sound of Gov's voice, then resumed his position and started snoring again. "Well, this is different than the last time Carli had a baby," she laughed to herself. She'd been at work when Carli went into labor with Ollie and had rushed to the hospital in a suit and heels. This time she was in Tahoe in her robe, with a man she hadn't known six months ago, watching a dog she'd fallen for almost as hard sleep. She'd had her heart broken, gone through a divorce and buried her grandmother. And it hadn't killed her. Ronnie would say there are no endings, only new beginnings. The tricky part was not getting hung up in the middle. So then why couldn't she finish the damn book? She was pulled out of her thoughts by Gov's disembodied voice.

"Laurel, do you want a chocolate or is it too early?"

"Too early," she called, feeling the smile that float-ed across her face settle in her heart. He remembered her affinity for a chocolate square with her morning coffee. It was not lost on her that he'd stayed with her every night since Grant's unbidden visit. They'd already fallen into a routine of checking in with each other at the end of the day, but now it was assumed they'd spend their nights together as well. And Laurel found herself liking it, counting on it. Maybe a little too much, she thought, as her phone pinged in her pocket. She grabbed it.

*We're in a room. She's at seven. Won't be long now, knowing her.*

*That was quick.*

*She could barely wait for Veronica to get to the house. The second she pulled up, we pulled out.*

*I'm thinking pink!* Laurel texted back just as Gov returned with two mugs of coffee.

*I tried my best there.*

*TMI*

"Thanks," Laurel told Gov, slipping the phone back into her pocket and taking the steaming mug from his hand.

"Any news?"

"She's progressing. Probably an hour at most."

"You weren't kidding when you said she goes fast."

"Typical Carli behavior. She's efficient above all else," Laurel commented, then switched gears. "Thanks for staying up with me."

"It's an exciting time. I wouldn't miss it."

"It'll be a long day for you," Laurel pointed out around a sip of coffee.

"Not nearly as long as it'll be for Carli."

"True. You put on a shirt."

"Boot will think it's potty time as soon as day breaks since we're up. You sound disappointed."

"I am, a little."

Gov set his cup on the end table, then did the same with hers. He gathered her in his arms and looked down at her with a twinkle in his eye. "I'm glad to take it off if you promise to do the same."

"Nice try," she told him with a brush across the lips. "But I'm basically on call."

"I know. Do they have names picked out?"

"Carli wants a Zachary, but Zack won't have it. No juniors for him. But it's irrelevant anyway because it's a girl. So she'll be Elise Rosalia Harper."

"That's pretty. Classic but not too old-fashioned."

"Exactly," Laurel replied just as her phone vibrated again. She immediately broke their shared embrace. "She's at nine," she informed Gov, reading the screen out loud. "Almost time to push."

"Wow. No messing around for our girl. I don't even have time for a quick shower, do I?"

"Not if you want to be here for the finale."

"Do you miss being there?"

"Not as much as I thought I would." Not as much as I would miss being here with you, Laurel suddenly realized, still a little awed that he'd stayed up with her. Grant never even came to the hospital when the boys were born. "But I'm thinking of going home for a few days. To see the baby and help with the boys." She wondered if he noticed that came out more like a question than a statement. She certainly wasn't used to running her plans by anyone, let alone seek permission to make them. She and Grant had been more independent than most couples. Obviously.

"Oh," Gov said in a tone laced with surprise. "I didn't realize that."

"I need to talk to Carli about it, make sure I wouldn't be more trouble than I'm worth. She has her family and my mom, of course, but I don't know if I can wait too long to see the baby. This is uncharted territory for us." As soon as the words escaped her lips, Laurel realized the ambiguity of them. "But myself aside, it might make more sense to wait until Zack goes back on the road. Closer to Thanksgiving."

"Right. Of course." They held each other impalpably for a moment until her phone signaled again. Laurel tore herself away. "Zack gave his phone to Rosa. She's starting to push!"

Fifteen minutes and what felt like hundreds of paces across the hardwood later, Laurel's phone rang. "Rosa?"

"It's a girl!" Rosa's high-pitched voice was watery. "We finally have *una niña*!"

Laurel felt her throat tighten and tears well in her eyes as joy and relief ran through her. She cleared the emotion from her throat and managed a phlegmy, "Everybody's good?"

"*Ella es perfecta* and my Carli is *buena*!"

"Yeah! Congratulations Abuela Rosa!"

"And to you, Tía Laurel! We will send pictures soon."

"I can't wait to see her. Does she look like the boys?"

"No, not really. More like Zack than anything—lots of blonde hair. But she will change a hundred times over. I must call your mama next."

"Yes, she'll be waiting with bated breath."

After she and Rosa exchanged good-byes, Laurel shifted her gaze back to Gov. He had a sappy smile on his face and his eyes looked a little misty. She closed the small distance between them in two strides and flew into his arms. "It's a girl!"

"I heard!" he exclaimed, picking her up and swinging her from side to side. "And all is well with mom and baby?"

"Perfect," Laurel told him as he set her on her feet. She grabbed his face and kissed him long and hard. He kissed her back with building passion, turning something that had started as impromptu and incidental into something poignant and heartfelt. The next thing she knew, his hands were in her hair and hers were wreathing his neck, drawing him closer as his mouth moved over hers. Every emotion swirling around in her body seemed to coalesce into the kiss. Elation, relief, even the guilt and disappointment of not being there for Carli. It was as if sharing Elise's birth deepened their connection, strengthened their relationship. It made Laurel wonder what it must feel like to actually share a child with someone, to experience that unbreakable, inextricable bond. When Gov finally pulled his mouth away, he rested his forehead against hers as if to prolong the moment. Then he tipped his head up and looked so profoundly into her eyes that she swore he must be seeing the inside of her soul. "Laurel…"

She silenced him by placing two fingers over his mouth. "I know. But that's for another day."

"Okay. But not too many more days."

She sent him a nod and blinked back the tears that had once again collected in her eyes. "Because today is for Elise Rosalia. Thanks again for staying up with me," she added, inching out of his embrace.

"Thanks for sharing it with me. It's quite a high. Might take me a while to come down from it."

"I have no intention of coming down from it. I'm opening some champagne. We'll have a toast to baby Elise to start the day."

"Champagne at sunrise. That's different."

"Ronnie used to call it a seesaw. A little coffee to wake you up, a little champagne to calm you down."

"I like the seesaw analogy. But I have a better idea along the same line." Gov's eyes danced with innuendo. "Another way to keep the celebratory mood going."

She sent him a coy smile. "You do, huh?"

"You get the champagne. I'll take Boot out for a quick pee and meet you in the bedroom."

~~~

March might have the reputation for coming in like a lion and going out like a lamb, but November was giving that adage a run for its money. And without the sweet promise of spring. The wind howled, turning the lake's gentle waves into tempestuous whitecaps and making the sun-kissed days of summer seem like a distant memory. Days like today reminded Gov of the story from his childhood about walking through the woods on a blustery day. He also likened it to the constant churning in the pit of his stomach. He and Laurel still hadn't, as Mac had put it, gotten any further.

Overall, the fall had been warm and dry. Gov had taken advantage of that, and to a lesser extent, Jack Brody's patience. Projects were on, if not ahead, of schedule. But he still hadn't executed the partnership agreement. And the end of the year, along with the approaching holidays, loomed in the back of his mind. Since no one hated loose ends more than he did, he knew the time had come to make a decision. So he did what he always did when his back was against the wall. He turned to his go-to, his greatest confidant, his life-long best friend.

His father.

"Thanks for meeting me, Dad." Gov stood and greeted his father with a hug. The restaurant was bustling with the lunchtime crowd, but Gov had managed to snag a corner booth out of the fray.

"Glad to," Jay replied, taking a seat across from his son. "It's been too long since you and I have done this."

He and his dad used to get together for lunch or a beer regularly, but between Gov moving up to the lake and his parents spending the winter in Palm Springs, the habit had gotten away from them. Gov decided he had to be better about that. His parents were both in good health, but weren't getting any younger. "Well, if you weren't busier in retirement than you were when you were working, maybe I could keep up with you."

"I like to keep busy, you know that. And if I don't, God knows your mother would find things for me to do. She's always got a project going, especially now with having two houses."

"As if you'd have it any other way."

Jay laughed, that booming laugh that hadn't mellowed with age. "That's true. I wouldn't."

Just then the waiter appeared with their drinks and took their orders.

"I went the safe route with an Arnold Palmer."

"Perfect." After the server left, his father asked, "What's on your mind, son?"

His father could read him like a book, something else that hadn't changed over the years. Gov decided not to state the obvious and mention that. "I wanted your advice about something."

"I'm honored to give it, especially at your age." Jay looked at him expectantly. "Shoot."

"It's about Laurel," Gov heard himself say, much to his own amazement. He'd fully intended to start by talking about the partnership opportunity, then move on to Laurel and what it would mean for their relationship. Freudian slip, as his mother would say. "We're at a bit of a crossroads."

"How so?" Jay took a sip of iced tea.

"I've been offered a minority partnership in Brody and Sons. A lucrative one."

"Good for you!" His father's voice was full of pride. "But I'm not surprised. You and Jack Brody are cut from the same cloth. I've never heard a foul word about the Brodys, in business or otherwise. And that says a lot in this town."

"Thanks, Dad."

"But what does that have to do with Laurel?"

Everything, Gov thought, or worst-case scenario, nothing. But he only said, "I'm not sure what to do."

"About Laurel or the partnership?"

"Either. Both."

"Then let's take one at a time. Winner chooses which one we tackle first." He reached into his pants pocket and produced a quarter. "Heads or tails?"

"Dad, I'm serious."

"So am I. There's not much that can't be decided by the flip of a coin. Most problems have one of two solutions. But first you have to figure out where to start. Heads or tails?"

Gov exhaled through his nose. "You know I'll choose heads because Kenzie always wanted it. She thought tails meant the tail of a snake."

Jay smiled at the memory. "Heads it is." He tossed the coin from palm to palm then covered it briefly to build suspense, reminiscent of Gov's boyhood days, before reading it. "Tails," he announced, returning the coin to his pocket. "I win."

"Hey! No fair," Gov protested, instantly suspicious. "You didn't show me."

"You're just going to have to take your old man's word for it," he said as their food arrived. After a few minutes of digging into their sandwiches and fries, Jay picked up the conversation. "So what's going on with Laurel?"

Gov took his own advice and started at the beginning. "She's only going to be here through the end of the year, Christmastime at the latest."

"I didn't realize that."

"That was always the plan and desultory she is not."

"That sounds familiar."

Gov thought of his mother. "Yeah. Anyway, neither one of us expected…We really hadn't planned on getting this involved or…"

"Falling in love?"

"Yeah." He took a sip of his drink. "Is it that obvious?"

"It was after your mother reminded me of the last time you brought a woman home for dinner."

Gov had no leg to stand on there. "True. I'd be fine with things staying how they are now, how they have been these last few months, but they can't."

"Because she has this plan."

"Right."

"So she's almost finished with her book, then?"

"No. At least I don't think so."

His father shot him a curious look. "You don't know?"

Gov put down his sandwich, wiped the corner of his mouth with his napkin. "Should I?"

"Yeah, probably," Jay answered with a shrug. "Seems kind of important. To her at least. And what's important to her should be important to you."

"It is important to me. She is important to me."

"Then the first thing I would do is find out about the book, where she is with it. According to your mother, that was her reason for coming to Tahoe in the first place. It sounds like you might have derailed that plan a bit. If she's as methodical as you're making her out to be, she might be feeling the same uncertainty about things that you are."

He'd never thought about it that way. Her way, from her perspective. "Maybe a little. But she still works on it most days. I mean I assume that's what she's doing when I'm at work or whenever we're not together."

"Have you read it?"

"No."

Jay jerked back a little. "Why?"

"I don't know. She hasn't offered."

"Have you?"

"Have I what?"

"Asked to read it?"

"No. I figured she'd ask me to if she wanted my opinion."

"Sounds like you two need to get on the same page." Jay chuckled, then added, "No pun intended."

"We are. I mean, I thought we were," Gov told himself as much as his father.

"Well, that's part of it. Making sure. So this cross-roads is about what to do come Christmas? When it's time for her to leave?"

Gov hated hearing the words spoken out loud even more than he hated thinking them. "Yeah. And the partnership only complicates that."

The waiter returned and cleared their dishes, refilled their drinks. After which time Jay put it, "Because you'd be committing to Brody and Sons, permanently entrenching yourself here."

"Right."

"And you guys talked about another possible scenario? In L.A.?"

Gov was starting to feel like he'd screwed up the future while still dealing with the present. "No. We haven't really talked about it at all. For some reason it's a sore subject, like the elephant in the room."

A look of concern crossed his father's face. "Oh. Well, then I stand corrected. You need to figure what you want, McGovern, before you do anything else."

"I do know what I want."

"Do you?"

"Yes. I want Laurel."

"Even if that means turning down the partnership?"

"Yes," Gov said unequivocally. "No contest."

A knowing smile replaced the concern on the older man's face. "Then you've answered your own question, solved your own problem. Everything else will fall into place from there, providing Laurel feels the same way."

"She does."

Now Jay shot him a look from under raised eyebrows. "You sure?"

"I'm sure," Gov reiterated, actually believing it for the first time. "I don't think I could feel this way otherwise. I'd like to think fate wouldn't be that cruel."

His father laughed without opening his mouth. "Not usually, no. But you've got to talk to her about it. You can't move past this, through it, until you do. You can't expect Laurel to put her life on hold based on assumptions."

"I've tried, Dad. I really have."

"Try harder. You already know that you need to, that you can, or you wouldn't be here, talking to me about it. You knew I would tell you what you needed to hear, not what you wanted to hear or what part of you already knows. You're more like your mother than you give yourself credit for. So, tackle this problem head-on, don't look for the easy way out and for God's sake, stop pussyfooting around. Make a plan and commit yourself to it, then go to her with it. Be steadfast, but open to compromise. If you two really are on the same page, hearing her out will only improve the outcome. The whole is always worth more than its pieces."

"What if it's too much, too soon for her? I don't want to rush her."

With an impatient sigh, Jay cocked his head to the side. "I don't think you have another choice here, son. You're running out of time. You don't have two decisions to make, you have one. You've made it. Own it. The other one will be on its heels and take care of itself, one way or the other."

Gov knew his father was right. Just like he knew why he went to Hues of Blue that night to bitch and moan to Mac. He could have easy drowned his sorrows at home. It was also not lost on him that Mac and his dad took the same slant on the situation, adding even more weight to the argument. He was overthinking things, underestimating Laurel, risking letting what was most important to him slip away. And for the first time in his life, he was scared. He needed to get over himself, he needed a plan and he needed it quick. But for assurance, or maybe insurance, he asked his father, "How did you know? With mom?"

The impatience on Jay's face slid away and was superseded by affection and reminiscence, as if the question transported him back in time. "I knew from the moment I met her she was the one for me. But reciprocation took some convincing on my part. I was pretty sure she loved me, so it was more a matter of making her realize it, accept it. I'm in your camp with the whole cruel fate thing. Trust me on this. Women like your mom and Laurel can't resist a solid plan and some heartfelt honesty."

Gov reminded himself how lucky he was to have come from them, to have been raised by them, to have them as an example. He hoped he could pass that on to a child some day. "Thanks, Dad. You know you're pretty good at this stuff. Making people realize what they already know. Why didn't you go into politics again?" Gov asked as the server returned with the check.

Jay swiped the check off the table before Gov could reach for his wallet. He handed the waiter a few bills and told him to keep the change. Then he looked back at his son with a gleam in his eye. "It didn't fit into the plan. The girl I loved didn't want me to." Then, smiling all the while, he stood and asked, "Ready?"

"Yeah," Gov told him, standing as that sunk in. He'd had no idea his mother was the reason his father had chosen a different career path. "Yeah, Dad. I'm ready."

# Chapter Seventeen

LAUREL WOULDN'T PRETEND she wasn't disappointed. But she'd acted nonchalant and hadn't let it show when Gov declined her invitation to go to L.A. for Thanksgiving. She knew her mother was expecting her and she was dying to see the baby in person instead of on FaceTime. Elise already looked like a different person at not quite six weeks old and Laurel didn't want to wait any longer to meet her.

Gov's reasons for refusal were perfectly understandable, gallant in fact. His sister and her family were coming into town. He hadn't seen them since last Christmas and his brother-in-law for almost two years due to his deployments. Coupled with that, the unseasonably warm, dry early fall had allowed several of his projects to advance and he had some loose ends to tie up later in the year than usual. And no one hated loose ends more than Gov.

To add to her disenchantment, the management company wasn't able to extend her lease in the long-term. Two additional weeks was all she was able to secure. She'd been surprised and, if she was being honest, more than a little disappointed. She still wasn't done with the book, although she'd made some progress. She'd written all but the last two chapters. She was pretty sure she knew what she wanted the ending to be, but she still had to figure out how to get there.

Maybe art really does imitate life.

She and Gov still hadn't discussed what would come next for them. She was admittedly dodging the issue and he hadn't brought it up again lately. He'd seemed just as surprised as she to learn the house wasn't available for rent into the new year and had immediately offered for her to stay at his place. As much as she appreciated and even expected the gesture, she wasn't sure it was the right thing to do. It seemed like every potential solution presented another challenge.

She'd decided to shelve the issue for the time being and concentrate on finishing the first draft of the book and enjoying Thanksgiving with her family. And of course spending some time with Elise, for whom she'd bought out nearly every online baby store as well as Tahoe Baby. She had one suitcase dedicated to those gifts as she'd had the online purchases sent to her mother's house. And, of course, she always remembered the boys. At present, Gov was loading that suitcase into his truck while she closed the other one.

"Almost ready?" he asked, returning to the bedroom. "The Tuesday before Thanksgiving is always crazy. Almost as busy as the Sunday after."

Laurel's bag landed on the floor with a thud. "Are you sure I shouldn't just drive myself? That way you wouldn't have deal with the airport traffic today or on Sunday."

"Nope. You're stuck with me." He gathered her in his arms. "I'll take any time I can get with you. I'm going to miss you."

Laurel actually felt her heart twist a little in her chest. "I'm going to miss you too."

He laid a kiss on her lips. "Thanks again for the invitation for Thanksgiving. I'm sorry I can't go with you."

"I understand."

"Besides, this will give you more time with Carli and the baby without having to worry about entertaining me."

He gave her a smile that didn't quite reach his eyes and she met it with one of her own. "Tell the boys that. They're quite smitten with you."

"They're quite smitten with Boot. I'm a sidekick at best."

"True." She paused for a moment, then let her heart do the talking. "I'm quite smitten with you, you know."

"If you're half as smitten with me as I am with you, I'm the luckiest guy in the world." He brought her against him and hugged her tight, then rubbed a hand up and down her back. She felt his chest rise and fall in a heavy sigh before he said, "We should probably get going."

"Yeah," she muttered, stepping out of his embrace. He grabbed her bag and she picked up her jacket and carry-on. As she walked out of the house and through the garage, a feeling of melancholy came over her. My God, you'd think she'd lived here for years instead of months. And she'd be back in five days. This time, at least.

They headed down the mountain toward Reno, winding through the forests of evergreens with their light dusting of snow, the deep emerald green of the trees a sharp contrast to the crisp blue of the sky. Laurel glanced down at the vast valley below, as the sun shone bright on the high desert hills speckled in color as autumn took its last breaths. Lost in thought, she suddenly realized they were almost to the airport.

"You okay?"

She sliced her gaze over to him. "Yeah, just thinking."

Gov took one hand off the wheel and laid it on hers. "Is it still only a penny for someone's thoughts? Or has that kept pace with inflation too?"

She couldn't help but smile. "I'll make you a deal, a quid pro quo so to speak. A thought for a thought. You go first."

After a moment of consideration he answered, "I was thinking that I wish it was Sunday and I was picking you up from the airport instead of dropping you off."

Laurel knew she had the upper hand here. More time to think about what to say and the advantage of temporizing rather than professing. She decided to split the difference. "I was thinking along the same lines. But that we'd be flying to L.A. together."

Nodding, Gov released her hand and pulled into the parking garage. "Yeah, I know."

"You don't have to come in with me." She'd expected him to drop her off.

"I know. I want to." He found a spot and maneuvered the truck into it. They got out and she started to take one of the bags, but he grabbed them both insisting, "I've got it."

They walked into the airport and checked the bags, then headed toward the escalators leading to Security hand in hand. "Well, this is my stop," she stated breezily when they reached the final corridor. Before she could lean in to kiss him, he drew her against him and covered her mouth with his. The kiss was long and deep, as if each layer was filled with something different. Love, passion, longing, promise, commitment. It was like a silent affirmation of everything between them.

He eased away with a peck on the forehead and a squeeze of the hand. "Text me when you land."

"I will."

"I'll be right here on Sunday, waiting for you."

She sent him an upward nod as her throat threatened to close and her eyes began to sting. This is ridiculous, she thought. It's only a long weekend. But they both knew it spoke to the uncertainty of things to come.

She pulled away from him, slowly releasing his hand, and stepped onto the escalator. When she got to the top, she turned and gave him a final wave before walking away. Out of the corner of her eye, she could see that he was still standing there as she started across the bridge leading to the terminal. She bit back tears and focused on the task at hand. When she got her phone out to show her boarding pass, she noticed a text from Gov. She stepped out of line to open it and let the tears roll down her cheeks. He'd sent it over an hour ago. He'd missed her before she was even gone.

~~~

A few hours later the tears returned, but this time they were tears of joy. Laurel sat in Carli's family room holding the most beautiful baby girl she'd ever seen. Elise Rosalia Harper had huge black eyes like her mama and a mound of blonde hair like her daddy. And rosy cheeks and a button nose and a perfect little mouth that smiled up at Laurel and melted her heart over and over again.

"She's taken to you already," Carli observed, returning from the kitchen with a cloth over her shoulder and a bottle in her hand. "Do you want to do the honors?"

"Absolutely. Anything special I need to know?" Laurel moved the baby from her lap to the crook of her arm.

"Not really," Carli replied, testing the milk on the inside of her wrist like a pro. "She's pretty cooperative. But I have to be careful not to overfeed her. I'm so used to the boys being ravenous all the time." She handed the bottle to Laurel, then draped the burp cloth over her shoulder. "Prop her up a little bit more. I think it helps with digestion."

Laurel obliged and wedged the nipple into Elise's tiny mouth. The baby sighed in contentment and began to suck. She leaned down and kissed the top of her head, then laid her cheek against it. She was the most precious little thing. "How are the boys with her?"

"Good. Really good." Carli bent down to pick up a plastic truck and a few action figures from the floor and threw them into the toy basket in the corner. "Ollie is nurturing by nature; I've noticed that before with friends' babies and Nick tries to make her laugh. They both want to know when she's going to be able to walk and talk and play. You know how active they both are."

"Yeah, they loved playing with Boot."

Carli plopped down on the couch next to Laurel. "Don't I know it. They're still soliciting for a dog. I said maybe in a year or two. And not a puppy. We'll adopt one from a shelter." She rubbed the top of one of Elise's pink-socked feet, then the other. The baby cooed and kept sucking. "Speaking of Boot, anything new on the Gov front?" Carli leaned back against the cushions and closed her eyes.

"No. Other than he reiterating his offer to stay with him when my lease runs out. I told you that, right?"

"Yeah. Have you decided what you're going to do?"

"No. Not really." Laurel gently removed the bottle and set it on the coffee table, then lifted Elise to her shoulder for a burp. She patted the baby's back with the palm of her hand a few times and voilà. "Good girl." She returned her to the crook of her arm and resumed the feeding. "He hasn't brought it up again. I'll deal with it after Thanksgiving."

At that, Carli opened her eyes and smiling over at her daughter, spoke in baby talk, "Auntie Laurel is equivocating. She's trying to avoid an issue that can't be avoided. The heart wants what the heart wants."

Of course Laurel knew Carli was right, but she had to come to terms with it in her own time, in her own way. And that was only the beginning. Then she had to figure what to do about it. "Mommy is using you to send a message," Laurel told Elise in kind. "Instead, maybe she should just tell me what she thinks."

There was a heavy pause, like when a pitcher is contemplating the game-winning pitch before throwing. Finally Carli said, "Mommy thinks Auntie Laurel is afraid to be happy."

Could it be as ridiculously simple as that? "No, Auntie Laurel is not afraid to be happy. Auntie Laurel is just…"

"Afraid." Carli blinked hard and looked at up at her. Then, speaking in her regular voice added, "And no one deserves to be happy more than Auntie Laurel."

Laurel held Carli's gaze for a long moment, then said, "I am happy. I'm just…"

"Afraid," she repeated. "Afraid of that rare and special kind of happy, the through and through kind, the forever kind, with all of its trials and tribulations and all of its unknowns. The kind of happy that isn't guaranteed, the kind that requires blood, sweat and tears from time to time. The kind that waxes and wanes like the moon, but is somehow always there, lurking behind the clouds. The kind some people look for their whole lives and never find, the kind some squander recklessly, the kind some people are never meant to have." Tears welled in Carli's eyes now. "The kind of happy—"

"Mommy is," Laurel finished for her. "The kind worth fighting for."

Nodding, Carli swallowed hard. "The kind worth fighting for. The kind Auntie Laurel reminded me I had. And now it's my turn to return the favor." Carli reached over and wiggled the empty bottle out of Elise's mouth. Laurel instinctively burped the baby, then set her back in the crook of her arm and rocked her gently. Was there anything sweeter than watching a baby drift off to sleep? "Here, I'll put her down for a bit, while it's still quiet." Carli reached for her daughter. "Zack will be home with the boys soon."

Laurel hated to give Elise up, but she did as she was told. After Carli left the room, she got up and stared unseeingly out the window. The backyard was freshly cut and bursting with family life. A swing set and sandbox stood in the center of the grassy area. Shrubs and trees of various colors and shapes ringed the lot, contrasting the rocky, barren hillside that sloped in the distance. A scattering of plastic toys and games were scattered around a couch and dining set on the paver patio. The day was warm and bright, like most Southern California days, yet Laurel found herself missing the cool mountain air of Tahoe, the crashing of the waves in the afternoon wind and the smell of pine and bark braided with sea and sand. And most of all, Gov.

"Zack is picking up a couple of pizzas on the way home." Carli's voice brought Laurel out of her thoughts. "Do you want to stay?"

"I'd better go home, see if Mom needs any help," Laurel replied, turning around to face her. "I'll come back tomorrow, though. I can take the boys out for a few hours or bring them back to the house to swim if that would help."

"It would. Zack has rehearsal tomorrow. He has a show in Anaheim on Friday night."

"Let's plan on that then. Or I can stay here with them if you want to run out for a while."

"They'd love to go to the house and swim. We'll be there on Thursday of course, but they'll be dressed up for Thanksgiving dinner. That way they'll have gotten the pool out of their system. And it'll wear them out."

"That works for me too because I can help Mom and Rosa when the boys aren't in the pool."

"Mom mentioned she was going over to the house tomorrow to help Veronica with the stuffing."

"So I'm told. But as usual I'm only allowed to set the table and bake the rolls."

"I got out of the whole thing this year."

"Giving birth has its benefits."

"Yeah," Carli laughed. Then she sobered a little and asked, "You okay? You seem sad all the sudden. What I said before—"

"Is food for thought. When I get to it, that is. Now I'd better head home before traffic gets bad. I'll touch base in the morning."

"Don't get an Uber after all. Take my car. You're coming back first thing anyway. I'm not going any-where tonight and Zack will be home soon if some-thing comes up."

"Okay. That makes sense."

Carli closed the small space between them and wrapped her arms around Laurel. "Thanks for all your help with the baby. And for coming here straight from the airport."

"I couldn't wait another minute to meet her. She's perfect. Looks more like you than the boys did at this age," Laurel told her, returning the hug.

"That's what my parents said."

"I know they're over the moon." Laurel broke their shared embrace.

"They are. And so is Jen," Carli said of Zack's mom. "Finally a girl to spoil."

"She's welcome on Thursday. But you already knew that."

"I know. Thanks. She has a boyfriend these days. I think they're seeing his family. I invited her for Christmas." She paused, then added, "Speaking of Christmas—"

Laurel held a hand up in the air, palm out. "I said I'd deal with it and I will. As usual, you'll be the first to know."

Carli cocked her head to the side and pursed her lips. "I don't know about that. This time I think I might be the second."

Laurel sat on the bed in her childhood bedroom, now redone in grays and blues, with her laptop open on her lap. Thanksgiving had been its usual huge success. Now with everyone gone home and the leftovers stowed, she was turning her attention to her manuscript. She'd thought writing would occupy her mind enough to take it off other things. She'd been wrong.

"Knock, knock."

"Come in, Mom," Laurel said without looking up. "And you know you don't have to knock. Especially when the door is all but open."

"Old habits and all of that." Veronica sat down on the bed. "Making progress?"

"Not in the least." Laurel closed her laptop and pushed it off to the side. "Dinner was fantastic. You outdid yourself, which I thought was impossible."

"Thanks, honey. Rosa and I make a good team. I think everyone enjoyed themselves. Thanks for all your help."

"Sure. Nobody sets a table and loads a dishwasher quite like me."

"You did a lot more than that. Thanks for coming home. I know this year is different."

To say the least, Laurel thought. "I wouldn't miss it. Did Mark leave?"

"Yeah. He's going to stop by and see his mother, bring her some leftovers."

"How's she doing?"

"The dementia is progressing. But she has periods of clarity. For his sake, hopefully tonight is one of them."

"I'm sorry. She was always lovely to me."

"Me too. Getting old can be a bitch. Feel free to remind me of that someday."

Laurel couldn't imagine not having her mother. "Stop." She had a feeling Veronica had more on her mind than a Thanksgiving recap. "But that's not why you're here. Because you've got to be exhausted."

"I am. But I wanted to talk to you about something."

Laurel scooted over and patted the bed next to her. "Come on, then."

Veronica settled in next to her with a tender smile. "We haven't done this in a long time."

"In here? Probably at least ten years. I think I crawled into your bed the night I left Grant."

"Yeah. And I think you stayed there for a couple of days. The bastard," she sneered.

"We've already established that. Spill."

Veronica started on a determined breath, "Mark asked me to marry him."

"Going for a baker's dozen, is he?"

Veronica acknowledged that with a self-deprecating grin. "I'm going to say yes this time."

Laurel sat up a little straighter. "Well, it's about time. Congratulations, Mom."

"I wanted to make sure you're okay with it."

"Of course I'm okay with it. Why wouldn't I be?"

"I know you're all grown up, but it affects you too. He'd sell his place, move in here."

"That's a long time coming. I assume he already stays here more than not."

"Off and on, depending on what's going on. But yes."

"Then why not make it official?"

"That's what I'm starting to think. Neither one of us is getting any younger. And he's a good man, loves me, us. He never had a family of his own and now with his mother slipping away…"

"He's already part of our family, Mom. Like Ronnie used to say, when you love somebody, you love the people they love. You love Mark and so do I. And not just by association. In retrospect, he was like the father figure I never had."

"And that was his choice. I made it very clear from the beginning that I wasn't looking for a father for my daughter. Remember your Prom? We had all the kids over beforehand for pictures around the pool. He fell in trying to get a panoramic shot!"

Laurel smiled at the memory. "Yeah. Everybody was horrified until he surfaced and started laughing. He held up the camera and said something about it being waterproof."

They shared a moment of nostalgia, then Veronica went on, "He's coming over tomorrow to help get the tree up. I told him I'd talk to you and give him an answer then."

Laurel's breath caught in her throat. Her dream the night before Elise was born. The Tahoe tree, the familiar ornaments, the indistinguishable faces. It was as if she was having the same dream again, but while she was awake. Almost like jamais vu and déjà vu at the same time.

"Laurel, are you okay with all of that?"

"Yes, of course. You just reminded me of something. A strange dream I had a few weeks ago." Coming out of the fog, she filled her mother in.

"Dreams are funny things, like a mirror into our subconscious. They tell us all the things we're afraid to think, let alone say. Even to ourselves."

"Yeah. It makes me wonder what I'm afraid to think and say."

Veronica took Laurel in discerningly for a long moment. "I bet you do know, somewhere in that beautiful head of yours. And being your grandmother's granddaughter, the only way to figure it out is to give yourself permission to find it, then pull it out and write it down. "

"Like the song Ronnie never finished," Laurel muttered, thinking back to her conversation with Mac.

"The one about Tahoe? She did finish it."

At that, Laurel's vacant gaze popped back to her mother's. "She did?"

"Uh-huh. For the most part, anyway. I was looking through the linen drawer for napkins the other day and I found a place card with some lyrics written on the back. It looked like the same song, or parts thereof. I'm sorry, I must have forgotten to mention it to you. So much going on lately." Veronica reached into her pocket and produced her phone. "I took a picture of it and put it off to the side." She found it in her photos and handed the phone to Laurel.

*But a lover won't wait forever. And I've got to make my own way, like that lover from long ago, who keeps comin' back around, never lettin' me down. I still think of that lover, as true as Tahoe is blue, through and through. And know he's there, making sure nothing keeps me down.*

Laurel looked up from the phone and into her mother's eyes. "The lover was Mac, wasn't it?"

"I think so."

"Why couldn't she let herself love him, be with him?"

"I'm not sure. She'd been unlucky in love more than I knew, I think. And she had a one-track mind when it came down to it. She could only do one thing at a time if she wanted to do it all the way, do it well. She chose her career, or it chose her, above everything else, even love. Other than us, of course."

No gray area, Laurel thought."But she never even cut a demo for this song, let alone tried to publish it."

"No."

"Why?"

"I can't say for certain, but I think she wanted to write her own happy ending because she knew she couldn't live it. And maybe whenever that got to her, she thought about that song, maybe even sang it. And in that moment, she had her happy ending. All to herself."

"And everything else the rest of the time."

Veronica's eyes filled with tears. "Yeah."

"Mac loved her too. I know he did."

Veronica nodded.

"You knew."

"I suspected. She never mentioned it. I never brought it up."

"So she stopped going to Tahoe because it was too tempting, hurt too much?"

"Maybe. But that was her choice and she had to live with it. And she did."

They shared a moment of understanding, a reckoning of sorts, before Laurel realized out loud, "You didn't really forget to send me these lyrics, did you?"

Veronica didn't confirm or deny, just kept her gaze steady as her eyes welled up again.

"You wanted to show me them in person, to see my reaction. Before I even told you about the dream. You know I've been stuck on the last two chapters, that I can't figure out how to get my characters to happily ever after." Suddenly Laurel saw it all clearly, knew what she had to do. "You knew all along that I...that he..." She reached for her laptop and opened the file and started typing.

Veronica patted Laurel's thigh and stood up. Then she spoke her daughter's name in a tone reminiscent of Laurel's teenage years. Laurel's head automatically shot up. "Tahoe got hold of your heart too. Don't leave it there. This one time don't be Ronnie. Don't just write your happy ending. Live it." Then she turned on her heel and walked out of the room, closing the door behind her.

# CHAPTER EIGHTEEN

LAUREL LANDED ON Sunday afternoon to a falling rain and unseasonably cold temperatures. She was coming from warm, sunny Southern California to a chilly, damp, overcast day. Way to go Reno, Gov, thought. Way to sell it.

Airport traffic was heavy, but not the nightmare Gov had feared. He'd had every intention of getting here early, but it had been one thing after another. And then some more. A prayer escaped his lips as he whipped the truck into the parking garage. Hopefully people were anxious to get home and there would be spots. And not just compact ones, he grumbled under his breath and headed up the ramp to the second level.

He had to get a handle on himself. He had too many balls in the air right now to lose focus and he needed to keep his composure on an even keel. Otherwise Laurel would see right through him, know something was up. That intuitiveness she shared with his mother was incredibly inconvenient at times. He hadn't been in the door five minutes on Thanksgiving before she'd pulled him aside and wanted to know what was going on with him. He'd told her only the bare minimum. When it came to this kind of stuff, his mother couldn't be trusted, as well-meaning as she was.

As he barreled up toward the fourth level, he reviewed his plan and firmed up his weekend story, admittedly filled with half-truths. He *had* spent Thanksgiving with his family, seen his sister, brother-in-law and the kids. The fact that he didn't stay all that long was irrelevant. As was the fact that he'd already been back in Tahoe for hours when he'd spoken to Laurel that evening. When she'd asked to speak to his mother to wish her a Happy Thanksgiving, he hadn't really lied. It was likely that she *was* in the backyard roasting s'mores with the kids. It's just that he wasn't there, so he didn't know.

"Yes!" Gov triumphed, as a Suburban started backing out of a spot at the end of the row. He stopped to give them a wide berth and continued his mental fact-checking. He *did* work on Friday, despite Brody and Sons being closed for the long holiday weekend. Moreover, he not only saw Jack Brody, but went to lunch with him. After which time he walked three projects that he hadn't gotten to on Wednesday. Why he hadn't gotten to them was immaterial. Sort of.

It *was* snowing up at the lake yesterday. He'd just exaggerated the extent thereof to explain his breathlessness. Laurel had no idea that Boot not only loved the snow, but had no problem taking care of his business in it. She also had no idea that the condo parking lot and sidewalks had been cleared before he and Boot went out. No shoveling necessary on Gov's part.

Details.

He maneuvered into the spot vacated by the Suburban and killed the engine. Then he grabbed the flowers from the passenger seat, zipped up his jacket and hightailed it toward Arrivals. He'd told Laurel he'd be waiting for her at the bottom of the escalators when she came back and that's exactly where he intended to be. He gave the monitors in the lobby a sidelong glance, noting her flight had landed ahead of schedule. He made it to the escalators about ten-seconds before the next group of people got on at the top.

He was huffing and puffing, his heart was racing, but he'd made it, he commended himself just as Laurel stepped on the escalator. Because of the configuration of the wall, she wouldn't see him for about five-seconds and Gov took every bit of that time to calm himself down. Smile etched firmly in place, he took a series of deep breaths and willed his pounding heart steady.

She spotted him about halfway down and lifted her hand in a hearty wave. Their eyes locked and the world around him slipped away. It was as if it was just the two of them in the crowded airport, like he was a horse wearing blinders only seeing the track ahead. And Laurel was the only thing on that track. She started walking down the escalator, snaking around the other riders, as if she couldn't get to the end fast enough. Gov skirted around a few people and carved out a spot at the bottom. She stepped off and rushed to him. Later, he'd remember how her purse hit him across the back, how the zipper of her coat scraped his chin and the way the flowers slipped from his grasp and fell to the floor. But now all he cared about was how good her mouth felt on his, how relieved he was to have her back in his arms, how she smelled like roses and tasted like mint and pretzels. He trudged his hands up and down her back as if doing so would somehow bring her closer. Breathless, he tore his mouth away and buried his face in her hair. He heard her sharp intakes of breath, felt her heart flutter even through the layers of clothes she wore. She muttered his name and when he finally pulled back, tears were escaping her eyes. He swept them away with his thumbs. "Hi."

She swallowed hard and gave him a weak smile. "Hi."

Unable to help himself, he took her face in his hands and kissed her again. "I missed you." No, he silently amended, he'd ached for her. "So much."

"I missed you, too." Her arms were circling his waist now and she rested her head against him, then hugged him again, even tighter this time. "So incredibly much."

And then he knew. He'd known before, or thought he had, but now there wasn't a shadow of a doubt in his mind that she was the one for him. All the running around over the last few weeks, the jumping through hoops despite the holidays, the white lies he'd told, sweating the small stuff so it didn't become big stuff. It was all worth it. And if this plan didn't work, he'd come up with another one. Being with her was all that mattered. However it happened, wherever it happened, by whatever means necessary.

"Excuse me." An orotund voice ended the moment. Gov looked up into the face of a middle-aged man wearing a TSA cap and a wide grin. "Are these yours?" he asked, displaying the flowers.

"Ah, yeah." Gov released Laurel and she turned in place to stand next to him. "Thanks."

The man handed the bouquet to Gov. "No problem." Then he tipped his hat at Laurel. "Glad she made it back to you safely. Merry Christmas."

"Merry Christmas," they replied in unison to his retreating back.

With any luck it would be his best one ever, Gov thought. He took Laurel's hand in his and started walking. They followed the corridor lined with slot machines and restaurants to the baggage claim area. A North Pole scene complete with Santa's sleigh and reindeer stood just inside the main entrance and Christmas wreaths hung behind the car rental counters.

"Oh, look! It's so pretty! All decorated for Christmas!"

Gov had been in such a hurry when he came in, he hadn't even noticed. "They don't decorate LAX for Christmas?"

"Of course they do, it's just not the same when it's ninety degrees outside and there are palm trees swaying in the distance."

"Well, you said you always wanted to spend Christmas in Tahoe. This is a preview of what it's like."

She looked around in wonderment, like a kid in the world's biggest candy store. "It's wonderful!"

They got all the way to the carousel before Gov realized he was still holding the flowers. Letting go of her hand, he passed them to her. "Sorry these are a little mangled. Welcome...back." Gov chose his words carefully, gauging her reaction.

"Thank you. They're beautiful. Christmas colors too." She took the flowers, then planted a kiss on his lips. "And that greeting was worth losing a few pedals."

He laid a kiss on the top of her head as she leaned against him, sniffing the flowers. "Speaking of Christmas," she said, shifting her gaze up to him. "Mom and I put up the tree. I mean, Mark technically put up the tree. He does all the heavy lifting and strings the lights. Mom and I just hang the ornaments. Anyway, I was wondering if you'd like to come to L.A. for Christmas."

Now she wants to talk about things? Make plans? When he didn't immediately respond, she quickly amended, "It's just an idea. I know we haven't gotten that far yet, but since I'll be leaving—"

She was interrupted by the sound of the baggage belt starting, announcing the arrival of the cargo from her flight. Gov decided it was some kind of divine intervention and gave silent thanks. He took advantage of the out and asked, "Do you have the same two?"

"Yeah, I brought the one that had the gifts in it back empty because I'll need it."

For packing up, he silently added. Her bags were among the first to arrive and Gov scooped them up and they headed to the parking garage. When they got to the truck, he helped her in and loaded the bags. The mood had clearly shifted and an awkward silence hung between them as they drove up the mountain. As tempting as it was not to, Gov stuck to the plan. This was an all or nothing situation for him. When he'd told her he didn't do things halfway, he'd meant it. Finally, he decided to break the tension. "Are you hungry?"

"No. Mom and I had brunch before she dropped me off. You?"

He hadn't eaten all day, but said, "I'm good. Maybe we can grab dinner later?"

"Ah, sure." Her voice was small, full of surprise and disappointment. "Do you have plans this afternoon?"

"Sort of. Errands, paperwork. I thought I'd drop you off at your place, then come back in a couple of hours. I figured you'd want some time to unpack, get organized. And you probably didn't get much writing done over the weekend."

"Actually, I finished the book."

That had him turning his head to look at her. He hadn't expected that."You did? That's fantastic. Congratulations."

"Thanks," she replied quietly.

He'd have thought she'd be more excited. "So what comes next? With the book, I mean," he quickly clarified.

"I've decided to self-edit. I can use the rest of my time here for that."

"Great."

They were coming into town now. The poles of the streetlights were wrapped in sparkling red garland and white bulb lights hung across the street. Christmas trees shone from behind store windows and a huge inflatable Santa Claus held up a sign informing everyone of local holiday happenings.

"What's the Northern Lights Festival?" Laurel wanted to know.

Gov knew it was an annual occurrence, but he'd never really paid much attention to the details or timing of it. Until this year, of course. It was an integral part of his plan. "Throughout the month of December there are holiday-themed events. A tree lighting, sip and shop, holiday food and drink specials at the bars and restaurants, a Christmas Village with a Santa, concerts." He paused for effect, then added, "Sleigh rides."

"Sleigh rides? Really? With horses?"

"Yeah. No reindeer."

"Obviously. Is there always snow at Christmas?"

"Usually."

"That's so cool!"

Stopped at a light, he took her in. She was over the moon about snow. Something he took for granted, something he often considered an inconvenience, something he would never have thought to appreciate. But it seemed that ever since he met Laurel colors were sharper, days were brighter, flavors more flavorful. His world was a better place because she was in it, had become such a big part of it. And he didn't want anything to change that. Ever. So this had to work.

"Would you like to do that? Take a sleigh ride?" he asked as the signal changed.

"Sure. But I'm not sure how long I'll be here." Her voice trailed off a little. "And with your schedule being so busy lately…"

Pulling into her driveway, Gov killed the engine and turned to face her. She was looking at him pointedly, a little fearfully. He might be flirting with overcorrecting here and he didn't want to give her the wrong impression. The last thing he needed was for her to doubt him or his feelings. So he went with his gut and hedged his bets. "For now, let's plan on you moving in with me when your lease is up. That will give us time to figure out the next step, make a plan for Christmas," he paused and cleared his throat unnecessarily before finishing, "etc. Will that work?"

She gave him a closemouthed smile and a nod of affirmation. "Yeah."

"Great. I'll help you in, then run out and be back in a couple of hours. Okay?"

"Okay." She unbuckled her seat belt and started to get out of the car, but he grabbed her arm. "Laurel." She turned back to him. He laid the palm of his hand on her cheek. "I love you. More than you could possibly know. "

"I love you, too."

We'll see about that, he thought. We'll just see about that.

~~~

Winter held the basin firmly in its grasp with morning temperatures in the twenties. But with clear skies and abundant sunshine, some afternoons hovered around fifty degrees. No snow to speak of, only the occasional flurry that melted with the heating of the day, but it was as close to winter as Laurel had ever gotten. Ronnie had hated the cold, let alone snow, so Laurel had spent every Christmas of her life in Southern California, opening presents in shorts and a t-shirt and eating breakfast out by the pool. And it looked like this year would be more of the same.

Gov had yet to commit to going to L.A. with her for Christmas, but of course she was always welcome in Reno with he and his parents if that didn't work out. Jay and Sheryl would be heading to Palm Springs in January and would celebrate with his sister and her family then as they were seeing Matt's family for Christmas this year. So Gov assumed they'd be together for Christmas, it was just a matter of location.

Neither of which was, ironically, Tahoe.

Writing outside was for the most part a thing of the past, but afternoons like today were warm enough for Laurel to sit on the deck in a heavy coat. She'd gone through the book once already, finding some typos and grammatical errors along with a hole or two in the story and a few repetitive phrases, but it had been pretty clean overall, which had come as a pleasant surprise.

She'd finished the last two chapters on Thanksgiving, writing through the night and falling asleep over her laptop only to be roused by her mother's knock at the door just before noon. After which came another awakening.

She'd written two endings.

And she didn't know which one to use.

But she'd finally named her male protagonist.

And that had been a wake-up call of another sort.

To make matters worse, she'd asked her mother to read both versions of the ending and Veronica had refused to tell Laurel which one she preferred. That was, her mother had insisted, for her to figure out on her own. Add it to the list. No endings, only new beginnings, she reminded herself, glancing at the wind chimes hanging motionless in the corner.

First and foremost, she was in love with the hero she'd created, whose name could only be McGovern Scott. She'd known she was like Whitney, every writer puts some of themselves into their characters, particularly in female-driven novels written by female authors. But she hadn't realized how much Whitney was like *her*. Independent, tortured, vulnerable and unexpectedly and hopelessly in love with a man who seemed too good to be true. Her male protagonist, larger than life and right out of central casting, was none other than Gov.

She shut her laptop and stared out at the denuded trees whose leaves only yesterday had been fluttering in the afternoon breeze. She took in the neighbor's house, now fully visible with the lushness of summer but a memory. They had decorated the evergreens at the perimeter of the property with lights and ornaments. It reminded Laurel of the giant department store tree with its oversized decorations she'd gaze up at while waiting to see Santa as a child. Tahoe sure did take its Christmas seriously. And she could use a little Christmas spirit herself.

She only had a few days left in the house, so there was no point in doing any holiday decorating. She'd been tempted to switch out the fall wreath on the front door with the Christmas one she'd seen in the garage, but didn't see much point in it. So the extent of her Christmas decorations would be the flowers Gov had given her at the airport—red roses and white carnations in a bed of pine branches. She'd be moving over to his place before she knew it, temporarily at least. She'd been thinking a lot about what Mac had said that morning on the beach, how life in Tahoe was often lived in an quixotic bubble, a parallel universe, that didn't always transfer to the real world. Would she and Gov be able to transition to a real life or would their relationship be exposed as nothing more than a fling? A romantic summer liaison in Tahoe that fizzled out as quickly as it had begun.

No, she told herself. She knew she truly loved him, believed he truly loved her. And she'd never felt as loved, as coveted, as cherished as she did when she stepped off the escalator at the airport. The way he'd looked into her eyes was the most heartfelt expression of emotion she'd ever known. He still seemed a little preoccupied, more stressed-out and busy than usual, but overall the aloofness was gone. They'd made love every night since she got back and once or twice again in the morning, as if to make up for lost time. Or maybe to prepare for it.

But was theirs the kind of love to last a lifetime? The kind that weathered all the storms, dodged all the curve balls, shared in all the triumphs, overcame all the disappointments? The kind Carli and Zack had? The kind Gov's parents clearly had? And maybe that older couple on the beach too? The kind she thought she might never have after realizing she'd never had it with Grant. Not even close.

In both versions of *Christmas in Tahoe*, Whitney and "Scott" ended up together. One scenario brought them to happily ever after, Laurel's intention from the start. The other took a more contemporary approach with a happy for now conclusion. Together, committed, playing the future by ear, a day, a month, a year at a time. Laurel's creative motivation had nothing to do with a potential sequel or a series; it was merely what poured out of her that night. But for herself, happily ever after was the only option. She knew deep down she couldn't settle for less, not knowingly at least. And she wouldn't bounce back this time if it didn't work out. Gov would be her last love, one way or the other.

In editing the book, Laurel had realized more than that she was in love with the hero she'd created. She hadn't only been writing about Gov, about them, she'd been writing about her journey to find herself, through falling in love with him. What had started out as therapeutic and introspective had become an autobiographical, self-fulfilling prophecy. *Christmas in Tahoe* had little to do with where she was and everything to do with who she was with. She might have always wanted to spend Christmas in Tahoe, but without Gov, it would be meaningless and empty. She'd found her sense of place here, the love of her life, her true purpose. She'd literally written her own happy ending and she needed to find a way to live it. Not just in Tahoe, not just at

Christmas, not just on paper, but for real, everyday. The only question was how.

And unbeknownst to Laurel, she was about to find out.

# CHAPTER NINETEEN

"TODAY?" LAUREL ASKED incredulously two days later. She was barely awake and only on her second sip of coffee. Gov, on the other hand, had apparently been up for hours. Showered and dressed and ready to roll as she stood half asleep in her robe in the kitchen.

"Sure. Why not?"

"For one thing, I have until tomorrow at five to be out. I need to do laundry and pack, then tidy up a little." She walked over to the island and picked up the checklist from the management company, then held it up in the air and read out loud, "I also have to empty the refrigerator, wipe it out, make sure all the drawers are empty in the bathrooms, clean out the pantry and dispose of any trash in the bins." She looked back at him with a mild grin.

Gov, unfazed, shrugged. "That's two hours, tops. We can divide and conquer." He joined her, taking the list from her hand and scanning it. "You can always do laundry at my place, so we'll cross that off the list straightaway. I'll take the refrigerator and the panty. We can take some stuff, like the condiments and frozen food, to my house. I have boxes and a cooler in the truck. While you pack and deal with the bathrooms, I'll do that."

He made it all sound so easy. Or maybe she just wasn't ready to leave quite yet. "But I still have to shower," she reminded him. "And I don't want to pack dirty clothes."

"Why not? It's no different than bringing your dirty clothes home from a hotel in one of those plastic bags they put in the closet."

She supposed he had a point. "But what's the rush? And don't you have to work? I figured that's why you're up and at 'em so early."

"Eventually. But I actually have more going on at work tomorrow than today. Plus you said you were going to take a break for a few days to let the book rest, so the sooner we get this done, the sooner you can get back to it for a final read. "

As much as everything he was saying made sense, Laurel had a sneaking suspicion there was more to it. She sent him a skeptical look. "What are you up to?"

"Nothing." He put down the paper and laid his hands on her shoulders. "I just want to get the move behind us. And the weather is clear today, no threat of snow or rain. Let's take advantage of it."

"But it's our last night. I thought we'd have a nice dinner, here." She put her arms around his neck and shot him a flirtatious look. "Maybe work out the bed one more time."

He circled her waist and drew her to him, slipping a hand inside the robe and resting it at the small of her back. He smelled like the soap from her shower and his cologne laced with petrichor. He'd not only been up and at 'em, he'd been outside. And not just with Boot. "We can do that at my place. And it's not our last night." He started to say something else, but swallowed it. "What do you say?"

Laurel let out a contemplative breath. He was right, she was taking a break from editing to clear her head. She'd planned to go Christmas shopping and follow-up with a cover designer and formatter today. All of which could easily be done tomorrow instead. "Okay," she heard herself say. "If you think it's best to get it over with."

"I do. Thanks for understanding." With a peck on the lips, he stepped out of her embrace. "And as much as I'd like to work out the bed one more time, why don't you go shower? I'm going to get started in here."

Nodding, she freshened her coffee, then headed out of the kitchen. As she was going down the hall, she heard the pantry and refrigerator doors open and close. The engineer in Gov was surveying, making a plan, determining where to start. And the writer in her was wondering why he so conveniently had boxes and a cooler in his truck. But she pushed that aside and got down to business.

Two hours later, the kitchen was cleaned out, the garbage cans emptied and the closets and bathroom drawers bare. Laurel's car was loaded up with suitcases and hanging clothes, Gov's truck with the food and supplies. And, of course, Boot. Laurel had already done a walk-through, but she wanted to look around one more time. "I'm going to double-check the bedroom, make sure all the doors are locked."

Gov shut his car door and fell into stride with her. "Don't you mean triple-check?"

"I want to make sure I don't leave anything."

"You'll be five minutes away if you do." But he took her hand and walked in with her.

She took in the kitchen, with its gleaming appliances and sparkling countertops and remembered the day she moved in. Describing the house to her mom on the phone, finding the old menus in the drawer, Gov showing up to check the house, then a few nights later with a pizza and one thing leading to another after that. She let go of his hand and walked out to the deck, thought about the countless hours she'd spent out there writing, editing, thinking. Talking with Carli about Zack, the boys playing with Boot in the yard, sipping wine as the sun set, watching the trees bud, then flourish, then shed their leaves and now sleep. Her gaze shifted to the corner near the bedroom window where the wind chimes hung silent in the still air. "I wonder if they'd sell them?" she thought out loud.

"The wind chimes?" Gov asked from the doorway.

Hand to her heart, Laurel spun around. "Oh, I didn't realize you were right there. Yeah, I'd like to have them."

Gov walked over, reached up and unhooked the chimes and then jingling all the way, brought them to her. "I'm sure it's fine. Old man Baker probably doesn't even remember they're here."

"Really?"

"Yeah, I'll throw them in the truck." He took her hand in his. "Let's check the rest and skedaddle. I'm starving and you must be too."

She sent him an upward nod, then followed him back into the house. They locked the deck door, checked the bedrooms and the front door before exiting through the laundry room. "Bye-bye little house," Laurel said under her breath as tears gathered in her eyes. "Thanks for everything."

"You okay?" Gov asked once they were outside with the garage door closing behind them.

"Yeah. It's silly, really. To be sentimental about a house that isn't even mine, that I only lived in for seven months."

Gov laid a kiss on her lips. "But what a seven months it was."

"Yeah," Laurel agreed.

"Let's head over to my place to unload the cars and drop off Boot, then go grab some lunch. I've got some work stuff to deal with this afternoon while you get settled."

"Okay."

Laurel spent the afternoon doing laundry and unpacking while Gov was at work. She was sitting in the living room having a glass of wine and exchanging emails with the cover designer when Gov called. "I'm going to be later than I expected. I had to run down to Reno and traffic is a bitch. Want to order a pizza? That way you can eat whenever and it'll be there when I get home."

Home, Laurel thought. She liked the sound of that more than she'd expected to. "Okay. What do you want?"

"I'll order it. I'm stuck in traffic anyway. The usual for you?"

"Yeah."

"I'll have it delivered so stay put. Oh, can you do me a favor and take Boot out, give him dinner?"

"Sure."

"Thanks. See you in a bit."

"Bye." Laurel was about to disconnect when she heard a commotion, then indistinct voices in the background. "Gov?" she said, but only got a click and dead air in return. Odd. He said he was stuck in traffic, not at a job site or in the office. She shook it off and dove into the samples from the cover designer, made some notes and suggestions, then replied to that effect. Moving through her inbox, she finalized the fee and schedule with the formatter and dealt with her messages from the last few days. By then it was time to walk Boot and before she knew it, the pizza had arrived. Gov had texted that he'd be home around nine, which was considerably later than she'd assumed. So she turned on the TV and ate as Boot snoozed on the couch beside her. News, Christmas movies, sitcom reruns, nothing really held her attention. She called her mom and got her voice mail. She and Mark were probably out to dinner. She hadn't talked to Carli in a couple of days, but knew this was a busy time for her, getting everyone to bed. Laurel put away her dishes and ran the dishwasher, figured out how to set the timer on Gov's coffee maker and got the coffee ready for morning. Then she poured herself another glass of wine and went back into the living room and settled on a rerun of *Modern Family*.

The next thing she remembered was hearing Gov's voice. "Hey, babe. I'm home."

Dazed, she opened her eyes to find him smiling down at her. He was sitting on the coffee table in front of her, gently shaking her shoulder, urging her awake. "Come on, I'll carry you to bed." He slid his arms underneath her, lifting her off the couch.

"What time is it?" she asked groggily.

"Late. Way past your bedtime."

"Did you just get home?" she asked, snuggling into his chest as he walked them toward the bedroom.

"Yeah. I still need to take Boot out. You were both passed out on the couch, pretty as a picture."

Boot, she thought as it all came rushing back to her. She'd been having that dream again about Christmas morning at the rental house. The huge tree, the ornaments, the present she couldn't manage to unwrap. But this time the people's faces were discernible. Gov, his parents, her mother, Mark, even Mac. And Ronnie. Somehow she knew Ronnie was there, but she couldn't really see her so much as feel her. Boot was there too, wearing a big red bow around his neck.

"I'm sorry I fell asleep," Laurel said around a yawn as Gov laid her on the bed and slipped off her shoes.

"Don't be." He sat down next to her. "I'm sorry I was so late."

"No problem. There's pizza in there."

"Thanks. Do you have something to sleep in unpacked? It's a little cold to sleep naked, but I'd be glad to turn up the heat."

She smiled up at him. "Yeah. I left stuff like that in my suitcase. I wasn't sure where you wanted me to put it."

He stroked her cheek. "Mi casa es su casa. You can put it wherever you want."

"You speak Spanish?"

"No," he chuckled. "What can I get you?"

"Nothing. I'll get up and change." She sat up, still a little foggy.

"You okay?"

"Yeah. I was just having the strangest dream."

"About?"

"I'm not entirely sure. It seemed like Christmas morning at the rental house. My mom was there and Mark, your parents, you and I, Mac and even Ronnie."

"Wow." Gov jerked back a little. "That is weird, especially the Ronnie part."

"It was like she was there, but then again she really wasn't."

"I'm sorry. I'm sure you miss her more at Christmas."

"Yeah, but what's really strange is that I had the same dream the night before Elise was born."

"Hmm," Gov said after a moment. "Maybe that's a good sign. Maybe something wonderful is going to happen tomorrow."

"Maybe," Laurel replied with a half-shrug. "But it'd be pretty hard to top that."

~~~

Gov was either clairvoyant or had the weather forecast memorized because the next morning Laurel woke up to overcast skies and gently falling snow. A quick check on her phone confirmed there would be snow off and on all day. This was Tahoe, so a few inches of snow was but a small inconvenience resulting in later school start times and a few slick roads. But to Laurel it was like an early Christmas present.

"I cannot believe you've never skied," Gov amazed, putting on his boots.

"Ronnie despised the cold, hated anything to do with winter."

"Another good reason to have moved you out of the house yesterday. Now you can stay home all day tucked under a blanket."

"I didn't say I shared her persuasion," Laurel replied, rummaging through her suitcase for a pair of socks. "But skiing isn't at the top of my bucket list."

"What are you up to today?" Gov walked over and hugged her from behind.

She leaned against him, indulging in his embrace and inhaling his familiar scent. "For one thing, I'm going over to the Christmas Tree Village to do a little shopping. Do you need anything while I'm downtown?"

"No. But remember we have the sleigh ride at six."

"I remember. I'm going to pick up a scarf and some heavy gloves while I'm out."

"Good idea. I've got to run." He twirled her around to face him, then clasped her face in his hands. "I'll be back around five. I love you. I love waking up knowing you're here. I love knowing you'll be here when I wake up tomorrow."

"I love you, too. And being here." She paused and biting her bottom lip, added, "But we still need to figure some things out. I need to let my mom know about Christmas. It's a miracle she isn't clamoring for an answer. She likes to have a plan."

"That sounds familiar."

"Seriously."

"I know. We'll figure everything out this weekend. I'll talk to my mom and Jack about schedules and logistics." He brushed his lips over hers. "See you later."

Laurel watched him take his leave out of the bedroom, then heard the door shut behind him. With a sigh, she sat down and put on her socks, then the boots her mother had insisted on buying her when she was home for Thanksgiving. Life in the mountains required a completely different wardrobe, Veronica had said. One that covered all the bases. And for now Laurel's life was here because Gov was here. He had become her life, not just a part of it, gradually, seamlessly, permanently. He was home.

She made the bed and opened the blinds just as the sun started peeking through low, gray clouds. She took note of a few things Gov needed, like decent coffee, real half and half and fresh fruit, then headed out. Incline Village was hopping this morning, full of the Christmas buzz only heartened by the morning snowfall. It was serendipitous that Gov had booked the sleigh ride for tonight as the snow was due to return by afternoon. She spent the next couple of hours shopping the locally-owned stores in town, such a welcome departure from the department store chains she was used to. She picked up several things for her mother, including a hand-sewn Christmas sweater light enough to wear in L.A. and some holiday placements. For Mark she bought Tahoe-themed golf club head covers and for Sheryl the Christmas pick for the chip and dip along with a serving plate in the same collection.

By the time Laurel accomplished all of that, grabbed something to eat and ran by the grocery store, it was time to get ready for the evening. She wasn't sure what to wear for a sleigh ride, but since she'd have her coat on the whole time, she wasn't going to worry about it. Gov had made a dinner reservation for afterward at a restaurant up on Diamond Peak known for its mountain views. Surely a sweater dress would do for both. She could switch into dress boots in the car after the sleigh ride.

Gov was home by five and changed into a fresh shirt and jeans. He seemed uncharacteristically antsy. "I'm going to take Boot out, give him dinner early so we don't have to come back here in between," he announced.

"Okay," Laurel said from the bedroom, securing an earring. She walked out to the living room to find Gov standing by the front door typing on his phone. Boot was on the leash next to him, waiting patiently. The second he heard her come in, his head shot up in alarm. "What?"

"Nothing. I just said okay."

"Right." He gave her a wobbly smile, then slid the phone into his back pocket and turned to leave. "Be right back."

She watched the door close behind him, then grabbed her long coat, another recent gift from her mother, and the scarf and gloves she'd purchased earlier. In the interest of time, she went to the hall closet and retrieved Gov's heavy coat. She knew he kept work gloves in his truck, but he surely must have another pair. She didn't find gloves, but she did find a small Christmas tree, what her mom would call a table tree, and a box marked 'Christmas stuff.' She wondered why he hadn't put it out yet and made a mental note to ask him if she could. Even though they wouldn't be here for Christmas, it would make the condo more festive in the interim.

Gov returned with Boot and once he was settled with dinner, they got going. "Excited?" Gov asked, reaching across the console to take Laurel's hand in his.

"Yeah. Thanks for arranging all of this." Just as Laurel was about to ask where they met the sleigh, Gov turned into the parking lot of the public beach. "We get on the sleigh here?"

"Yep. Your chariot awaits."

Laurel looked up to find an old-fashioned carriage pulled by a horse with a long blonde mane. A man in a top hat and a bright red coat and black riding boots stood next to it. "Oh, it's wonderful! Just like a fairy tale!"

"I'll have to take your word on that. But it is pretty cool."

"I love it! Have you ever done this before?" she asked, as they got out of the truck.

"Nope." He took her hand. "It's my first time too," he told her with raised eyebrows.

She sent him a knowing look. "Ah-ha."

Gov and the driver exchanged pleasantries and Gov helped Laurel into the carriage. They covered up with a huge plaid blanket and the horse started trotting. The evening was cold, but so far clear and the rising moon cast beams of bright, white light over the water. They meandered along the lake and through the meadow just outside of town as moonlight sliced through the pines and Christmas lights illuminated the hillsides. Laurel decided it had to be the most magical night of her life. After about an hour, they turned back toward the lake. But instead of returning to the beach parking lot, the carriage headed up into the hills.

"Where are we going?"

"I guess the ride's not over quite yet."

The next thing Laurel knew, they were entering a residential neighborhood. A familiar one. The sleigh came to a stop in front of the house she'd called home for the last seven months. A Christmas tree twinkling with lights stood in the front window. She turned to meet Gov's gaze. He gave her a furtive smile and squeezed her hand. "Merry Christmas, Laurel."

"What's going on?"

"You'll see."

The driver helped them out of the carriage and taking her hand in his, Gov led her up the walk to the house. When they got to the front door, he turned to her. "Before we go in, I want to ask you something."

With a portentous feeling brewing in her stomach, Laurel sent him a confused look. "We can't go in. I don't live here anymore."

"Hear me out."

"Gov," she breathed. "What did you do?"

"Nothing that can't be undone. Well, there is one thing that can't be undone. The fact that I love you. That is never going to change. But if this plan doesn't work for you, we'll come up with another one. I'm up for whatever as long as we're together. But I'd like to make it official either way." He reached into his pocket and produced a box. A tiny silver box topped with a red bow.

Laurel's hand flew to her mouth with a gasp. The dream. The box. The bow. Her eyes found his again.

"Laurel, I love you more than I thought possible. I never knew what love was, never understood it, never experienced it, until you. I want to go on loving you for the rest of my life. You and only you." She looked on as he got down on one knee on the wet stoop and lifted the lid of the box. Inside was the most beautiful diamond ring Laurel had ever seen. A halo of miniature diamonds surrounded a large, round solitaire stone, resplendent under the coach lights of the house. "Will you give me the chance and marry me?" He lifted the ring out of its velvet bed and held it up in the air between them. Shocked and awed, she slowly dropped her hand to meet his. He removed her glove and slipped the ring on her finger, then with her hand in his, stood. "Laurel?" he asked after a long moment. "I'm on pins and needles here."

"What?" she said vaguely, tearing her gaze away from her hand. "Oh! Yes! Yes! Yes, yes, yes!" she screamed, jumping into his arms. "A million times yes!" She laid a sloppy kiss on his mouth, then turned her attention back to her hand. The ring shot out beams as bright as a supermoon shimmering off the lake on a summer night.

"Thank God. You scared me to death, the way you reacted at first with the gasp. Like it wasn't a happy surprise," Gov said, putting his arms around her waist as she lost herself in the ring.

"Oh, no! I mean I was surprised, but it was the dream, the one I told you about, that threw me. There was a present I couldn't open, no matter how hard I tried. In a small, silver box just like this. I tried and tried, but couldn't get it unwrapped." She paused, then meeting his gaze, realized out loud, "Because I was afraid to let myself be happy. But you opened it for me. And now because of you, I'm not afraid anymore." She looked deeply into his eyes. "Because I never knew what love was, never understood it, never experienced it before either. Not until you. And I want that, and you, for the rest of my life. You and only you." She fell back into him then, suddenly spent as he kissed the top of her head and held her tight.

They stood there holding each other in the cold, still night for a moment until Laurel pulled back in alarm. "Gov!" she said in a desperate whisper. "There are people in there! I can hear them! We have to get out of here. "

A clever grin replaced the tenderhearted smile on his face. "No, we don't."

"Yes, we do! The new tenants already moved in. There's tree in the window!"

Eyes glued to hers, Gov reached over his shoulder and tapped his knuckles against the door. It flew open.

"Well, it's about time! How long does it take to ask a question?" Veronica mocked annoyance. "Get in here, the both of you. It's freezing out there."

Laurel felt her jaw drop and her breath catch in her throat. Standing there in the bright light of the living room was her mother and Sheryl. Behind them was Mark and Jay and rounding out the makeshift triangle was Mac. Beyond, a fire roared in the fireplace and stockings hung from the mantle. Pulled inside by Gov, Laurel could only look around in wonder. The tree in the window was the one from her dream. It was tall and full and freshly cut; she could smell the pine needles. On it hung the ornaments of her childhood, along with some other vintage ones she didn't recognize. And at the top sat their family heirloom angel. Still in a daze, she dropped Gov's hand and walked over to the tree. She had to touch it to make sure it was real, to make sure that all of this was real.

It was.

She turned back around and looked first at her mother, then at Gov. "What's happening?" she muttered around a breath.

"I didn't get to tell you about the rest of my plan," Gov answered, joining her next to the tree. "I wanted to lock down the most important part, the proposal, first. The rest is negotiable. I figured I could always ask for forgiveness later. Please keep that in mind as we go through this. I bought the house."

"You what?"

"I bought the house," he repeated, removing her other glove and taking both of her hands in his. "Old man Baker finally decided to sell it and Jack convinced him to sell it to me. We don't have to live here all the time. I know we haven't gotten that far yet. And we can always rent it out or sell it if living here doesn't work for you at all. But you can write anywhere and you really seemed to like living here. And this is where we started. I know L.A. will always be home, but maybe we can get a place there too." He took a breath, then resumed his rant, "I'm trying to work out something with Jack about work. He offered me a partnership in the business. We'll get to that too. I didn't want to commit to anything until I talked to you. It would keep me here more than not and there are plenty of job opportunities for me in Southern California." He paused then finished wryly, "I think."

In what had become second nature, Laurel reached down and petted Boot who had appeared at her feet as Gov barreled on, "I know you always wanted to spend Christmas in Tahoe. We still can if you want, but your mom thought it might be nice for all of us to spend Christmas in L.A. this year. She wants to throw us an engagement party on Christmas Eve. That way we could all be together, even my sister and her family could come. And Zack and Carli and the kids and Rosa and Javier. Mac even said he'd ask off and make the trip." Gov tipped his head at Mac, then went on, "It'll be our first Christmas together and that's the most important thing, not where we spend it. But if you agree to all of this, or at least to some of it, and since a lot of us are here now, we could have an early Christmas. Here, tonight. This could be your Christmas in Tahoe," Gov ended on a hopeful note.

Laurel's head was spinning, but she pushed up from Boot and somehow managed, "Is that why you did all of this? Bought the house, moved me out early, brought my mother and yours in to decorate, had the guys do God knows what—"

"Help him get the tree, put it up," Jay supplied under his breath.

Nodding, she gave Jay a sideways glance and continued, "Just so I could have Christmas in Tahoe, one way or the other?"

"Yes. Well, the house is not Christmas-qualified but the rest, yes."

She went to him, cupped his face in her hands. "Thank you." She laid a kiss on his lips. "Thank you for going to all that trouble. No wonder you've been running around like a chicken with its head cut off for the last month. Thank you for understanding how important my mother, my family, is to me. Thank you sharing yours with me. Thank you for knowing before I did how much this house means to me. Thank you for having faith in me, in us, when I didn't always give you reason to. Thank you for loving me and giving me the most beautiful ring. And thank you for making all the dreams I didn't know I had come true." She hugged him as tears rolled down her cheeks. Then she leaned back asking, "But how *did* you know?"

Gov dried her cheeks with the tips of his fingers. "It's in your book."

Laurel was stunned. "You read my book?"

"Yeah. A little bird told me to. Actually three little birds told me to, each in their own way."

Laurel looked around the room, then settled her gaze on her mother. "Really?"

Veronica just shrugged her shoulders and looked away.

"When you were gone for Thanksgiving. You left the printout here."

She returned to him. "But I hadn't even written the ending yet."

"I know. And since I couldn't get it out of anyone." Gov looked briefly at Veronica, then back to Laurel. "I went with my gut." He looked down at her with shining eyes. "How'd I do?"

She looked around at all the glowing faces, now so clear, at the tree adorned with her childhood creations and thought of all the memories they held and of the lifetime of memories she and Gov would make here. She took in Boot by her side, the ring sparkling on her finger. Then she met Gov's gaze again. "You nailed it," she declared, hugging him as her eyes filled and her heart overflowed with joy. And then, just as everyone gathered around them with happy tears and congratulatory hugs, the breeze picked up and the wind chimes began to clang merrily on the deck.

The End

*About the Author*

Martha O'Sullivan has loved reading romance novels for as long as she can remember. Writing her own books is the realization of a lifelong dream. She is a graduate of Illinois State University where she wrote for the school newspaper and was a member of Zeta Tau Alpha. She is also a former Acquisitions Editor at MacMillan Computer Publishing. Martha writes contemporary romances with M/F couples and happy endings. A native Chicagoan, she lives her own happy ending in Florida with her husband and two daughters.